Redemption

Redemption

N.F. STEINER

For information, contact bluevirgapublishing@ANVpartners.com.

Book and cover design by Blue Virga Publishing in association with ANV Partners. Additional publishing assistance by Alicia Harrison and Sasha Harrison.

ISBN-13: 9781943743001
ISBN-10: 1943743002
Library of Congress Control Number: 2015910687
ANV Partners attn: Dave Harrison, Denver, CO

First Edition: April 26, 2015

Dedicated to my beautiful wife

pas de deux
noun (French; literally "step for two")
\-'də(r), -'dü\

1: a dance or figure for two performers
2: an intricate relationship or activity involving two parties or things

-- A dance duet in which two dancers, usually a man and a woman, perform steps together

-- Characteristic of classical ballets such as Swan Lake and Sleeping Beauty, it is often considered the highlight of a ballet

-- Perhaps most notably: *The White Swan Pas De Deux* (Act II) of *Swan Lake*, in which Odette and Prince Siegfried fall in love for the first time and *The Black Swan Pas De Deux* (Act III) in which the Black Swan Odile seduces the prince away from Odette, leading to her tragic death.

Table of Contents

Chapter 1   The Dream · 1
Chapter 2   The Ballerina ·11
Chapter 3   The Businessman ·15
Chapter 4   The Bar · 28
Chapter 5   The Call · 34
Chapter 6   The Distance ·39
Chapter 7   The Encounter · 43
Chapter 8   The Scheme · 60
Chapter 9   The Aftermath · 66
Chapter 10 The Press ·82
Chapter 11 The Obsession ·92
Chapter 12 The Spiral · 112
Chapter 13 The Rebellion ·122
Chapter 14 The Breakdown ·130
Chapter 15 The Transformation ·137
Chapter 16 The Setup · 157
Chapter 17 The Trap · 162
Chapter 18 The News · 177
Chapter 19 The Chill ·193
Chapter 20 The Discussion ·195
Chapter 21 The Plea ·198
Chapter 22 The Evidence ·203

Chapter 23 The Opening· ·211
Chapter 24 The Payoff· ·216
Chapter 25 The Call ·227
Chapter 26 The Finale· 234
       Acknowledgments ·241
       About the Author ·243
       Fiction· ·245

One

THE DREAM

Christina

I AWOKE WITH A START, WITH MY HEART HAMMERING wildly. I saw from the clock that it was three o'clock in the morning. Beside me, Adam snored quietly. I rubbed my eyes, willing the dream to leave me. I generally dreamed of dancers and of dancing, and this one had started out with me on stage at the Met with the members of my present company, thrilled by the opening measures from the orchestra. Then, one by one, other dancers on stage peeled off until it was just me.

And then the man ran on stage; he was so strange and frightening that I fled. And then the stage disappeared, and I was suddenly in a strange forest. The trees were so tall and old that they blocked out the moonlight, and everywhere there were shadows and creatures, and there was a taste of malevolent magic. I somehow knew that the man behind me, who was still on my heels, was the source of that magic. He was some sort of sorcerer, and for some reason, he wanted me and me alone.

I could not move fast enough. My dance was abandoned. Branches whipped at me as I passed and caught at my beautiful tutu and ripped it. In my panic I could feel myself changing; my arms ached and stretched out until they were useless appendages at my side. My skin itched, and sharp barbs began to grow.

1

I was growing feathers.

I was frightened, of course, but hopeful. Perhaps I could fly away from the man who was so close behind me that I could hear him grunting and swearing as he tripped in the underbrush in the dark.

More feathers came in. I began to flap, but there were not enough feathers. Still, I was changing and changing fast. After a few more moments, I was certain I could leave the ground completely.

I could fly away. But first I felt his outstretched hands around my neck.

"My beautiful Odette," I heard the man sigh, even as he crushed me to him. "You know you cannot escape me. Sometimes I think I accidentally turned you into a silly goose."

I tried to scream, but my voice came out strange to my ears and inarticulate. At that moment, death seemed better than captivity. I did not know the man, and yet somehow I had always known him.

I was confused for a moment when I woke up. Then I felt upset.

I wondered how many artistic directors had nightmares about the ballet that they were producing. It couldn't have been a good sign.

The shadows in the bedroom frightened me, so I turned on my light.

I told myself it was just a dream, just like I told myself that the problems with the company were all in my head.

Adam stirred briefly and sat up, squinting his eyes. "Why is the light still on, Christina?" he said.

"Sorry—bad dream," I mumbled.

He kissed me and then rolled over and pulled the covers up to his ears. "Go to sleep, darling," he said, yawning.

I wanted to hold him, but I couldn't. I felt like my nerves were all on fire. I needed to move. I mumbled an apology, turned off the light, put on my robe, and walked downstairs. I padded from room to room in the house—our dream house—and looked out the window at the rain that had started falling. Why did I feel such an ache?

A few years ago, Adam would have coaxed me to sleep gently with sweet kisses and lovemaking. I told myself he had another huge day in front of him and needed his sleep. That everything was okay.

He had been working a lot lately—driven by a new baby, a mortgage, and a wife to support.

I worried that he was disappointed by the problems I'd been having with the ballet company. He had made it clear over the past few days that he wanted me to be more than a mother. That he believed in my dream.

My dream had been to assemble a ballet company right here in Lockville—one that was innovative and would survive. I knew traditional ballet from the eighteenth and nineteenth centuries would not succeed in a midsized town like ours. I had solicited a group of dancers from the area to audition for the new venture. I was not going for false emotionalism but for something that rang truer. I wanted to move beyond dancers as "flowers," which is what my mentor had called them, though it had been hard to tell if he was being witty or merely profound.

When the candidates had arrived at the studio I had rented for the auditions, I had announced my vision. The show, *Swan Lake*, was a classical favorite, an icon. It had first been performed by the Russian Imperial Ballet at the Bolshoi Theater in March 1877. But it had undergone changes since its initial debut. The production as we know it was first performed in Saint Petersburg in 1895. It had played to American audiences for the first time in 1940 with Russian choreographers and mostly American dancers. The Metropolitan Opera House had presented the "Black Swan Pas de Deux" from act three in 1944. Our choreography would be modernized with a new format that retained the classical flavor. But the costumes would be more tantalizing, more provocative, more modern. We had to keep up with the big Broadway musicals that were proving so popular. Every time my husband and I went to see a show, it seemed like the dancers were showing more skin. The production of *Hair* had been shocking but also inspiring. We needed to keep up with the times. Nostalgia would not keep us afloat.

The dancers had looked at me curiously when I had announced all of this. I knew that they needed work; it was hard to maintain a living in Lockville, and we had all moved out of the city for one reason or another. I knew they would be invested in making a new vision work; I just hoped that they would pull hard enough.

Then I had announced the clincher: the show would show a tasteful element of the erotic but would be nuanced enough to really attract the attention of critics and the cultured who would normally drive to the city to see these things. We needed to have something exciting to keep them at home.

"The selection of the female dancers will focus on finding those whose figures are curvy," I had announced. My voice sounded a bit too soft and shaky, I realized, so I lifted my chin and dared anyone to question me. I saw the dancers look around the room at each other; some of them were shaking their heads. A few of the older dancers who had obviously had babies and were approaching that dreaded age of forty, which is when most dancers retire, looked brighter. They had probably wondered if they even had a shot at the audition.

Then one of the fellows, Michael Griffin, spoke up. He was one of the top dancers there, and I really wanted him to be part of the company. I was happy he had shown up. "Is this really a ballet or something else?" he asked.

I just smiled and said, "Think of this as a new and evolved ballet."

The dancers broke into a buzz of excitement and were talking among themselves. I let them go for a moment and then opened it up to a brief question-and-answer session. I tried to keep my answers brief and enthusiastic. It wasn't that I didn't want to give too much away; the vision was still forming, and I wanted to put it in a hothouse for the moment until it had roots and blooms.

"If you're done with questions, I'll ask those who believe in the vision to stay for tryouts and those who don't to leave."

A silence followed. I watched while five of the dancers walked out of the room. I looked at Michael. He shrugged his shoulders and smiled slightly. He was staying. For the time being.

I took a deep breath. "Let's begin."

I had gotten through the auditions and several weeks of practices, but it still didn't feel like everybody was on board. The tension between me and the principal dancers, Michael Griffin and Jill Curtiss, another professional who had trained in Russia, was evident. Both of them, of course, were heavily invested in the original form of *Swan Lake*. I was staying the course, but I was worried.

Somehow the fact that Adam believed so earnestly in me made my worrying worse. Truth be told, I had a nagging feeling that our marriage depended on things going well with the company. I was afraid of what would happen if it didn't go well. I knew it was silly, but I was afraid Adam would fall out of love with me. It happened to many women.

Yet without some connection to dancing, I felt unmoored.

There in the living room, I saw that the rain had stopped and the clouds had parted. Staring out at the wet yard, wild and wonderful in the light of the moon, I felt a sudden inspiration.

I would take the company even further in the modern direction. This would be a new, never-before-seen version of *Swan Lake*. I pulled out a sketchbook and started drawing. Dancers took flight; their movements were bold and modern. The costumes were not demure or traditional; they celebrated the female form. I was going to take my cues as much from Las Vegas and the Rockettes as from some of the more innovative dancers and choreographers doing fresh work in jazz. I began to get excited.

I walked back upstairs to the bedroom to find Adam sprawled diagonally across the bed, dreaming deeply. I stood awhile and looked at him, feeling pangs of love and sadness. He looked so young at the moment—so much like the man I had been dating when I had begun to gain ground as a principal dancer.

Restless, I grabbed a quilt and decided to go sit with my son. I settled into the rocker in his room. The streetlight illuminated the rain, which had begun again, falling fast. The wind had picked up and rattled the gutters and the trees. My son woke and said, "Is that you, Mommy?"

"Yes, darling," I murmured.

"Are you sitting with me?"

"For a bit," I said.

When I woke some hours later, feeling stiff from falling asleep in the chair, I found that my husband had already headed to work. He had left a note wishing me a great day and saying that he would pick up Chris from my mom's.

I thought about calling him and telling him about my big plan, but I suddenly felt shy.

"It's better to surprise him," I whispered to myself. "He'll be so amazed by how the show turns out."

I put aside the twist of fear—that feeling that things were going to fall apart somehow—and went about my morning routine of getting our son up, fed, and dressed. I did some finger painting with little Chris until it was time to drop him off at my mother's house and head into rehearsal.

For the past few weeks, our company had moved into our new rehearsal space at the civic center. It was home to several other established arts organizations including two theater troupes, an improvisational company, a writing work-shop, and, of course, the arts commission. When Mark Turner, the director of arts and culture for the city, offered us the space, I was thrilled. We had the stamp of approval from the city, though I half expected someone to stop me every time I walked into the center. We hadn't pulled everything together. We were short on funds. But it simply had to work.

I took a deep breath, elongated my spine, and walked with purpose down the main hallway to the rehearsal studio in back. Body language is important to dancers, but it's even more important to artistic directors. If I was going to pull this off, I had to steel myself for the job—and managing people was something I was beginning to fear I wasn't very good at.

When I walked into the studio, most of the dancers were already there working on their choreography, though they had broken into two groups. Sandy Segal was standing at the far corner of the room, talking to our two principal dancers, Michael and Jill. *Good God*, I thought. *What's she doing here?*

Michael had the kind of glower on his face that I might have found allur-ing when I was a kid just starting out. Jill's hand went up to her mouth as though she were covering a smile. Sandy immediately walked over to me, her boots making tiny staccato noises on the wooden floor that I could hear above the music.

I had only met Sandy a couple of times at art fund raisers, but she had always been a little cool. Her husband had died young and had left her an obscene amount of money, I had heard, but having misfortune along with her fortune seemed to have made her permanently peeved. She was one of the governing board members who had voted against taking in the ballet company when Mark Turner had recommended us as a pet project. Her presence there on that day of all days rattled me.

I looked around in a panic. Where was Anna? My partner in crime, my very best friend, was supposed to help out with rehearsals. *She* would know what to do with this unexpected visitor.

"Ms. Segal, what a pleasant surprise," I said. "What brings you here today?"

"Please, Christina, call me Sandy," she said. "We're all friends here."

I hoped my smile didn't look as fake as it felt, and I wished my voice wouldn't quaver when I was feeling threatened.

"I heard through the grapevine that you had a big announcement to make," she purred, and then she leaned forward and whispered, "You know I love surprises."

Since I had just called the members of the troupe that morning to make sure they were in attendance for my announcement about the first production date, I was a little startled that she had heard about it. Moreover, who had told her and why?

Don't be paranoid, I told myself. *She's just bored. You should feel sorry for her, having so much time on her hands, rather than threatened.*

"We just have some routine business to take care of," I said, hoping Sandy would go away and bug somebody else. "Talking about our scheduling and the like."

Sandy raised her eyebrows. "Routine, huh?" she said. "Then you don't mind if I stay?"

I took in the dancers, who had not stopped the music, and we got into our normal circle. Michael had taken one group of dancers and was working them through some of the new steps we had talked about. Jill was with another group of dancers trying to get their pointe work down. Some of the moves were stiff, and I could see a few of them struggling with pain as they danced. I could see them strain to keep up with her; she didn't have the sunniest demeanor in the world, but she made everything look easy. I watched her gluts flex as she took tiny steps across the floor, and I felt a pang of jealousy and insecurity. I missed dancing.

Sandy was watching me watch the dancers with a small smile on her lips as though she could smell my insecurity. It didn't matter, really, if I failed that day or not, because I had already failed in her eyes. I would have to give it a shot, even if I couldn't get rid of her.

"Not at all," I said to Sandy.

I love ballet. I love the way it challenges me, the way it makes me think, and how it's like a puzzle. I love pushing my body and making it form the story of each individual dance, each gesture adding to its meaning. I just had to use the mind-set that had made me such a great dancer and the pick of the artistic director for the Metropolitan Ballet to convey this story.

I called the dancers together, unfurled my sketches, and explained my ideas. Some of the dancers looked intrigued while others looked a little skeptical.

Jill, who was standing at the back of the room and leaning against the bar, finally spoke. "You're turning this into a burlesque show, then?"

"No, not completely," I said. "Anyway, people love burlesque. It's very hot right now."

I could see that a few of the ballerinas looked dubious but were going to let it go. I saw Michael standing off to the side, looking amused.

"Michael," I said. "Surely you can see the merit of taking some artistic chances," I said. "Let's do something we could never get away with in New York."

Michael grinned. "This is going to be interesting."

I cleared my throat nervously.

"Interesting is good, though I was hoping for…revolutionary," I stammered. "This is something that will attract the general public."

Sandy, who had been silent the whole time, spoke up. "I don't think you've really thought this through."

My throat tightened, and I couldn't even speak. My beloved idea felt sad and ineffectual, even to me.

I didn't want anyone to see me cry, so I took a deep breath and tried to pretend it was opening night, any opening night, and the performance was about to start. I imagined that the music was swelling; I traced the floor with my pointe shoes, counted the beats, and prepared to lead the rest of the danc-ers. I stared Sandy in the eyes and felt the pounding of a migraine begin, but I smiled anyway.

"Thanks for your input, Sandy," I said, nodding a little too much and kicking myself mentally for always being so darn agreeable. "Dancers, let's get back to where we were, shall we?"

"Christina, why don't you let me lead rehearsal this morning?" Jill asked. "I'd love to be able to do that for you."

I hesitated a moment. "Michael will help me," she added.

After a moment, I nodded. I left them in charge of the rehearsal and fled to my office.

I can't say I was surprised when Mark Turner called later that afternoon.

Mark Turner was a loud, boisterous man who seemed like the sort who would be just as happy running around with a group of kids at a summer camp as he was herding around a bunch of art organizations. Normally I enjoyed our conversations.

"I'm not going to beat around the bush," said Mark.

I straightened my back and tried to connect the top of my skull to the heavens. "I would expect nothing less."

"Sandy has recommended that the city pull the plug on your use of the civic-center facility."

Breathe, I told myself. *Just breathe.*

The clock on the wall said 4:30 p.m. Anna had not shown at all, and soon it would be time to get going. I needed to go to the grocery store to pick up some food for dinner. I wanted to make Adam a memorable dinner. I was hoping that Chris would be worn out from playing with Grandma and would go to sleep early. I liked my plan—I would put on candles and pick up some good steaks and maybe even flowers. For a guy, my husband sure liked flowers. He'd been working a lot, and I needed to be the one to make sure the spark was still there.

I was so deep in reverie about a dinner with Adam that it took me a few minutes to register that Mark was saying my name. "Christina? Are you okay?"

"Sorry, Mark," I said. "I'm just so shocked and saddened to hear that."

"It's not the end of the world," said Mark.

"But it is," I said softly. "It's the end of the program—the end of my dream of directing a company. It's the end of my world, and it would mean the end of bringing the world a new and rejuvenated ballet."

"I know this means a lot to you," said Mark.

I stood up from my desk. I needed to move.

"It's not just me, Mark," I said, my voice rising with emotion. "I have a new format that could rescue ballet from being a dying form of entertainment. If you shut us down now, it will kill the opportunity for Lockville to become a noted player in the entertainment world."

Mark said nothing. I looked at the clock. I hoped Adam wasn't running late that night. If he was, I'd have to pick up Chris. What a day.

"Look," I said. "Don't take it all away. I can fix things. I promise."

I could hear Mark sigh. "You've got until the end of the month, Christina."

"What do you mean by 'the end of the month'?" I said.

"If you can't demonstrate some progress by the end of the month, the arts commission is going to ask you to leave the space," he said.

My heart hurt. "What kind of proof do you need?" I asked dryly.

"That's up to you," said Mark.

I was silent. I could feel my throat close up, and it was hard to talk.

"Christina?"

Finally I could speak. "Thanks, Mark," I said. "I'll have something pulled together for you soon. You'll see."

"I wish you luck," he said. "I really do."

"Thanks," I said.

After we hung up, I sat there massaging my temples.

I had no choice but to give it my best. I knew I only had one shot to impress him, and I was going to give it my all.

It was show time.

Two

The Ballerina

Christina

CHRISTINA WAS BORN AND RAISED IN THE CITY OF LOCKVILLE, a midsized city in upstate New York. She was the daughter of David and Gloria Parker. She was an only child.

Her mother, from a wealthy, upper-class family, was a beautiful, cultured, and loving lady who had attended a New York finishing school as a young lady, and was a university graduate. Her father came from a blue-collar background. He was a handsome man with a gregarious personality. He was a successful stockbroker.

Christina was a beautiful and loving child, who grew up to acquire the grace, beauty, and cultured personality of her mother. Christina possessed personality traits that she acquired from her mother. She was a naïve and trusting person. She could not possibly see or think anything negative about anybody, and would never confront a "wrong" at the risk of offending. As her mother before her, she attended a New York finishing school.

Christina became fascinated with the ballet and began lessons at the age of eight. In time, this activity came to dominate her life. At the age of seventeen she moved to a nearby city so she could attend a ballet school full-time. After a year of dedicated training and graduation from high school, she went to New York City and joined the Metropolitan Ballet Theater Company. She was a natural performer and quickly became a "principal dancer" and was cast in leading roles where she achieved rave reviews.

It was during her third year with the company when she returned to her hometown for a vacation break. And while at home on vacation she met Adam Cramer. He was an aggressive, ambitious man who worked for an investment banking company. He was often out of town as his work required a significant amount of travel.

THE FIRST TIME I WAS TAKEN TO THE BALLET I WAS six, and my father had deemed me "old enough" to go to the New York Metropolitan performance of *Swan Lake*.

Though *Swan Lake*, with its tale of an enchanted girl, an evil sorcerer, and a love-struck prince, thrilled me, I was even more thrilled by my father's attention. My father was often away at work and was tired when he came home. Even though he had a blue-collar background, he supported my mother's zeal for the arts. The evening of the show, my mother dressed me in a blue-velvet dress she had sewn herself to match my eyes. My mother was a quiet, sophisticated woman who had gone to a finishing school and was very cultured. I could tell by the way she combed my hair, giving it vigorous strokes, and by the way her eyes seemed to dance that she was extremely excited by the evening. My father smiled and held both of our hands; he held mine in his left hand and my mother's in his right one. I felt intimidated and shy when we arrived at the opera house, which felt cavernous in the hallway and even more so when we stepped inside, where the ceilings soared to the very heavens. I was in awe when I saw so many people dressed in such finery. When the music started and the dancers started coming onstage, as graceful and as light as fairies, I was enthralled. I forgot my velvet dress, my quiet mother, and my strict father—I forgot the many people, I forgot the cavernous building, and I forgot my shy and clumsy self in the grand sweep of the performance. It was *Swan Lake*, and no one could fault me for applauding during the wrong moments.

We stayed up long past my bedtime, and I fell asleep in the car on the way home and dreamed of the dancers.

A short while later my mother and father signed me up for dance lessons at Mrs. Tolliver's Dance Company. I worked hard all of those years, juggling college and work, until I eventually became a principal ballerina with the New York Metropolitan Ballet Company.

Then I met Adam Cramer. He was sharp, ambitious man five years older than me who worked for an investment-banking company. The fact that he had been traveling a lot and was a catch added to the excitement, but what really set him apart was the depth of his passion for life—and for me. He believed in me. I hadn't dated very much at all, having always been a little shy, but Adam made me feel special. Every chance he could get, he drove down from his house in Lockville, which was 150 miles north of the city, to see me. We didn't have much free time between my demanding rehearsal and performance schedule and his work schedule.

One night, he brought a beautiful bouquet of yellow roses backstage to my dressing room. "I have reservations at the Tavern on the Green," he told me. I had been there with my parents and their artistic friends but never on a date. I felt all grown up and in my element that night as Adam kept up a steady stream of charm. I loved him so much at that moment. He was dapper looking in a tweed vest that looked straight out of an old movie. The waiter brought out a bottle of champagne and set it on the table. Adam swiftly came around to me and dropped to his knees. I was surprised for an instant at his actions, but I was even more surprised when I saw in his outstretched hand a most exquisite vintage diamond ring.

I hadn't thought it possible, but the passion I felt for him eclipsed my passion for the music of Frédéric Chopin's *Les Sylphides* and the score of *Swan Lake* that rings daily in my ears. It eclipsed the curtain calls, the final rounds of applause, and all the other bouquets I'd received.

I also knew I was getting older; I had escaped serious injuries, but I knew what a demanding career ballet is and that it only lasts a few years.

And good men—like Adam—are rare.

Still, I hesitated. Then I gave him a counterproposal of my own. "Adam, I love you very much, and I love the ballet as well." I paused and took a deep breath. "Would you be willing to move to New York? Then I could have you and the ballet?"

Adam said nothing for a moment, and in those few beats, my heart sank. I had blown it.

Then he stood up and took me into his arms.

"Christina, darling," he murmured. "Let's get married and bring the ballet to Lockville. You don't have to choose."

I felt a sense of relief, which bloomed quickly into joy.

"That's a great plan; I'll do it!"

Adam gave me a look of mock consternation. "Do what? Start a ballet company or marry me?"

"Let's do both," I said.

Adam was true to his word. We rented a rehearsal studio and upgraded it with mirrors and barres, and I began operating a small school for adults and kids. Then I got pregnant, and Adam got promoted at work. I was happy. We were happy. But I began to feel this inexplicable sense of worry creep over me. I sensed that I needed to push my dream ahead. I didn't want to stray too far from the accomplished artist that Adam had fallen in love with.

Three

THE BUSINESSMAN

Christina

I MADE MY WAY THROUGH THE THRONG OF shoppers in the grocery store, trying to sort out my thoughts on my surprise dinner. Dinner posed an easy problem. Saving the ballet company would not be so easy. I lingered in front of the meat counter, but when one of the butchers asked if he could help me, I shook my head and stepped back, motioning for the woman next to me to go first. I needed a moment to decide. Would Adam want steak or salmon? I wanted to make my husband something special to show my gratitude for his support—to bulletproof our marriage.

Mark Turner's ultimatum had sent me into a panic.

I wasn't even sure what I could do at that point to impress the arts commission. My stomach tightened as I remembered the expression of disdain on Sandy Segal's pretty little face. And where had Anna been anyway?

"Ma'am, do you know what you'd like yet?"

I jumped. I had to pull it together. "The filet mignon looks great," I said. "Please give me three good-sized steaks."

I put the steaks into my cart and continued working down my list. It was nearly 5:30 p.m., and the store was packed. Adam would have picked up Chris from Mom's by then and would be on his way home. I knew that if I hurried, I might be able to beat them home. I scanned my list; I still needed pick up some milk and coffee for the morning. And I had my heart set on some flowers.

I picked up my pace.

I swear I didn't see the guy coming around the corner with his cart until it was too late.

He slammed his cart into mine with enough force to jerk it out of my hands and into the display case of potato chips. The bags went flying everywhere.

The man looked at the bags with a displeased look on his face. I felt heat rush to my cheeks. "Oh, I beg your pardon. I am so sorry," I said, scrambling to pick the bags off of the floor and to stack them on the back on the display case.

The man bent down to help me, a smile on his face. I was glad to see his irritation turn to amusement. "I'm sorry," he said. "I'm in a hurry to get to work."

The man was dressed in khakis and a black turtleneck. I quickly placed the last few bags back on the rack and patted them lightly.

"There," I said. "Nobody's the wiser."

The man grinned. "You have some crazy stacking talent."

I shook my head and stole a peek at my watch. It was nearly six; Adam and Chris would be home already. I started pushing my cart down the aisle he had come up. "I need to get some crazy shopping skills going, or I'm going to be late getting dinner on the table," I said.

"I've got important things to do, too," he said.

I sighed and hustled to get the rest of my groceries and decided I didn't have time to get flowers after all. It was already dark out. I booked it through the checkout line and out to the parking lot. I had parked way in the corner because I don't like parking my car anywhere it might get dinged. As I fumbled with my keys in the car door, I heard a low whistle behind me.

"That's some ride you have there," said a man's voice. "You can run into me any day with that."

I turned to see the man from the store standing behind me and looking like a cat with a canary.

"You ran into me," I said.

He laughed. "Whatever you want to think," he said. "You can't put one over on me. I'm a lady magnet."

I rolled my eyes.

"And the car—it's sweet! You want to sell it?"

"Thanks, and no, I'm not selling," I said. "My husband bought it as a birthday gift for me last summer."

It was a brand-new 1962 Ford Mustang that was painted a candy-apple red and had a white hardtop convertible. It sure was fun to drive. Anna had called it a "babe magnet," but since I owned the car, it seemed to me that guys were the ones who were most obsessed with the make and model. They were always talking me up, and a few men had tried to make me a couple of offers. I steeled myself for another somewhat tedious conversation about my "wheels." I always tried to be polite to those guys, as it was clear they were reliving their glory days of high school.

"Is this a special edition?" he asked, running a hand along the front fender.

"My husband ordered it," I said, though he was looking at me as much as the car. We stood and talked about the car awhile, but it was getting cold, and I really needed to get home. Little Chris needed to get to bed at about eight, and Adam probably had some paper work to do after supper.

I didn't want to be rude, but I needed to get going. And he made me feel uncomfortable. I rubbed my hands and hugged myself.

"Oh, you're getting cold," he said. "And you have that husband to feed."

"And a child," I said, regretting it the instant I said it. I felt like he was overly interested in me.

"Well," he said, winking. "Catch you later."

He turned around and walked away, and I got into the car and turned on the engine. I sat there for a moment, letting the engine idle since it was a little temperamental and needed to be coaxed along. The man walked back up to me and knocked on my window. I rolled it down.

"Did you say you were a dancer?"

"Yes," I said. This guy was pushy.

"Where do you dance?" he asked. He looked oddly hopeful.

"I'm not that kind of dancer," I said. He looked puzzled, and I added, "I started a ballet company, if you must know."

"Oh," he said. "That's super!" He started turning around and then turned back around again, making me jump.

"What did you say your name was?"

"I didn't," I said.

"Right," he said, looking at me sheepishly. "Nice to meet you."

I smiled politely but muttered "hardly" under my breath and started the car. When I pulled out of the space, he was still standing there, looking at me.

By the time I got home and walked from the garage into the kitchen, Chris was already in a high chair scooted up to the table and was being fed by Adam. "Mama, you're home," cried Chris, banging his spoon on the table.

Adam got up to hug me, a big smile on his face. "Hey, babe," he said. "I missed you!"

I confess that I clung to him a little longer than I needed to, burying my face in his sweater and drawing in the scent of him, which comforted me so much. Adam wasn't a cologne man. He smelled soapy, clean, and sweet, just like his personality.

"Darling," he murmured, running his hand through my bun and taking it out. "Is something wrong?"

"The company," I groaned into his shirt.

"What's new with that?" he joked. I must have looked crestfallen, because he changed tactics. "I'm sorry," he said. "Care to talk about it?"

I hesitated. I wasn't ready to talk about the horrible conversation with Mark Turner just yet. I took a deep breath, stepped back so I could see my darling husband's beautiful face, and deftly changed the subject.

"Yes, that stupid birthday present you gave me attracts all sorts of attention."

Adam laughed. "It's not the car that's attracting the attention."

"Please," I said. "A guy at the grocery store was admiring my car. I didn't want to interrupt him, because he was so nice, but he made me late."

Adam swatted me playfully. "You need to be more assertive, my dear." Then his expression turned serious. "You also need to be more aware of the motives of others, especially since you're as beautiful as you are."

I felt a sense of sadness sweep through me. Adam was always trying to get after me to "assert" myself. If anybody was a women's libber in the family, it was him. Anna was always out with her women's groups, canvassing for the vote and other such activities. She was a regular suffragette. I was a little more traditional, I guess, though I felt disparate pulls on my heart and my time. I wasn't the type of girl who was going to get loud mouthed, but I sometimes thought Adam would appreciate me more if I were a little more ambitious and a little more opinionated, like some of the girls he worked with at the office. The other night, when we'd gone out to the Chop House, my steak had come out a bit overdone. Adam had wanted me to return it, but I hadn't wanted to offend the waiter and the chef. Adam thought I should stand up for myself more.

Of course, I hadn't stood up for myself very well with Mark Turner, had I?

"Oh, Adam," I murmured, "You just don't understand."

But he did understand, didn't he? I just wasn't sure I could live up to his expectations—to be the kind of wife he wanted me to be.

Chris was trying to get out of his high chair, so I picked him up and hugged him. He smelled soapy and clean, too. My mom must have given him a bath, bless her.

Adam walked over to me and put his arms around the two of us. "I know you can do it, Christina. You have mad skills."

I pulled away from him and gave him a smile that I hoped didn't look as sad as I felt.

"Do you want to play with Chris and get him ready for bed while I cook dinner? I'm making you a surprise."

"What's the surprise?" Adam said, taking Chris from me and pretending to look in the grocery bags I'd set on the counter.

"Get away, you," I said, laughing. "You'll have to wait."

As I seared the steaks, I thought more about my plan. Maybe if I could get some additional help and attract some donors, I could turn this thing around and get an extension from Mark. If they saw that people in the arts and business communities around Lockville believed in the company, they would have to buy in.

After dinner, I found myself sitting at the kitchen table, trying to work out the choreography for the second act. The White Swan Pas De Deux was giving me particular trouble. I just couldn't see it in my head: the innocence, the delicacy, the harmony of the two dancers. It wasn't like trying to choreograph something for a single dancer or even a group of dancers. There is something particularly challenging about a dance for two. Adam was reading to Chris when the phone rang. I figured it was Anna calling with some new drama about her mother or her latest love interest. Anna had moved back to Lockville at the same time as we had, not because she was getting married but because she had to take care of her mother, who was dying of cancer. Of course, she'd been dying for a few years and kept making miraculous recoveries, and Anna was beginning to chafe under the constant care her mother required. She didn't want her mother to die, but her ability to find a suitable man while she was knee-deep in chemotherapy treatments, cooking, managing her mother's medicines, and getting outside nurses to come in was nonexistent. The situation was killing her love life. Or so she said. In my opinion, she had plenty of suitable suitors at her door; despite working full time, being in the company, and taking care of her mom, she had a surprising amount of free time.

I was just steeling myself to give her another pep talk when I picked up the phone, and I was a little disappointed when I hard a man ask, "Is this Christina?"

"We're not buying this evening," I said. "Please take us off your list."

He chuckled. "I'm not selling you anything. Well, I am, but I think you'll like it."

I felt a little put off. "I'm sorry?" I said. "Do I know you?"

"I'm being rude," he said. He had a smooth, deep voice. It was almost sexy. "My name is Buck Johnson. I serve on the board of the Lockville Symphony, and I was just talking to Mark Turner about your company."

My throat tightened. "Oh?" I said. So now Mark Turner was running me down in front of everybody. And in front of Buck Johnson, of all people. I'd heard about him and had seen him at some arts-organization fund raisers. He had come into money at a young age and was a fierce supporter of the arts. He was a heavy hitter in our little community.

I wasn't sure I was up to talking with him.

He laughed. "Look, I know Mark can be a little bit…blunt, but he has good intentions. He called me to ask if I could help get your ballet company on the right track."

I hesitated. It was my company, and I wanted to get things going myself. I needed to prove that I could do this.

But still, what harm could it do to talk with this man?

Plenty, as it turned out. But I'm not psychic at all, and I read nothing more into the man's voice than the fact that he was a smooth, sophisticated businessman.

"Sure," I said. "It'd be interesting to talk with you and see what ideas you might have."

"Good," he said. "Mark says you have rehearsal tomorrow down at the center. Do you mind if I stop by and check things out?"

"Not at all," I said smoothly.

We made arrangements, and I hung up the phone, feeling a little agitated. I couldn't say why. Surely having someone come in who knew the arts would be a good thing.

I walked into the bathroom and sat on the toilet, watching Adam splash around with Chris. "Who was that?" he asked.

"Salesperson," I lied. I didn't really want to get into the whole thing with Mark Turner and the fact that I sucked as the manager of a fledgling non-profit. And then there was somebody else poking his nose into my business.

"I hate it when they call so late at night," said Adam.

"Me too."

The rest of the night went quickly. By the time I got Chris to bed, I was so exhausted that I went to bed by myself. My husband stayed up into the night working on some report due for work, and I didn't hear him come into bed.

In the brightly lit dance studio the next day, the dancers took their places on the wooden floor of the studio, which was marked by tape. I started the new music we had picked out: a pop version of the first dance that was just daring enough to encourage some new freedom.

I stood at the front, watching the dancers in the mirror, and started swaying my hips.

"We're going to get a little creative," I called above the beat. "Let's see if you gals can keep up with me."

I was the same age as them, but I had not had many injuries in my career, and I hoped that what I had lacked in practice during my few years of marriage and childrearing, I had made up for in experience. I had been trained by some of the most exacting teachers in New York—teachers who had studied with Mr. Balanchine himself.

"And reach. And hold. And turn," I called. The studio was chilly, but sweat had already trickled down my neck and cleavage and into my black leotard. I had to blow some hair out of my face. I wished I had taken a little bit more care pulling my hair into a bun. I was hitting every step with power and precision, and it felt good. I loosened my hips a bit and did a few moves straight out of *Chicago*.

"And double. And hold," I called.

Jill, a dancer with long legs and a bouncy ginger ponytail, had no problems keeping up. She had studied jazz in LA before she had moved to Lockville. I knew I could count on her as well as a couple of the other younger ones who had also done some competitive couples' dancing. A couple members of the troupe seemed to fall behind, and I walked over to stop the music. I heard a few murmurs of complaints but nothing serious.

"I know this is a bit of stretch for you," I said. "But these moves will begin to feel more natural as we keep practicing."

Anna, who had been working with the male dancers in a separate space, came up to me at that moment and tugged my arm. "I need to talk to you."

"Now?" I said, raising my eyebrows.

"There's someone here to see you," she whispered. She jerked her head to the side. "It's him," she hissed.

"You're jumpy as a cat in a room full of rocking chairs," I joked, but when I followed her gaze, I shut up and stood a little taller.

It was Buck Johnson. I had only just glimpsed him at events, but close up and by the light of day, he was surprisingly handsome and young looking.

I had been planning on seeking out donors, but maybe this was my lucky day.

My hand flew to my hair. "How do I look?" I said out of the corner of my mouth to Anna.

"Like the director of one of the hottest up-and-coming ballet companies in the state," said Anna. "Go get him, tiger."

"Can you take over here?" I asked.

"Sure," she said. "What are best friends for?"

I walked over to the visitor, who was standing by the entrance of the studio, taking it all in, and looking awkward, as if he might bolt at any moment.

He gave me a shy grin. "Christina, uh, I'm Buck Johnson. I hope I'm not imposing."

He took my hand and gave me a kiss on the top of it European-style. He gave me the once-over but then quickly looked away.

I felt self-conscious, standing there in my form-fitting leotard and dance tights. My dance shoes had seen better seasons. He said nothing more, and I rushed to fill in the silence with talk. "Well, Mr. Johnson, thanks for coming. This is our group, and we meet several times each week. I'm working to choreograph a condensed version of the ballet *Swan Lake*. It's a lot of work, but it's fun work." I paused and then added, "It's my passion. Is it also yours?"

I folded my arms and smiled. Adam would have been proud of me for being so very assertive.

Buck looked a little nervous. "Um, of course," he said, "I read this piece in the *Business Journal* about your grand scheme to build a first-rate ballet company in Lockville. As it happens, I'm a supporter of the arts."

I looked at him dumbly. He wasn't what I had expected; he was quite charming and a little awkward.

He cleared his throat and nodded at some chairs at the end of the rehearsal studio. "Can we talk? I'd like to know how your goals for this effort are progressing. What's the plan, and what do you need to get things going?"

We walked over to the chairs, and my heart was racing. If I could put together a coherent pitch, I thought, perhaps we could be in business. But then my honesty, or perhaps my timidity, got the best of me.

"We don't have a detailed plan yet, and we don't have any money," I said. I was talking, but I wanted to pinch myself and start over. "Right now, we're just taking it week by week."

I hesitated. He was looking at me strangely. "Go on," he said.

"We're hoping the community will support us. We need so many things… I don't know where to start."

He said nothing, but he looked up to the ceiling and put his hands together as if he were praying. In fact, he looked rather pained.

I sat very still, watching Anna practice with the dancers. I concentrated on watching to see if the new choreography we had created really took the particular movement to the next level. Was the music perhaps just a bit too slow, I wondered. I purposely did not look at Buck Johnson, though out of the corner of my eye, I could see him moving his lips as though he were muttering to himself. I didn't want to seem too eager.

Finally, he turned to me, his expression inscrutable, though his ears were a little pink.

"Pardon me for asking, but do you at least have a business plan?"

"No," I said, slowly exhaling. I smiled cheerfully, hoping that it would distract him.

"Insurance? Do you carry insurance?" He smiled apologetically.

"Actually," I said, "we haven't crossed that bridge yet."

I made myself look him square in the eye, even though I was sure I was blushing bright red. I've never been much of a salesperson, but I wanted to at least appear confident. Adam said I wasn't much of a bluffer and advised me never to play poker, but I had to try or watch the company—my dream—die.

Buck Johnson took a deep breath. "You've bitten off way more than you can chew," he said.

"We're going to make it," I said smoothly. "With or without funding."

Buck got up and paced around with his hands in his pockets. He appeared to be deep in thought. "This is a long shot," he said. "I've been involved in supporting arts communities and nonprofits before. I've even served on the advisory board for the symphony. And frankly, it seems like you need to lay the foundation for making this company work. "

I stood too, feeling the knots in the back of my neck tighten. I reached out my hand toward his, and he looked at it wordlessly and then grinned and clasped it.

"Well, thanks for checking us out," I said. I felt as though he surely wasn't going to fund us.

Buck gripped my hand tighter and didn't let go.

"Christina, you don't understand," he said. "What I'm trying to say is that I'm prepared to come on board as your business manager."

I stood there, feeling shock and relief roll over me.

"Say something," he said. "Before I feel awkward."

"Yes," I said. "Yes! Thank you!"

He released my hand and ran his fingers through his hair. I sensed it was gesture caused by habit. He regarded the dancers.

"Why don't we plan a meeting for someplace that's a little less distracting," he said. "I can't hear myself think in here."

"Certainly," I said.

He pulled out a business card, scribbled something on it, and pressed it into my hand.

"There's my private number," he said. "But I'll give you a call."

I stood, speechless. He smiled and said, "This is going to be great, isn't it? Bringing some culture to this city—putting it on the map."

He gave me a mock bow. And then he was gone.

I stood there, gaping after him. Anna came up to me and clutched my arm. She was doing a lot of that lately. I knew I would bruise, so it was a good thing I wasn't in the show.

"Are we saved?" she said.

"I hope so," I said.

"Good," she said. Then she gave me a steady inquiring look. "Are you sure he's trustworthy?"

I told her who he was, and she said she had heard of him. She already figured that out.

"He seems legitimate, so you need to show up with some ideas," she said. "Let's go to tea."

"Okay, let me close up here first," I said.

I wrapped everything up with the dancers and told them we were going to break a little early. I thanked them for all their hard work, though, to be honest, I wasn't sure that our principals had had their hearts in the practice. I thought I saw Michael rolling his eyes, but when I shot him a look, he merely winked at me. I froze when he did it, because I didn't know what to do. Did Balanchine have this many problems with his dancers? I didn't know many women dance directors, and I was beginning to wonder if I had overreached. Perhaps my mother was right, and I needed to just appreciate where I was and concentrate on raising Chris.

I talked myself into being glum by the time Anna and I reached the teahouse. It was tucked into a corner off of Broadway—a different one, not the one in New York. But still, its location on that fantastic namesake cheered me. We stood at the front entryway waiting for the host to seat us. Since it was midafternoon, plenty of ladies were out with their friends, eating watercress-and-cucumber sandwiches and drinking tea in tiny cups with flowers and gold trim. The murmur in the vast room sounded like a distant waterfall, and I smoothed the wrap skirt I had thrown on over my dance leotard, feeling as though it didn't quite measure up. Everyone there had on a hat, and a few wore gloves.

"They'll think we're hippies," I whispered to Anna. "Maybe we should have gone to get a hamburger."

"Nonsense," she said. "Anyway, maybe we can shake them up a bit."

"I don't much feel like that," I said.

"Sure you do," she said, giving me a knowing look. "Otherwise, you wouldn't be doing such a risqué production of the ballet."

"Oh, hell's bells," I said, my stomach sinking. "I'm not doing this to shock people."

The hostess gave us a surreptitious sniff when he crossed our names off of the waiting list, but he seated us.

"Sure you are," said Anna. "You really are a women's libber at heart."

I didn't want to encourage her, so I said nothing. I ordered my tea, and Anna managed to talk the waiter into bringing her a highball from the bar.

"We're going to get kicked out," I said.

"Nonsense," she said. "Now tell me about Buck Johnson."

I told her about how he wanted to get together to talk business and about how he had actually volunteered to help us. "Can you believe it?"

"Yes," said Anna. "Now what's he like? He's a handsome fellow, do you need me to help you reel him in?"

"He seems shy," I said. "I think you'd scare him off."

"I can be demure," she said, pursing her lips and batting her eyes.

"I can handle it," I said.

"You might not be able to," she said, suddenly blunt.

"Why do you say that?" I asked.

"Because he likes you," she said. "I saw the way he was looking at you. And I can read body language."

"Body language?" I asked.

"Yes. It was clear from his posture and the way he was so nervous that he digs you."

I took a sip of my tea. Clearly Anna had men on her mind.

"I'm a married woman, and this is purely a business proposition," I said. "Don't be scandalous; it doesn't suit you."

"It suits me just fine," she said. "Anyway, if you want to disregard what I saw, go ahead. But I think you ought to let me handle any negotiations with him. I can handle that tiger." She gave me an evil grin.

"Now stop that," I said. "This is simply business, and it's important business. We need this business."

"Well, don't say I didn't warn you," she said.

"What about your boyfriend?" I asked her.

She just smiled. I sighed, and we continued to talk about the company, hashing out some of the details of what we needed to cover in rehearsals. All the while, a little voice in the back of my head wondered if it was a good idea to do business with this man and if my husband would like my working with him. But he had seemed shy and respectful, and I ignored it.

Four

The Bar

Buck

THE MINUTE I WALKED OUT OF THE REHEARSAL SPACE, I had a spring in my step. Christina was even lovelier in person than she was in the newspaper. I knew I was smitten, but I ignored the signs because, frankly, I didn't care. I needed something fresh and new in my life—someone who appreciated what I had to offer and could heal the pain of my recent loss.

Christina had been so perfect, so beautiful, standing there in the rehearsal space, that I ached to hold her. I wanted to see her dance, and I wondered if she ever would dance for me.

It was with those thoughts running around in my mind that I returned to my office, shut the door, and dialed up Frank Wichman.

Frank was a buddy of mine from college who had done quite well for himself in the business world. He had struck it rich with some great oil investments down in Texas and had recently invested in transistors and electronics. I knew that if anybody could get the funds quickly for the ballet company, it would be him. I wanted to move on it because the sooner I had the funds, the more time I could spend with Christina.

I called him on the phone and told him that I had a great deal on the table and needed his help. He didn't hesitate. I'd bailed him out of a tight spot or two, and he knew my instincts were good.

"So this ballet company sounds like a great deal," he said. "You know I love the arts."

I laughed. "Thanks, buddy," I said.

"But I want to know if there's a dame involved."

That last one hit me like a sucker punch. If anybody knew me, it was Frank. So I had to come clean. "Yes, and she's a beauty. Really classy lady."

"Is she worth it?"

I didn't need to wait to answer that.

"Yes, she is," I said. "Definitely worth it."

"Let me have my people check her out," he said. "At one hundred fifty thousand dollars, you're asking for a pretty penny."

I hung up the phone and let myself feel victorious. I liked making deals, and I liked making things work. Once Frank checked her out and saw that it was legitimate, I was sure he would fund the project. He had to.

Still, I felt like I needed to blow off a little steam, and I decided to head over to talk to my favorite bartender.

Within a couple of hours, I was nursing my…my third? Fourth? I'd lost track because Zack, bless him, just kept them coming. My mind kept going back to Christina. She was so beautiful, with that black full-body leotard that showed off her figure, a nice high rear, and perfect breasts. She had fine features and big eyes, and I confess I felt a certain satisfaction at the way she looked at me when I offered to help with her company. She was also utterly, impeccably charming and perfectly poised. My mother, had she been alive, would have loved her. She would have fit right in with the circles my family had run in. Hell, my father might even have liked her.

I took a sip of my drink and chuckled to myself. I liked the chase. It was true. I was a man who liked to experience the finer things in life—food, drink, art, women—and I turned my fine taste and disposable income into collecting. My ex-wife had accused me of being shallow, but the fact is that she just didn't understand me like she should have, and to be honest, I had married her before I had known my own worth.

This dancer, though, was something else. She was a woman who would appreciate everything I had to offer.

"What's her name?" Zack asked. He stood in front of me, rinsing and wiping out glasses with a practiced flourish.

I snorted. "Whose name?"

"You get that same look on your face whenever you're onto someone hot. Kinda like a cat that just caught himself a nice juicy canary," said Zack.

I knew Zack wouldn't let up. That's one of the things I liked about him. I'd been coming to the Good Times Club for at least five years and considered Zack a good friend, though we hadn't done anything together except go golfing a couple of times. Zack was about the same age as me and was an "out-there" guy. He wasn't like the stuffed shirts in the Lockville Chamber of Commerce and in the Arts Council. Zack understood that I sometimes liked to party.

The Good Times Club itself was a little dated, with its dark-wooden floors and booths that hadn't been redecorated since the big bands were touring regularly. It attracted lots of classy single women who were not immune to my charm. It didn't attract too many regulars, since it was attached to a hotel and people came in and out. I liked my anonymity. My work was high profile, and I was a big shot in arts circles. The town, which had three hundred thousand people, was pretty small; it was nothing like Manhattan, where I had grown up.

"I guess I need to talk with you about my latest obsession, then," I said.

"That's part of my job," said Zack. "You come into my place and drink my spirits, and I help you with your problems. No extra charge." Zack swept my drink away, and another appeared. "Her name?" he prompted.

"Christina," I said. "I walk into her dance studio, and there she is, in this hot little black leotard. Zack, she is stunning. Just stunning."

"Go on," he said.

"She has this perfect body—curves in all the right places. Calves that won't stop. And the way she moves."

"What do you mean?"

"Zack, you ever been with a professional dancer?"

Zack grinned and leaned against the bar. "I've been with a stripper or two, if that's what you mean."

I frowned. "The way she moves is very"—I searched for the right word—"poised."

Zack's eyebrows shot up.

I leaned forward. "And Zack, based on my observations during our brief meeting, she's totally unaware of her sexuality."

I stopped for a moment and realized that I really, really had to have her. Christina. She had had a strange effect on me—one that I didn't quite understand but already craved. I felt a stirring inside me—a longing I hadn't felt for a long time. I wouldn't have admitted it to anybody, but sometimes, despite the fact that I was living the high life, I felt like something big was missing.

Zack was talking to me. I snapped back into focus. "So, Buck, you know how to have your way with women." His blue eyes looked amused. "What's the problem?"

Out of the corner of my eye, I saw a pretty brunette sit down at the far end of the bar. Our eyes met in the mirror, and she smiled.

"Well, a conquest usually takes time, and it's not always successful."

"Sure," said Zack. "Uncertainty is part of the fun."

"Also, it's going to be difficult to work with her on the development of the company—hard to concentrate," I admitted. I was surprised to hear myself blurt out, "I've never gotten so wrapped up in a woman before."

His eyes narrowed. "You're really into this chick?"

"Don't know," I said, putting on my poker face. "I haven't sampled the goods."

"Tell you what," he said. "Have her over to lunch at the Classic Hotel. Have a couple of glasses of wine, and then invite her to a room where you have something important for her to review. Important financial papers. Fund-raising plans. Stuff like that."

"Then?"

Zack grinned. "And then have sex." He leaned over and lowered his voice. "With your skill and charm with the ladies, she'll be yours for the taking. Like low-hanging fruit."

My stomach tightened, but part of me filled with joy. Yes, I had to have her. In my exuberance, I smiled at the lady at the end of the bar. She smiled back.

Then I realized that a liaison with Christina wasn't a done deal.

"What if she refuses?" I asked Zack.

"Have sex regardless," said Zack. "She'll enjoy it, and you'll be on your way."

"I don't generally need to force myself on a lady."

Zack's grin looked a little more mercenary than cheery. "Going to a hotel room with you is implied consent. She would have zero recourse."

At that point, I felt a presence beside me. I turned. It was a woman dressed in a miniskirt and white boots. "You two appear to be in a deep discussion," she said, wagging her finger at both of us and touching my chest ever so softly. "You got my curiosity up. What're you two talking about?"

"We're doing some business," I said smoothly. I let my eyes travel down her neck to her breasts, which were bouncy and big, then all the way down to her toes and back up. I realized I wasn't interested.

"Aren't you forward?" she said, giggling.

"Not really," I said. "Look, I don't mean to be rude, but I'm in a relationship right now."

"All the good ones are taken," she said, glowering slightly before walking away.

When she was out of earshot, I said to Zack, "What I'd really like is an ongoing relationship with her. But she might refuse me. That would be hard for me to deal with."

Zack lowered his voice. "I have a plan B to deal with that eventuality. Remember Britney, my assistant bartender?"

Sure, I remembered her. It wasn't hard to remember a knockout who had worked there for about two years. I hadn't seen her for about half a year, which was a pity.

"I was never able to score with her in spite of every approach I tried." Zack made a sad face.

"No," I said in mock horror. I was beginning to enjoy his story.

"About a year ago, it was discovered that the bar was experiencing an ongoing cash shortage. Maybe fifty dollars a week or about five hundred over a two-month period."

I whistled. "That's a pretty chunk of change. What'd you do?"

"So I mounted one of those surveillance cameras in the bar and caught her red-handed on tape, pocketing money." Zack smacked his hand on the bar. "I gave her a choice: one-time sex or get charged with theft."

"And she chose jail?"

Zack rolled his eyes. "We had sex, she enjoyed it, and it became consensual. You see what I'm saying? You need a scheme."

I downed my drink. "So you're suggesting some form of coercion?"

Zack didn't answer me. He merely pulled a camera out from behind the bar and gave it to me.

"You have a twisted mind," I murmured.

"Who has a twisted mind?" The lady with the white boots was back. She settled herself into the barstool beside me and crossed her legs. I sighed.

"Our bartender," I said. "He's a dark soul."

"I like dark," she said. "What's with the camera?"

"That's my business," I said evenly. "Enjoy your evening."

I took a wad of bills out of my wallet and threw them on the counter. "Keep the change, buddy."

"Buck, let me know how it goes," said Zack. "And remember—my fee is that I'm entitled."

"I don't know about that," I said dryly.

Behind me, I heard Zack yell, "You're welcome!"

I drove home, and the instant I hit the door, I went straight for the phone and dialed Mark Turner. He didn't seem surprised that I'd called him at home, probably because we'd worked on projects together before, and he knew I was the type of person who didn't like waiting around. I told him my plans and asked him for a reprieve.

Mark seemed surprised. "So you're sure that you think this company is going to be viable?"

"Yes, I am," I said. "And I like Christina. I think she's got a good head on her shoulders."

Mark was silent awhile. "I don't know what you're up to, but I trust your judgment. She has more time."

"Thanks, Mark," I said. "You won't regret it."

Five

The Call

Christina

"YOU'RE LEAVING AGAIN?"

That had come out a little more petulant than I had wanted it to. I was sitting in bed hugging a pillow, admiring Adam as he changed out of his work clothes, and trying not to sound shrill about the prospect of another business trip. He stood there in his underwear, seeming not to be bothered by the chill, hanging his pants up. He rolled his belt up and put it away. Then he looked at me with mischief. "You admiring the goods, lady?"

"No," I stammered, feeling myself blush. "Yes. Maybe?"

He walked over to the bed, jumped in it, pulled the pillow out of my arms, took both of my hands, which were clenched, and unfolded them.

"You're tense," he said. "What's wrong?"

I felt myself tear up. I didn't want to burden him—didn't want to tell him that I missed him terribly when he went on those long trips. I couldn't tell him that I missed the camaraderie of being part of the corps and that now, since I was the director, I felt somehow separate from it. I couldn't tell him I didn't know what I was doing with the ballet company and that I was afraid it was all going to slip through my fingers.

Instead I sniffled and said, "I have a donor lined up who's willing to help with the business end of things." My voice sounded quivery. I didn't want to sound like such a baby. I bet his office girls didn't boohoo like that. I lifted my chin and wiped my eyes.

Adam stroked my hair and smiled. "You make that sound like a bad thing."

"It's not," I said. "It's a good thing."

My darling husband pulled me into his arms and kissed the top of my head and down my neck until my pulse quickened. I caught my breath.

"I'll be back soon. It's only a few days, and I'm just going to California."

"A few days is forever," I said, turning my head and catching him full on the lips. Then I tasted beer. I pulled back.

"Did you stop by the bar on the way home?"

Adam grinned. "Caught me. Erick and I had a few beers after work."

I tried to smile, but the effort felt fake.

"You don't mind, do you? It's just some hangout time with the fellows."

Just then, I heard the Chris calling from his room. "I don't mind, dear," I said, slipping out of his arms and out of bed. "You need some time with your friends."

I kissed him on the cheek, forcing myself to linger, to be tender, but I couldn't meet his eyes. I didn't want to start blubbering. "Baby's up!" I said brightly.

"Aw, Christina, don't be that way!" I heard Adam say. I kept walking down the hall and wiping the tears that were flowing once again down my cheeks.

"It's okay, honey!" I called back. "I'm not upset. I'm just a little tired."

I walked into the nursery and picked up Chris, who had already escaped from his crib and was sitting on the floor, looking at a board book. He was outgrowing the bed after sprouting up so much even in the last few weeks. I mentally added "buy a toddler bed" to my list of things to do.

"Mommy," he cried. "Read to me."

I sat down on the floor and pulled him onto my lap. I loved his sweet smell and the feel of his little body pressed against mine. "Patty-cake, patty-cake, baker's man," I said, pulling him into a game of patty-cake. He squealed in delight.

Adam walked into the room and sat on the floor beside us. I could tell that he was doing his best to make sure I felt comfortable, but he didn't even ask me who the donor was. I wondered if the ballet was as important to him as he made it out to be, or if he was just humoring me.

I decided that I wouldn't be clingy and would wait for him to call me in the evenings when he was done with work. And I would be fully prepared for my meeting with Mr. Johnson. I idly wondered what I could wear that would make me seem very professional and businesslike, and not like the washed-out ballerina I feared I was becoming.

"You seem like you're feeling better," Adam remarked, leaning in to me.

"Yes," I said, looking him straight in the eyes. "I'm feeling much better."

"Good," he said. "That's what I like to hear."

That night we made love, and it was so tender and sweet that I could hardly bear the thought of his leaving. I lay in bed awake long after I heard his steady snoring. I told myself that everything was going to be okay.

The next day, Adam kissed Chris and me good-bye and drove himself to the airport. He would arrive at San Francisco in the afternoon.

I sat for a long time at the kitchen table sipping my tea, trying to put my head around all the things we needed to prepare for the show, and trying not to think about Adam's absence. If I filled my days, they would not loom empty in front of me. And I had legitimate stuff with which to fill those days.

The ringing of the phone made me jump. "Jeez, Christina. Get a hold of yourself," I muttered to myself. I answered the phone. "Hello?"

"Hello, Christina, this is Buck Johnson calling."

My heart started pounding. I really wanted to make sure my plan fell together. I cleared my throat nervously. "Hello, Buck—it's great to hear from you."

"Christina, I want to get things moving with the ballet company. I just spoke to Mark Turner, and he's agreed to lift your end-of-the month suspension. You and I are going to put on a great show."

Wow, this guy is a take-action man, I thought.

"Yes, that sounds great. I'll do whatever you want to do to get it going."

"That's good, Christina," said Buck. His voice sounded approving. "We need to prepare a business plan. There are several parts of the plan that we need to develop together, including organization, administration, finances—you know, fund-raising."

My throat tightened. As a dancer, I had never developed a business plan before. In fact, I had just kind of gone with my intuition when we were planning our company and show. I felt a little foolish for not having gotten more involved with the details of the business end of things.

"Sounds great, Buck," I said.

"Could you meet with me at noon tomorrow for lunch?" he asked. His voice sounded pleasant.

I thought about it. Surely my mom could watch Chris for a little while.

"Yes, certainly," I said. The more I thought about it, the more it sounded like a great plan.

"Let's meet at the Classic Hotel," he said.

I'd gone there often with my mother and aunts, but mostly we went to the tearoom. They served a high tea complete with watercress sandwiches. "It's a date," I said, laughing nervously.

"Yes, a date," said Buck. I thought he sounded amused. "See you tomorrow, then."

After I hung up the phone, I did a little celebratory cha-cha around the kitchen. It felt good to move. It felt like we were going to be in business…if I could seal the deal.

On impulse, I called Anna.

"What's up, hon?" she asked.

"I just got a call from Buck Johnson."

"And?" asked Anna.

"We're meeting for lunch tomorrow to review a start-up plan for the company. He's going to raise money for us. Isn't that exciting?"

"Oh, Christina, that's so fantastic!" said Anna. "We might just get this company going and be able to perform once again." Then Anna's voice turned soft—almost pensive. "I know that you miss the dance, the music, and the curtain calls as much as I do."

I needed to cheer her up. "Yes, Anna. It'll be great."

"Anyway, you are so lucky," said Anna.

"Lucky how?"

"You're lucky you get to meet with Buck. He's pretty hot. It looked like he was flirting with you the other day."

I rolled my eyes. "I'm a married woman. He knows that."

"Humph," said Anna. "What if he comes on to you?"

"That's all you think about—men and sex!" I said. "Buck and I have a business relationship. And I have my handsome husband. So get your mind out of the gutter."

"Well, you never know," said Anna. "If he does, and you're not into it, let me know. I'm ready."

I laughed. "Well, I'll keep it mind."

"Seriously, I'll go if you don't want to. He's a catch."

I was amused by the idea of her and Buck together. That would never work out.

"I've got it handled," I said. "Thanks anyway."

When I hung up with Anna, I decided that I was going to impress the heck out of Mr. Buck Johnson. I might have been a neophyte when it came to running a business, but I knew dance. I just had to convince him that my ideas were worthwhile.

Six

The Distance

Adam

THE AIRPORT WAS BUSY DESPITE the fact that it was on the smaller side, and I was happy to shut the door of the business club and leave the blare of the planes being called over the loudspeakers behind me for the calm order of the lounge. I sat down at the bar and ordered a double martini—I'd be in the air awhile, and my meetings wouldn't be until the next morning—and felt my troubles slide away.

I watched the bartender, a woman sporting modest makeup and a navy-blue suit, make my drink, admiring how she shook it and dropped in a few olives to seal the deal before sliding it my way.

"Thanks," I said, sighing and rubbing my eyes. It had been a hard few weeks with Christina. She no longer seemed to sleep at night, instead tossing and turning and finally getting out of bed to slink around our house like a stray cat in the middle of the night. She seemed both distracted and clingy, and poor Chris had responded by being unusually fussy and clingy as well. Sometimes when I came home after work, dinner wasn't even made, and Chris was running around with a dirty face and dirty clothes. Christina didn't even seem to notice.

Sure, I'd had to work a lot at the firm to make it as high as I could on the corporate ladder, but Christina had known I'd be a company man when she married me.

She'd given up dancing at the ballet because we had needed to live in Lockville, and it just hadn't been possible to drive back and forth. She'd been very depressed, but I had convinced her that trying for a baby was just the medicine she had needed.

And having a baby had worked, for a while. But I'd had to work even harder at the company to ensure our financial stability, and she'd become even more withdrawn and listless.

One night last fall, we'd been sitting outside in the yard, enjoying an Indian-summer evening, and I'd recklessly suggested she start a ballet.

She had started it with a vengeance. But since things hadn't worked out as well as she'd expected them to, she appeared to have fallen back into her old helpless ways.

I felt a little exasperated just thinking about it. I sighed again, sipping my drink.

The lady bartender leaned over the bar and gazed at me with amusement. Her eyes were strikingly green, and I felt a flash of attraction for her, followed by a flash of guilt. What was I thinking?

"What's up, doc?" she asked. "You look like you've lost your best friend."

"Oh, it's nothing," I said lightly. I checked my watch and wondered if I had time for another martini. I had actually left for the airport earlier than I had needed to just to have some time to myself to think. I loved being a father and absolutely loved Chris to pieces, but in between Christina, her folks, the baby, and all the demands of work, I felt positively suffocated with responsibilities.

She quirked her lips in a pouty smile that looked undeniably attractive. "That's what they all say," she said. "Does your flight leave soon, or do you have time for another?"

"I have a few hours," I said without thinking.

Her smile grew broader. "Ah, it's your wife, then."

I reddened, but she pretended not to notice, instead merely whisking my glass away and replacing it momentarily with a fresh one with even more olives in it.

She leaned over once again, giving me a good shot at her breasts, which were suddenly showing through her crisp white blouse. Had her uniform been so tight earlier? I tugged at my tie.

"Let me guess," she said. "You have a new baby."

"Well, he's hardly a baby anymore," I said in protest.

The way she laughed made me realize that she'd deliberately provoked me, and I had fallen for it.

"Still not sleeping through the night?" she purred.

"He is," I said. "It's my wife who isn't. She roams around all night, keeping me up."

She gave me a curious look, and something inside me snapped. I thought, what the hell? So I told her about my wife and the ballet. Christina would have been really sore if she had known how much I was talking about our life, but it all poured out of me at once. Really, it was as though someone had popped my cork.

It was a relief, to be honest.

I told her that she'd started a ballet company and that it seemed to be floundering because she had no administrative or managerial experience. And just as I said that, I felt guilty because I could have—no, should have—been helping her with all of it. But I hadn't. It was as though I had made the suggestion and then had somehow begrudged it and was sitting on the sidelines, waiting for her to fail. What a heel I was.

And the cute bartender was looking at me with her nose a bit wrinkled nose as though she knew what a heel I was.

I felt like I couldn't get a break. I rolled my eyes and waved my hands dismissively.

"We've got a good marriage," I said.

Priscilla, the bartender, gave me a doubtful look and shook her head. "I guess you know what you're doing, then," she said. "I see all types in my line of work, and it isn't my job to judge them."

I nodded as though I wasn't the judgmental type either. For the briefest moment, though, I thought about cancelling my business trip and rushing back to the house to be with my beautiful wife. I realized. I could really surprise her and all that.

As I was mulling it over, she leaned back over again and whispered, "Just to be safe, I'd woo her a bit. Send her flowers and the like."

"I will," I said, laughing. "Thanks for your advice."

But the suggestion, for whatever reason, had the opposite effect on me. I decided not to go home. I dismissed the idea of wooing my wife. She was, after all, already mine.

On the flight and at the hotel later, I thought about our conversation and about Christina's dalliance with her ballet company and rationalized my position even more. We were fine. It was just a bump in the road. If I bailed Christina out of her troubles with the ballet, she'd never learn to do things on her own. If I rushed in, it might even impact our marriage negatively.

Seven

THE ENCOUNTER

Christina

I DROPPED CHRIS OFF AT MOM'S AND WAS TRYING NOT TO feel flustered as I drove downtown and found a parking space. I paused when I got out of the car to admire the Classic Hotel, which was one of those grand buildings from an earlier era. My mother and her friends had taken me there plenty of times when I was a kid. The building was four stories tall and brick with arched windows and a green-tiled roof. A stately veranda ran around the building. I loved history, and I liked the idea of meeting there because I hoped to make a new kind of history in Lockville with my ballet company. I squared my shoulders.

Inside, I walked through the lobby with its elegant cherry staircase and into the hotel restaurant, where I found Buck Johnson already seated at a table. He stood when he saw me, his eyes gleaming. He looked me up and down. I felt myself flush slightly at his scrutiny; I had dressed in what I had hoped was a sophisticated, businesslike outfit: a white blouse that was slightly sheer but not too provocative, my favorite blue skirt, hose, and high heels.

"Christina," he said, extending his hand to me. "What a delight to see you!"

I took his hand, gripped it firmly, and shook it up and down once. "Thanks so much, Buck. It's kind of you to take an interest in the ballet company."

"My pleasure," he said. "It's certainly the kind of project I enjoy getting involved in."

He pulled out my chair, and we settled in at the table. We perused the menu. When the waiter came, I ordered a chicken-salad sandwich and a cup of tea. Buck frowned. "This is a celebratory moment—an auspicious beginning for the ballet in Lockville. We should have a glass of wine to celebrate."

"Oh," I said. "Certainly." If he was going to lend his considerable expertise and finances to the ballet project, it wouldn't do to look like some sort of prude or teetotaler. Besides, a glass of wine wasn't going to hurt anything. I thought it might even help me relax a little—and I did feel a little intimidated.

When the wine arrived, Buck raised his glass and looked me in the eyes as though he were trying to divine my deepest secrets. "Here's to our collaboration."

"To our collaboration," I echoed him, meeting his glass with mine. I took a sip of wine that turned into more of a gulp. I wished I wasn't so nervous, but I felt like so much was at stake, and we had to receive funding.

"So," Buck said, putting his glass on the table and leaning forward. "You're young to be so accomplished and talented."

"I'm hardly that," I said. I was already beginning to feel flushed from the wine. I wished I had taken the time to eat some breakfast instead of spending so much time on my clothes, makeup, and hair.

"Well, I think so," said Buck. "I read the article about you and your company in the *Journal* and was quite smitten with your project. I confess that that's why I sought you out."

"Well, thank you," I said.

"So tell me all about yourself."

"I'm hardly the subject at hand," I said, laughing uneasily. "I'd rather discuss the company."

Buck nodded. "Business it is."

Just then, the waitress delivered our lunch. We settled into eating and talking about dance. I was happy to learn that we had a lot in common. He had been a New York boy as well, and he'd grown up going to the ballet, the opera, and the museum a lot, which had driven his business interests. Plus, he was such a great listener. He kept laughing at my little jokes and puns, my observations about the New York arts culture, and even the way I gushed over Balanchine. (As if nobody had ever gushed over Balanchine before.) I felt myself start to open up.

That feeling made me perhaps too bold. "What about Mrs. Johnson?" I said. "Does she like the arts, too?"

I hadn't known my new sponsor for very long, but I could tell by the way he stopped eating, by the way he held his fork in the air with a bite of food on it, and by the stiff way he sat that I had struck a nerve. His expression gave nothing away, but I thought I detected a hint of sadness, perhaps even remorse, in his eyes.

"There is no Mrs. Johnson," he finally said, putting his fork down and patting his face with his napkin. He spoke stiffly. "At least not anymore."

"I'm sorry," I said, feeling the heat of embarrassment flush in my face.

"My mother—Mrs. Johnson—passed away of breast cancer when I was twenty-one," he said briskly. "There has not been a 'Mrs. Johnson' since then who could hold a candle to her."

He sat there, looking balefully at me, but I decided not to challenge him. I had stepped in it enough for one day, and there was still the business of the ballet to be discussed. I did wonder why a man of his status who was good-looking, cultured, and obviously successful hadn't married, but I didn't think it seemly to ask. I would come to regret my decision to not pry further into his personal life at that very moment, because I didn't realize then what the lack of a partner in his life signified or how much it would impact me.

"You must miss her," I murmured.

"Every day," he said. "But life goes on. As it should."

We continued to talk during the rest of the meal, but the mood had been spoiled. While Buck was gracious and, on the surface, affable, he seemed a bit distant. His mood had worked me up into a state of worry by that time, and I was sure that his interest in the ballet had waned because of my big mouth, so I was relieved when he suggested we get on to business.

I was so nervous that I didn't notice that the restaurant had been emptied of all of the other customers. The manager came over with our bill. "I'm sorry," he said. "But the restaurant is closing up for the afternoon. We need to get ready for a special event. Otherwise, you could linger for as long as you wish."

"That's okay," Buck said. "We're going to go upstairs to finish our conference."

It was only when we stood at the elevator that I asked him what we needed to take care of.

"I have a pile of paper work for us to look at, and it will be easier for us to focus on the important issues if we're not distracted."

When he said "upstairs," I had automatically assumed there would be conference rooms. A voice in my mind scolded me: *Christina, this is not a good idea.* I ignored that voice; I was always feeling a bit anxious about something since I'd become a mother. There's nothing like running around after a toddler and keeping him from hurting himself or choking on something to put you on constant alert. I was just being a worrywart.

I wish I had taken that niggling feeling more seriously.

When Buck stood before a regular room and took out a key, I balked.

"What's this?" I said.

He turned the key in the lock.

"It's where I conduct my top-level secret business meetings," he joked, smiling at me. He did have a megawatt smile.

"But this is a regular room," I said dumbly.

"This, my dear Christina, is *not* a regular room," he said.

He opened the door, stepped just inside, and bowed to me in an over-the-top manner, holding his arm out in a flourish.

"Madame," he said.

I gave a gasp and walked into the room. It was not just a regular room. It was a full-blown suite with rich, paneled walls, a golden chandelier, and golden carpets. The windows were framed by lush brocaded drapes and the couches were a fine pale leather with dark-wood appointments. A fireplace took up one end of the sitting area. It had a stunning white-marble mantle and was flanked by four ornately carved half-naked women formed from the same marble. I estimated the fireplace was from the 1890s, which was about the time the hotel had been built. I walked closer to the fireplace to get a better look at the painting above it. It pictured Diana on the hunt with an entourage of nymphs, and sylphs. A dying white stag had one of her arrows protruding from it, and its face bore a look of agony.

"Is that a…" I asked, groping for the name of a lesser-known but well-respected artist of that era whose paintings had recently become popular among collectors and the well heeled.

"Yes," Buck said, grinning rakishly. "I thought this would please you."

I walked around the room, letting my hand wander over the massive oak partner's desk, which had some of the finest burling and inlay work I had seen. It held reams of paper, envelopes, folders, and an old-fashioned manual typewriter. I walked into the kitchenette, if one could use that diminutive term for something so massive. It had been updated with sleek cupboards and marble countertops that echoed the marble in the fireplace. A bottle of wine sat chilling in a silver ice bucket.

I studiously avoided the bedroom and the massive four-poster bed that sat in the far section of the room, which was separated from the rest of it by half-open curtains also of some sort of lustrous brocade.

"This looks like a museum," I finally said. "It's exquisite."

Buck simply looked smug and pulled out a chair.

"Sit," he said, tapping the back of the chair. "Look over that pile of papers. I'll get us some libations."

I hesitated a moment before sitting down. My gaze went around the room again, and I noted many items that had to have been personal, like silver-framed family photos on the end table; an ornate Spanish acoustic guitar leaning casually against one of the chairs, and a hall tree with jackets, sweaters, scarves, and umbrellas. I suddenly realized that Buck spent a lot of time there.

It didn't seem like it was proper for Buck to be entertaining me in the suite, even as tastefully appointed as it was, even if it was his home-away-from home or whatever it was. I felt like I had entered Batman's secret lair high above the city of Lockville. Who was this man?

I knew, with a sense of discomfort, that I would be unable to tell Adam that we had met there simply because Adam would not have approved.

So what if Adam didn't approve? He would have hated the place—would have called it stuffy and pretentious. My darling husband preferred modern architecture, with its lack of ornamentation and nod to austerity and utility.

And then I felt a little bristle. It wasn't the nineteenth century, and I wasn't living inside some sort of Edith Wharton book. I was a modern, liberated woman. I could work, I could drive, I could vote, I could drink, and I could run a company. I could even join the old boy's network and smoke cigars, if I so desired.

In fact, Buck clearly was one of the old boys. I was joining the network. I was in.

Buck walked over, sat down next to me, and poured us each a glass of wine before handing me mine with a flourish. He was handsome.

"So, I want you to tell me all about yourself, beginning with your childhood and ending with, say, us sitting here at the Classic Hotel." He smiled broadly. "I would be honored to know more about you. You, Christina, are a treasure."

I felt a little taken aback, and then I felt flattered. The wine was going to my head, so maybe I talked too much. I told him about my childhood, my early attraction to the ballet, and the finishing school I had attended for about a year, where I had learned how to host a social event, how to write thank-you notes, and how to eat sophisticated cuisine like oysters and caviar. I had also learned a smattering of French, Italian, and German and had taken riding lessons. "Although my ballet instructor had a fit when she knew my parents were packing me off twice a week. She thought I would fall and break a bone and be unable to dance," I laughed.

As I talked, I began to feel more relaxed. I told Buck about my experience as a principal dancer at the New York Metropolitan Ballet and about how I had danced with the finest dancers from all over the world.

"And what about your husband?" Buck said abruptly.

For a moment I remembered that Adam was off on his business trip to California, and I felt a spasm of pain. I realized I didn't want to look as though I were being evasive about my husband. "Oh, he's great," I said, giving Buck my biggest smile. "His name is Adam. He works for an investment-banking company that buys and sells other companies. He travels a lot so that I can spend time with the ballet rehearsals, which works out okay."

I stopped because for a moment, Buck had an odd expression on his face. "Are you quite well?" I asked.

He frowned.

"I don't mean to intrude," I said. "It's just that it looked for a moment as though you were in pain."

"Oh, it's nothing," said Buck. "I was just remembering something I had forgotten to do at work—that's all."

"Perhaps we should get to it, then," I said as I pulled the first paper off the stack.

I soon became engaged by the rough business plan that Buck had drawn out. Buck pulled his chair over so we could sit side by side, and he pointed out the company's organizational structure and financial projections. We looked at the schedule. Buck suggested that we have our first performance in September.

It was a warm spring day, and a breeze came through the open balcony doors. I was feeling sleepy from the wine and the numbers, and I struggled to pay attention. With Adam traveling so heavily, perhaps I hadn't been sleeping well. I missed him.

"For our next meeting, I would like you to bring a list of company expenditures." I must have looked at him blankly, because he added, "You know, a list of where the money is to be spent. We'll then create a formal business plan. The money people will want to see that."

He told me that his proposed fund-raising program was projected to raise five hundred thousand dollars in the first year of operations.

At the sound of that number, I nearly fainted. With that amount, we would be able to do ample publicity and even advertise in some of the larger newspapers that covered the arts. I could pay the dancers a healthy salary, which would surely put down their minor rebellion. I could pay Anna a decent salary, which would help with her mom's care. I might even be able to contribute to my family's coffers, which would make me feel more independent. Less like a child.

Buck abruptly stood up from his chair. "With that amount of money— and there will be more—your knowledge and experience with the ballet, and my administrative guidance, we'll build a first-class company right here in Lockville."

"Christina," he said. "Do you realize that this is going to be groundbreaking? We're going to infuse the arts with some modernization right here in Lockville. We're putting this town on the map. If we play our cards right, we can invite luminaries from all over the place. Top journalists in the arts will want to get in on this story."

His speech was over; his face was flushed with excitement. I was suddenly struck by how boyish he looked. When he dropped his serious businesslike demeanor, he looked like any young man in his late twenties: full of life and vitality, the world his to explore and savor. For a moment, I saw my own young boy in my mind's eye, and I wondered how he would look like when he reached Buck's age. The years seemed like they would go by quickly, and my heart was filled with thoughts of youth and sadness.

"Gee, this is so exciting," I said. It was all happening so fast. I felt myself talking too fast like a little girl, but I didn't care. I hadn't felt that happy about something besides my son in such a long time. And it was Buck who was making it all possible. "I appreciate your help so very much. How could I ever repay you?"

I stood and realized we were standing very close to each other. Impulsively, I reached out and hugged him, surprised by how muscular and solid he felt. Without thinking, I stood on my tiptoes and gave him a kiss on the cheek. I could feel the beginnings of afternoon stubble on his cheek, and I smelled his subtle cologne.

Startled by my impetuous behavior, I stepped back.

Buck reached out and grabbed me by the arms, pulling me into him. I could see something fierce in his eyes, and it made me shiver. Just as quickly, he leaned over and brushed his lips against mine, softly at first. Then again he pressed down gently yet with a firmness that gave me a small involuntary thrill.

My brain was still a little groggy from the wine, the warm afternoon, and the barrage of numbers and details. It took me a moment to realize he had taken my silly hug and kiss as an invitation.

I tried to pull away, but he held me firmly. "Buck," I said. "You misunderstood me."

Buck held a finger up to my lips. He looked solemn. "We work hard and we play hard," he said. "And now it's time to make love."

Make love? I thought. I wasn't sure I had heard him correctly. "I beg your pardon?" I said.

He came in for another kiss, but I turned my head.

"You know—let's have some fun," he said. The expression in his eyes was one of amusement, but I felt wary as I sensed a hardness in him and a relentless aspect to his nature that, until that moment, I'd not noticed.

"I can't—I don't want to," I said. I wanted to shout, but it came out as a whisper. "Buck. It would be wrong."

Dancers are strong, and I was able to twist out of his grasp. I grabbed my purse and headed toward the door.

"I'm sorry," I said. "I can't."

Buck stepped in front of me and engaged the chain and the lock on the door. "Don't make me do it this way," he said.

My heart was pounding like a scared bird in my chest. The wine had come up in my throat as bitter bile, and the easy drowsiness I had felt moments before felt like a maddening sluggishness. It was as though I'd been drugged. *Think, Christina*, I told myself. *Think.*

I backed away from him, though there was nowhere to go.

"Surely you can't be serious?" I said. I tried to say it as coolly as I could, although I felt like crying.

Buck smiled and took my left arm gently by the wrist. He took the purse out of my right hand and set it carefully on the end table. He then trapped both of my wrists effortlessly in his left hand, and with his right hand, he reached over, caressed my cheek, and then ran his hand down my neck.

"You must have known," he said, his voice deliberate, "that coming to this room with me, drinking wine with me, and flirting with me implied consent."

He then walked across the suite toward the bed on the far side, dragging me along after him. He spun me around until my back was up against one of the broad wooden bedposts; the ornate carving dug uncomfortably into my spine. He kissed me passionately.

"So now, we will make love," he said.

He moved my buttons and undid them effortlessly. My silky blouse fell open.

My mind was going fast, and I was wondering how I was going to extricate myself from the situation. I briefly wondered if he was a murderer. I could feel my pulse throb in my throat and my temples.

"I'll make sure this is a positive experience; I promise that you'll find it enjoyable."

The final buttons on my blouse succumbed to Buck's administrations, and he abruptly let go of my arms. I pulled away, and my blouse slipped off of my arms. He was holding it in his hands, giving me an odd look.

"You really must relax," he said.

I blinked back tears and tried to gauge whether I could make it to the door quicker than he could.

The room darkened. I saw through the windows that gray clouds had rolled in while we had been talking, and they then covered the sun. The breeze coming in from the open balcony door was then brisk and cold on my skin. I felt gooseflesh.

And if I reached it? Was I willing to go outside in my half-naked state?

One of my secrets, something I had not shared with anybody, was my extreme modesty. Even though my body had been displayed on the stage, I had always disassociated myself with it, putting up a barrier between my mind and my body, over which raked the hungry gazes of the audience members. Disassociating was harder in the dressing room, where I changed with my fellow dancers, the indelicate smell of sweat mingled with sweet perfume. I would pretend that I didn't care—that my body was just a container. But of course, I did care.

In the bedroom with Adam, I always insisted on turning off the lights. I was not one for afternoon trysts. Adam, who liked his objects predictable, spare, and uncomplicated, had not insisted on anything else. Since he was a few years older than me and didn't have the fine, taut body the male dancers had, I sometimes suspected he felt that he didn't measure up. But it was one of those topics we danced around.

But with this stranger, I felt naked—exposed.

Buck must have seen an expression of despair, or perhaps resignation, wash over my face. He proceeded to fold my blouse very carefully on the bed, walk over and pick up his briefcase, and bring it back to the bed.

He sat it on the bed and placed my blouse in it, smoothing it until it was flat and unwrinkled. I stood there impassively. He looked at me steadily and then closed and latched the briefcase. Then, clearly making sure I saw what he was doing, he spun the tumblers on the lock.

I bit the inside of my cheek so I wouldn't cry.

Buck walked over to me and put his palm against my face. He did so in a gentle, almost loving manner, though I sensed nothing but steel and want underneath his façade.

"Cristina, you *must* understand that extramarital love is a positive and exhilarating thing. It's a natural part of human nature."

He placed his hands on my back and undid my bra. The cups swung in front of me. I tried to back up, but he held me.

"It's false thinking to consider it improper. If it's done discreetly, it's harmless and will actually improve your marriage and your love life with your husband. Variety adds to the experience for everybody."

He removed my bra, placed it with care on the bed, and looked at my breasts with approval.

"You must not be concerned. I promise that you'll enjoy our time together," murmured Buck. "We'll work together to develop the company, and it would be so awesome if, on occasion, we could enjoy ourselves like this together."

He must be joking, I thought.

He nudged me toward the bed so the back of my knees hit it, and I nearly lost my balance and fell onto it.

"Please, I don't want to." I finally found my voice, but it seemed inadequate. "Please let me go. I don't want to do this."

Buck frowned and then rubbed my face with his. He reached in to kiss me. I felt wooden and stiff, though his lips plied mine expertly.

"It's all right, baby," he said.

He looked at me like a cat contemplating a bowl of cream. I swear I could hear him purring, and I hated him, just a little. I felt myself redden, and I knew without looking at myself that a mottled blush had run all the way from my breasts up to my hairline.

"If you don't undress," he said, "I will do it for you."

I felt fear. I knew Adam would not understand my actions—my going to his hotel room, the wine, the small talk. How could I have been foolish enough to put myself in this situation?

I felt tears leaking out from my lids and running down my cheeks.

No one would believe he had forced himself on me. They would think I was complicit in the situation.

Buck had removed his shirt, shoes, and socks, and he stood there, bare chested and barefooted, clearly waiting for me to start undressing. He held his belt in his hand and flexed it in a menacing manner.

I mechanically stood up, slipped off my pumps, and shimmied out of my skirt. I turned so I wouldn't see him watching me and tugged off my panty-hose. I decided not to remove my panties. I couldn't bear to. *Let him beat me or choke me or whatever he's about to do*, I thought. I was trembling then, from the cold and the fear. My teeth chattered.

I thought about screaming my head off. I wondered, in the paneled room, if anybody would hear me or even bother to investigate. If Buck brought women there often, and I had begun to suspect he did, the people who worked in the hotel would probably think it was business as usual.

Hot tears ran down my face, and I felt my nose run, too. I wiped it with the back of my hand.

I felt strong hands on me, turning me around and lifting me back on the bed—that time, gently. He stood there, gazing at me, his expression rapt.

He crawled on the bed and suspended himself over me, his face hovering inches from mine. I turned my face so I wouldn't have to meet his gaze.

"You are a beauty to behold," he whispered in my ear. He then moved backward and, still straddling me, lifted me up and started tugging my panties over my hips and down my thighs.

"Turn off the lights," I muttered.

"It's day," he said with amusement in his voice.

I closed my eyes and could feel his weight leave the bed. I could hear him moving about the room and closing the balcony door, and then I heard the sound of curtain rings being drawn along rods. I heard him close the curtains in the room.

When I opened my eyes, it was not pitch dark, but it was darker. There were, blessedly, no windows in the bedroom portion of the suite.

I felt the bed shake as he got back into it. I felt his hand touch my forehead as though he were checking me for a fever.

"You're cold," he pronounced. "Christina, get under the covers."

I obeyed, crawling under the covers. I noticed Buck playing with some sort of gadget on the bedside table, but I was so overcome with distress and was feeling so wrung out that I couldn't even begin to imagine what he was up to.

That day is filled with regrets that have only partially faded.

Buck crawled into bed with me and manipulated his legs between mine. I felt open—vulnerable to him.

"Please don't do this," I repeated. My voice sounded flat, and I felt like I was a million miles away.

"It's okay, baby," he said, his voice husky.

I lay there mutely, willing him to do his business and to get it over with. But instead, he moved his lips and mouth across me with deliberate, careful attention. He kept murmuring about how beautiful I was.

He acted like a coach, a teacher, and a lover. "Isn't that wonderful, baby," he'd say. "How about this?"

There was Buck, encroaching on my body in ways I had not imagined. And my fear and revulsion mixed with pleasure as my body betrayed me.

"How are you doing, baby?" whispered Buck. "Are you okay? Are you okay, doing this? How does this feel? You are fantastic, baby!"

I felt the wine and his lovemaking wear down what was left of my resistance.

Buck had, apparently, finished his tour of all the sensitive parts of my body and was done instructing me on the finer nuances of pleasure. He had become silent. I had stopped protesting.

When it was over, Buck slumped on top of me, kissing my then-sweaty forehead.

I realized, dimly, that I had given up trying to get away.

He whispered, "How are you doing?"

"It felt good," I said softly, more to myself than to him. I felt the answer was honest, and I was deeply troubled by what I had discovered, what I had just admitted, and what that admission might cost me.

I was aware that the afternoon was speeding by. My mother would be wondering when I was going to pick up Chris. I was aware that I smelled like sex and another man. I wondered if my baby would smell someone other than his father on me. I wondered if my mother would take in my surely disheveled appearance and the makeup that had been smudged on my face from tears and illicit sex and become suspicious.

I felt a cold fear crawl into the pit of my stomach and take refuge there.

Abruptly, Buck grabbed me by the feet and pulled me and the covers toward him, standing me upright.

We were standing there naked together against the side of the bed, my pale white body framed against his, when a flash repeatedly lit the room, blinding me.

"What was that?" I cried in a panic, grabbing the bedclothes and pulling them to me. "Are you taking photos? I don't like that."

I sounded petulant and childish, even to myself. I was guilty. I was there, naked. In the photos, would I look as though I had been satisfied?

Buck began strolling slowly around the room, seemingly unperturbed by his nakedness, picking up his clothes and mine. "Don't worry," he said, his tone soothing. "I knew this would be a special moment and such a beautiful experience. I wanted to have something for me to remember it by. Something just for me."

Adrenaline sent my senses on full alert.

Buck smiled at me. He was so beautiful and charming, and yet he did not understand me. "You don't have anything to worry about," he said. "I really hope that you don't mind."

I knew better than to respond about what I did and didn't mind.

Buck walked over to me and took me by the arm, pulling me down on the bed with him.

"Christina, that was the most beautiful and satisfying experience of my life," he said. He looked a bit sad. "I'm sorry that you were reluctant. I was hoping that you would be willing and ready from the start."

He had a wounded look. "I thought you would be excited."

I smiled thinly.

He didn't seem able to read my true emotions; or perhaps he didn't care. He continued. "I'm pleased that you seemed to enjoy the experience once we got things going."

I realized with a start that he had really wanted it to be pleasurable for me. Somehow he had managed to delude himself into thinking that it was something I had wanted.

I must have looked stony at that, because he then spoke quite firmly and without the cloying tone he had used for his pretty little speech. "I do want you to know that it would be foolish to tell your husband. What was his name—Adam?"

I nodded slightly despite my good intentions.

"Or even the police. That would not go good for you."

He waited. I nodded again.

"All of the circumstances support a consensual encounter."

He sighed and drew me to him roughly. He kissed me full on the mouth, his tongue briefly intruding between my lips, before he pushed me back on the bed and stood up.

"My greatest desires are for us to continue to work together, to launch the company, and to share time like this together."

"I think it's time to get dressed now," he said. "I wish we had more time together." He nonchalantly pulled his business shirt on and stood there without his pants on, buttoning his shirt, as though it were the most normal thing in the world. It was as though we were husband and wife, and he was simply getting himself ready for work, acting out his normal routine.

I gathered my clothes and held them in front of me, covering myself.

I waited for him to remember that he had locked my blouse in his briefcase. I did not want to risk his ire. I realized I was very vulnerable.

"May I have my blouse?"

Buck looked at me. "Oh, I'm sorry. I forgot," he said.

Please, God, get me out of here safely, I prayed to myself. *Please make him let me go now.* He pulled on his boxers and then his dress pants, and then he carefully threaded his belt through his belt loops before he picked up his briefcase, walked it over to the bed, and pulled my blouse out. Then he held it up and shook it as if he were helping me with my coat. I stood frozen.

"Well," he said. "Don't be shy."

I didn't bother pointing out to him that I normally would have put my bra on first. I put my clothes back on the bed and held my arms out as though I were a child. That seemed to please him, and he chatted to me while he slid my blouse on and buttoned it starting from the bottom. He kissed me again.

Buck abruptly let me go, and I stood there stupidly, watching him. He picked up the camera, which I then saw he had cleverly hidden on a shelf by the bed, and started taking photos of the wine bottle and the glasses. He aimed the camera toward me and took a few photos of me standing there, my breasts probably showing through the sheer blouse, which was not long enough to cover my thighs.

He then placed the camera in his briefcase along with the papers and a few magazines and locked it up. Then he carefully tied his tie, put on his jacket, pulled a comb from an inside pocket, and combed his hair. He looked impeccably put together and as though nothing untoward had happened.

"Christina, I'll call you in a few days to set up our next meeting," he said. His voice was friendly, though he looked at me with yearning and as though I had hurt him. "Don't forget to make a comprehensive list of company expenses and any other details for our business plan. Next time, we'll finalize the input for the plan."

He grabbed the ice bucket and the two glasses and took them to the kitchen sink. He dumped the ice into the sink and rinsed the two glasses before upending them on a crisp white dish towel. Then he turned and gave me a grin that didn't seem to reach his eyes.

"Together we're going to be a great team, and we will make things happen."
Then he strode to the door, opened it, and left.

I stood there, feeling as though my legs were going to give out. The room spun, and the horrible expression of the dying elk in the painting across the room caught my attention. I could almost feel his agony.

And then I ran to the bathroom and threw up.

Eight

THE SCHEME

Buck

I WALKED OUT OF THE CLASSIC HOTEL FEELING LIKE A MAN who had the world by its tail. Christina—my Christina—the lovely ballet dancer, was more irresistible than I had imagined. The encounter had been everything I had hoped for and more. She had been so shy, and peeling her out of her clothes had been like watching a flower unfold and bloom.

I walked to the car, got in, and sat at the steering wheel before I put the key in the ignition. For just a moment, a shadow passed over the sun, and my thoughts darkened with the day.

I remembered the stricken look on her face. The paleness of her skin. The look in her eyes of…fear? Panic?

I felt a twinge of guilt and worry. The bile rose in my throat.

I had everything I wanted—all the trappings of success: a Porsche; two condominiums, one in Lockville and a small one for entertaining in the city; and my own small airplane. The previous year I had traveled to Italy, Spain, and even the Galapagos. And yet just a hint of a thought lingered: I hadn't really had Christina—not in the way I had wanted her.

I realized just then that if I did not command her heart and soul, all those things would not matter very much.

I had to harden my resolve. She had clearly enjoyed our lovemaking. It had been more than just sex; a woman like that was not into one-night stands. She was classy, sophisticated, and probably too good for that husband of hers. I had to laugh at that. I had probably just improved their sex life. For a moment I allowed myself to imagine them in their little suburban house—in their bedroom that was probably all feminine and frilly, him undressing her. I couldn't get him right; was he short and skinny or big and fat? Was he older than her? Probably yes, I decided. He must have been older. A lot older. Old enough to be her father.

Then I imagined them together in the act, the golden light from the setting sun catching her face, her eyes closed, her lips parted in pleasure, calling out my name.

The sound of a garbage truck driving by startled me out of my daydream. *What are you doing?* I could feel myself sweating into my shirt. The leather of my steering wheel felt sticky in my palms.

I took a breath and started the car. I loved how the engine sounded throaty yet refined. I pulled away from the curb and wondered if I should go back to the office.

I had come early to success, and during the last year, I had realized that I had paid the price. I lacked friends. Peers. Men I could trust. Sure, I had drinking and cigar-smoking buddies, but they were just hangers-on sniffing around for business or contacts or to learn how I had managed to build my business.

Zack was not a hanger-on. By pure definition, he was stuck behind the bar, and I, who came in almost nightly after work, was the hanger-on. That's one of the reasons I liked Zack so much. For a bartender, he was pretty smart; he was surprisingly well read and articulate and had even had an ongoing correspondence with a famous author, Truman Capote. I remember being very impressed when he showed me the letter. I had thought about hiring him away from Good Times more than once and giving him an entry-level position in my firm, but then I would have lost my counselor. We always joked about him taking the bar exam.

Talking with Zack and holding court at the bar felt right to me. I would not go to the office. I felt awesome about my encounter with Christina, but I also felt a certain tightness building in my gut that I needed to deal with. Zack was my man.

The Good Times Club was pretty dead when I walked in, and I felt a surge of disappointment when I saw Dave, the owner of the bar, behind the bar. I figured Zack was out and about. Maybe had gone up to see his brother, who was in the county jail. He did that about once a month, and though I thought his brother was a scoundrel, I didn't judge Zack by his family. You can't help blood; it's the company you keep that matters.

"Hey there, Buck," said Dave.

"They got you working today?" I asked, sitting down at the bar.

"Somebody's got to keep things in line around here," he said. "What'll it be?"

At that point, Zack came walking out of the kitchen, hauling a keg of beer. "I got it, boss," he told Dave. "Thanks for covering for me."

He put down the keg, wiped his hands on a bar towel, and gave me a crooked grin. His expression said that he was up to no-good and loving life.

"Hello, Buck, the usual?"

"Yes, but make it a double,"

"A double, eh?" said Zack. He made my gin and tonic with Tanqueray as I liked it and slid it across to me. He leaned over the bar and gave me a quizzical look. "Something has happened, my friend."

I nursed my drink and nodded.

"It's about Christina…We made love this afternoon."

Buck straightened up and did a little dance behind the bar like he'd just scored a touchdown. He was damn odd sometimes. "You scored. That's fantastic."

He walked around the bar and sat down on a chair next to me, taking off his apron in the process.

That made me raise my eyebrows. "Aren't you going to get in trouble from the boss?" I asked.

"Nah, I ain't scared of him. This place would die without me."

He took an unopened pack of cigarettes out of his shirt pocket. I watched while he took off the plastic, opened them, and shook one out in a move that I could tell was well practiced. He offered one to me.

I shook my head. "Prefer Cubans myself," I said.

"They're practically impossible to procure. You are man of impeccable taste, Buck," he said, shaking his head. He took out a matchbook, tore out a match, and lit it with a quick flick of his wrist. The brief flare of the flame made something in his eyes look, for a moment, sad, but it was a fleeting impression. I wondered if I had imagined it. He sucked on the cigarette a bit, and we sat there in companionable silence, neither of us having any need to speak.

He finished his cigarette at about the same time I downed my drink, and after flatting his cigarette on the bar and dumping it in my glass, he said, "Let me refresh that." He patted me on the shoulder as he walked past. "I want to hear all about it."

I wanted to boast a little about how lithesome, petite, warm, alive, and eager she had been. But the truth was, she hadn't been eager, and my stomach tightened a bit when I thought about it.

"It wasn't consensual," I found myself blurting out.

"Of course it was," said Zack.

"No, I had to force the issue," I took a swig of my drink to steady myself. "I don't feel good about it."

I didn't tell Zack just how full of shame I felt. I didn't tell him how innocent she was and how part of me felt like I had just corrupted her.

For pity's sake, she wasn't a virgin, another part of my brain told me. She'd had a child.

The notion, once it was in my head, made me feel sour.

"Are you saying she didn't like it?" Zack had this shit-eating grin on his face. I envied the way he seemed like nothing bothered him. He reminded me a little bit of Peter Pan about to crow—about to take on Hook.

"Well, it was probably the best sex either of us has ever had," I admitted.

"That's what I'm talking about," said Zack.

"We both went the distance," I added.

"So what's the problem? Why are you so down? You should be on top of the world."

"I'm just bothered by the fact it wasn't...perfect," I said. "I don't know how she's going to handle things going forward."

Zack leaned on the bar, looked both ways, and dropped his voice to a whisper. "Well, did you use the camera?"

"Sure," I said. "I got some good pictures." I hadn't looked at the pictures yet, but I remembered the flash going off. I got aroused remembering how sexy Christina had looked. Then I felt a pang of guilt again. "But I don't know if I'm going to be able to use them; that's a little too much."

"Hey, if you're not going to use them, let me have them," he said.

I felt sour at that, and I gave him a look.

"Okay, okay," he said. "But if you change your mind, holler."

A couple of more guys sat down at the end of the bar—middle-aged guys with their shirt sleeves rolled up and their ties loosened. I gave them a nod and waited while Zack took their orders.

I thought of Christina and wondered what she was doing at the moment. I wanted to taste her lips again, to hold her in my arms, and to feel the way she had belonged to me and how right it had felt. Then I wondered if her husband was off traveling, or if he would be at home when she got there. Would he be able to smell our lovemaking? Would she be that transparent?

I needed to get a grip.

The two guys at the bar bothered me for some reason. I tried to peg what they did and decided they must have been car salesmen. They probably had ugly, fat wives to go home to, I decided. Their houses probably stank of dogs and kids and pot roast.

I thought about my own condo, which was right smack in the downtown area, in the most expensive real estate I could own. I wondered if I would ever be able to take Christina there.

Zack came back and wiped his hands off on his apron. "Where were we?" he said. "Here's my speech: I think you're on track for a great run. Give her a couple of days, and she'll realize that you're the best thing that ever happened to her. Trust me on this."

"And if not?" I asked, keeping my tone even and devoid of emotion.

He shrugged. "You need to go with plan B. After two or three sessions, she'll be calling you and begging you for more."

I got up, pulled out my billfold, took two crisp hundreds out, and laid them on the table.

I felt a little tingle of satisfaction when I saw Zack's surprised reaction; his eyebrows went up briefly, and his lips pursed slightly. I noted the quick movement of his Adam's apple as he swallowed. Then he quickly recovered and put a hand over his chest, feigning pain in his heart. As though he had a heart, the bastard.

"Oh, Buck, you flatter me," he said. "What have I done to deserve this?"

"You make things sound so easy," I said. I knew I sounded curt, and I didn't know why. It wasn't his fault that I felt torn between feeling high and feeling terrible. "I have to go home and sleep it off and clear my head."

"You know you still owe me," he said, waving the bills around. "This doesn't even begin to settle things if she's that much of a prize."

"She is," I said. I walked toward the door and called out over my shoulder, "Good night, Zack!"

"Good night, you old devil," he called back.

As I stood on the sidewalk, the sun was finally setting. I knew I needed to hook Christina again, and good, before she managed to slip away. I decided that what I needed was more leverage on the company. That was her vulnerable spot. That was the first vulnerable spot I would hone in on. At least at first. I told myself that I was fully prepared to exploit all the advantages I had in the situation.

Nine

THE AFTERMATH

Christina

YOU CAN TRY TO LIVE HONESTLY, but in a moment you can slip into a double life—into living in two different worlds, like an actor playing two different characters in the same play.

That's how I felt that afternoon, driving away from the Classic Hotel, from my inadvertent tumble into bed with Buck Johnson, though I didn't know entirely what door I had opened and could not have imagined how it would alter my life. I had walked into the situation as a wife, a mother, a daughter, a ballerina, and an aspiring businesswoman. What was I after?

I couldn't bear the memory of that man on me—of the scent of him on my skin; my hands trembled on the steering wheel, and I could feel my nose run. I couldn't even keep track of what was going on. My mind was in a panic, and I drove aimlessly around town, past the library, past the park where I had played so many times with Chris in the mommies' groups, past the private preschool where Adam and I had already reserved a spot, and again past the Classic Hotel. It was as though I couldn't find my way home. It was as though if I kept driving, I could wind back time.

It would be my husband's worst nightmare. If he found out.

Would I tell him?

At that, I felt my stomach heave a little bit. I needed to get something to settle it. Some crackers, perhaps? Or a soft drink?

Then I realized we hadn't used protection, and for a moment, the street in front of me turned red and then black, and the next thing I felt was a lurching as the car went up over a curb. I slammed on the brakes when I was inches away from hitting a tree. I counted the days since my last period.

I was sitting there, feeling my heart skittering, when someone pounded on my window. I saw a guy out of the corner of my eye. I pretended I didn't hear him. He kept knocking on the window. When he stopped, I saw that the man—he was young—was peering in my window.

I rolled down the window. "No, don't worry," I called. "I'm fine."

He paused and looked at me suspiciously. "You're sure you didn't hurt yourself?"

"No," I said. "I just…had a spell."

"A spell, eh?" said the man. "You okay to drive, or do I need to call someone for you?"

"It's okay," I said. "It's just that I'm pregnant."

Holy mother of God, I thought to myself. I felt myself starting to sink into a whopper of a story, telling lie after lie until I buried myself in it.

The man looked suitably embarrassed and wiped his brow. At least that had done the trick.

"I just need to get a little bite of something to eat," I said.

His face brightened. "Hold on a sec," he said. I watched him run to his car, which he'd parked just down the street.

I decided I needed to get my car off the sidewalk before a cop came by and ticketed me. That would be just what I needed. With a start, I remembered that I was supposed to pick up Chris—I looked at the clock in the car—a half hour ago.

I started the car, waited until it was clear, and then backed gingerly into the street. At least I hadn't hit the tree. That would have been hard to explain.

I straightened the car up on the street, and the man came running back with a bottle of Fresca and some crackers. He thrust them through the window at me. "The soda is a bit warm, but the crackers are saltines," he said, grinning at me. "My wife is pregnant."

"Congratulations," I managed, feeling very odd. "And thank you."

"Congratulations to you too!" he said. His happiness could no longer be contained. "Do you know if it's a boy or a girl?"

I smiled weakly. "I want it to be a surprise."

"Yeah, surprises are good," he said.

"That's great," I said. "Well, I have to be going. Thanks again."

I pulled away without bothering to wait for his answer. *Pregnant,* I thought while I tried to steer. *That would be just peachy.*

I stopped by a gas station on the way to my mother's house, parked around by the side, and ran into the bathroom to try to make myself presentable before I landed on her doorstep. She could always spot a lie. She would have made a great private investigator and could have been a regular Dick Tracy if she had lived at the right time and in the right place.

The bathroom was cold, and the floor was dirty and strewn with paper towels. I almost didn't recognize myself in the mirror. My makeup was all smudged, and I looked like I'd been crying. Then I remembered I had been crying.

I washed my face, but the cheap soap from the dispenser got in my eyes and stung. I tried to scrub the mascara from under my eyes with the paper towels. My eyes were quite red, I thought. I wasn't going to pass my mother's inspection. She always looked calm and put together, and she reminded me very much of Jackie Kennedy. She was one of my mother's heroines. My mouth felt like cotton, and I looked pale. I fished around in my purse and found a bit of lipstick. I pinched my cheeks for good measure, ran my fingers through my hair, and straightened my blouse. There. It would have to do.

I went back to the car. It was late in the afternoon then, and I had to come up with some sort of excuse. I couldn't say I'd been at a business meeting. Could I? Did I look like I'd just had sex?

I collected myself by thinking calming thoughts. When I pulled up to the house, it was such a beautiful evening that I almost missed my mother, who was sitting in the shadows of the front porch and half-hidden by the trellis, which was already bursting with morning glories.

"Chris has had his nap already," she said. "Grandpa's taken him for a walk in his stroller; they should be back soon."

"Thanks, Mom," I said.

"So where were you?" she asked. "You didn't answer your office phone, and Anna said that you had an appointment."

"Sorry, Mom," I said.

She chuckled. "With Adam gone, I figured you were taking some time for yourself." She paused and took a sip of her iced tea. "You know, you have to schedule intimacy, or you lose it."

"Mother," I said, unable to hide the shock in my voice.

"We're both adults here," she said. "And with Adam traveling the way he is, you need to keep your romance alive. Plus...I noticed you've been letting yourself go."

She spoke kindly, but I felt myself flush. Goodness knows she knew my history. Keeping my weight down as a ballerina had always been a challenge. I wasn't a natural stick like most of the other girls. My directors often liked dancers tall and thin, and since I wasn't tall, I had to be thin.

"Anyway," she continued, "I approve. And I told Adam as much this afternoon when he called me."

"Adam called?" I asked, trying to keep the worry from my voice.

"Yes," she sniffed. "Sometimes when he's on the road, he calls to ask how you're doing."

"That's nice of him," I said.

"You ought to spend a little more time thinking about being a wife and a mother. I sometimes worry that you're too involved in the ballet."

"What time did Adam call exactly?" I asked, not taking the bait. She had supported the ballet like a stereotypical stage mother right up until Adam had come on the scene. Then she had showed an equal amount of enthusiasm for getting me to drop my career and get married. The baby could be said to be just as much her doing as ours. If I went a few days without letting her put her hands on her grandson, she had a fit.

"What difference does it make?" she asked. I could tell I'd hurt her feelings.

I didn't have an answer to that. I imagined that somehow Adam had figured out that I had been with another man that afternoon, and I felt myself grow faint.

My mom got up abruptly from her porch swing. "Oh, look," she said. "Here come the guys."

I saw my dad tooling his way up the sidewalk with Chris in the stroller. "Mommy," he cried as they got closer.

"This kid's a runner," said my father, looking proud. "He's going to be a standout with the Giants. You mark my word."

"Grandpa chased me!" Chris said, leaning forward and clapping his hands.

"What've you two been up to?"

"Ah, we just had a little game of hide-and-seek in the park," said my dad. "Then I had to catch him."

"You let him out of your sight?" I asked. I knew my voice sounded tremulous, and I didn't want to set my dad off. Our neighborhood was fairly safe, but the park at the end of the block was backed by some woods. Plus, it was easy enough to lose a two-year-old, and Dad wasn't as fast as he was.

"Don't make such a fuss," my mom said.

My dad shot me a petulant look and jammed his hands in the pockets of his pants. "I did keep an eye on him," he said. "We raised you, and you turned out just fine. I have this handled. I'm a pro."

I sighed and leaned down to get Chris out of the stroller, which he was outgrowing. I picked him up—he was getting heavy—and inhaled his sweet scent. "Hello, darling," I murmured. "Don't you be running away from Grandpa again, okay?"

"Now, Christina, don't be silly," my dad said gruffly. "We were fine."

"It's okay, Dad," I said.

"Kid's been crying for his mother."

"Now, dear," said my mother. "She had a little alone time. It's hard work being a mother, especially when your husband is never home."

"You're a half an hour late. You could have called," muttered my father. He leaned over and kissed Chris on the head. "See you later, pumpkin," he said. He kissed my forehead too and patted me awkwardly on the shoulder. "You too, pumpkin," he said, and then he turned around and shuffled into the house.

I felt a swell of pain hit my chest and expand. My eyes welled with tears. I loved my parents more than anything and wanted to make them proud. If they found out how stupid I'd been, trusting Buck Johnson…Well, I would never be able to face them again. They loved Adam as though he were their own son.

My mom shook her head. "Well, he'll be asleep in the chair shortly. Good thing I've got a good book." She looked at me, and then I could see the expression on her face sharpen. She looked me up and down. "What's wrong?" she abruptly asked.

"Nothing," I stammered. But then the tears started falling.

Chris patted my face. "Don't cry, Mommy," he said helpfully. "It's okay."

"Honey," said my mom. "What's going on?"

"I don't know," I said. I wiped the tears from my face and tried to smile. "I'm just feeling a little sad that the production isn't going smoothly."

My mom pursed her lips and gave me look that said she didn't believe me.

"And Adam has been gone a lot," I said.

My mother shook her head and sighed. "Darling, I think you better get home," she said. "You need to keep your house in order. Remember that your real job is being Adam's wife. Don't forget that."

I felt miserable. "Thanks for watching Chris, Mom," I said.

"Don't worry. I'll talk to your father about being more careful with him," she added. "Now, you better go home and get some dinner on, honey."

I put Chris in the car. "We going to see Daddy now?" he asked.

"Daddy's on a trip, sweetie," I said, straightening up and bumping my head on the roof of the car.

"Ouch," he said.

"Ouch is right," I said.

I slid in to the car and turned the ignition. It had been a long day. For the first time, I was glad that Adam was gone.

My mouth felt dry. I licked my lips. I wondered if I should just come clean with Adam when he arrived home from his trip. Could our marriage survive my indiscretion? Or would he ask for a divorce? My mind raced, and I came to the conclusion that he would divorce me. He valued fidelity above all else. I imagined my husband standing there in front of me, cold, hard, and telling me to get out of the house.

Or worse, I imagined him weeping.

I didn't want to hurt him or to jeopardize our marriage. I couldn't possibly tell him. That would be a decision I would come to regret. Many times over the next few months of that summer, I would wish I could rewind time back to that moment and make a different decision. I had no idea what kind of road I had stumbled upon in the dark. I was so naïve.

I would simply have to find a way to get Buck Johnson to back off. I hoped that doing so wouldn't mean I'd have to scuttle the company. I would call him the next day and end this thing.

"Okay, sweetie pie," I said. "Let's go home!"

"Let's sing!" he cried.

So we did.

Later, after I put Chris down for the night, I went into our bathroom and turned on the shower. The bathroom was all steamy, and I jumped in and scrubbed and scrubbed and scrubbed. It wasn't enough. I believed that I could scrub all I wanted, but I would never be clean.

I had to make that phone call the next day.

I awoke the next morning to my child patting my face and the doorbell ringing. Chris had taken to clambering out of his crib at night. Most mornings, I didn't mind the company. The person ringing the doorbell was Anna, who was going to pop by that morning for a talk. "I'll get it," said Chris, clambering off the bed and running out of the room.

"I'll help you, buddy!" I called after him.

Chris had managed to open the door, the little imp, and was dragging Anna by the hand into the kitchen. "I want some pancakes," he said. "Mommy won't make them for me."

"Is that so," she said, laughing. Then she saw me, and her eyebrows shot up as she looked me up and down. "Well, good morning to you," she said. "Hard night at the office last night?"

I could feel the heat creep into my face, and I'm sure she noticed. If the CIA had known about her stellar observational and intelligence skills, they would have been recruiting her.

"I think I'm coming down with something, and I'm probably contagious."

I elbowed past her into the kitchen and grabbed a mug from the cupboard. I usually drank tea, but that morning, some coffee seemed like it was in order.

"Ha," said Anna, laughing. "I'm pretty sure I can't catch what you have. Why don't you pour me a cup, too."

I frowned and opened the fridge, looking for the milk.

"Or I'll just help myself," she said. "Thanks for having me over."

"Are you making me pancakes now?" asked Chris. "Or do you want to watch Elmo first?"

"It depends on how cute Elmo is," said Anna. "Does he have a girlfriend?"

"Aunt Anna, Elmo is a puppet," said Chris, smacking his hand on his forehead. "On *Sesame Street.*"

"Then I'll make you some pancakes, pumpkin, while you watch the show. Unless your mommy doesn't approve of television so early in the morning." She turned to stick her tongue out at me.

"Mommy is okay with television this morning," I said. "Just not too loud."

"Yay," said Chris. I could hear the television turn on in the living room and Chris laughing.

Anna fixed me a look. I was spared by the sound of something falling in the living room, followed by Chris's crying. I ran into the living room. A crystal vase we had gotten for our wedding lay broken on the floor.

"I brooooke it," wailed Chris. I swept him into my arms.

"I'll get a broom," said Anna from beside me.

"That was bound to happen," I said. "We should have put it up somewhere."

"I've got this," said Anna. I was too upset to say anything else. I just walked in a circle from the living room, through the dining room, through the kitchen, and back again, trying to shush Chris. "Hush little baby, don't you cry," I sang.

His sobs had turned into sniffles by the time Adam called from his trip. He heard that Chris was crying and sounded concerned. I told him what had happened, and I could hear that he was taken aback for a moment by the fact that I'd been negligent. "I'm sorry," I automatically said.

Adam sounded cross. "You don't have to be sorry. It wasn't your fault."

"But it is," I said. I almost told him the whole thing right then and there—that it was not only the vase, but also our marriage. And I'd done it. I'd jeopardized everything. I stifled a sob myself.

"Look, try to forget this, and have a great day," he said, "I miss you, and I promise I'll come home as soon as I can."

I knew he wouldn't come home very quickly. And I wondered how much of that was my fault.

I sighed and cradled the phone in the receiver. Chris patted me on the cheeks.

"How about we see what Elmo is up to," I said. Chris immediately became enthralled with Elmo, Cookie Monster, and Big Bird, and his sobs turned into intermittent hiccups.

Anna had already taken care of the broken vase and was whipping up batter for pancakes.

"You forgot to buy blueberries," she said.

"I know." I sat on a stool in the kitchen, sighed, and rubbed my temples. "Somebody rammed me at the grocery store, and I got distracted."

Anna poured some batter into the pan. She was able to make perfect silver dollar–sized pancakes. She could have been a chef.

I was glad to see her, but I didn't want to talk about what had happened just yet. Actually, I didn't ever want to talk about what had happened—not with her, not with anybody.

I felt sick just thinking about it. About him. All naked and on me.

"Trouble in paradise?" Anna said, looking at me thoughtfully. "Are we starting out this morning with hair of the dog?"

"I don't have a hangover," I snapped.

"But then what?"

"It's nothing," I said.

"Don't give me that," she said. "I wasn't your college roommate for nothing."

The phone rang. I jumped when it did, but I didn't move to answer it. I was hoping it was Adam, calling to tell me he would miss me for real. But I wanted to give myself some time to figure things out. To get my head on right.

Anna answered the phone before I could stop her.

"Lockville Ballet Company," she said, smiling at me. "This is Anna speaking."

I frowned at her and shook my head "no."

"Oh, of course she's here," she said. "I'm really just the crazy auntie—don't mind me."

Then Anna shoved the phone in my hand. "It's that Buck fellow," she whispered, grinning.

"No," I whispered, trying to shove the phone back in her hand.

"Don't be silly," she said. "Talk to him. He called you."

I felt like I was going to faint. My hand shook, and I didn't think I could speak.

I would like to think that I had come up with a million ways of telling him off. After all, I had been planning on calling him that morning. But they all fled out of my head in a sudden flood of emotion.

"Yes?" was all I could muster.

"Good morning, my dear Christina, and please don't hang up on me. What I have to say is critical for the future of our ballet company" Buck sounded sure of himself. Happy.

I sure didn't like the way he had said "our ballet company," but I had brought him on board, hadn't I? I needed to get it over with. I took a deep breath. "We need to talk."

"That's why I'm calling," he said.

I let out a sigh of relief. "You are?" I asked. "I mean, I wasn't sure. Yesterday was all a—"

"I have big news," he said. "Are you sitting?"

"What are you talking about?"

I bit my lip and turned away from the Anna, who was standing in front of me, her eyes flashing in curiosity. "What does he want?" she whispered.

I waved her away. Buck was talking about one of his friends, a fat cat who supported arts organizations. "Frank Wichman has more money than he knows what to do with," he said.

"Oh," I said cautiously.

"He's willing to donate one hundred fifty thousand dollars if you serve as the artistic director and I agree to be the business manager."

I didn't speak for a second. It was wonderful news, and the whole process was going so fast. And then there was the acid in the back of my throat when I thought of being in the same room as the man who was speaking to me on the phone.

"The man is a marketing genius," said Buck. "He wants to announce the news at a press conference."

My head was spinning. I leaned against the counter for support. I thought I might pass out.

"You need to be there for this," he said. "It's on Friday at one o'clock sharp. You need to be there thirty minutes earlier."

I just couldn't do it.

"Christina? Where'd you go, baby?"

I felt tears rising in my eyes, and my throat constricted. Why was he pushing me around like this? And how dare he call me baby, especially after he had forced himself on me.

But what would happen if I said no? What if he told Adam what we'd done? I remembered the flash of the camera's light going off. Had he kept the photos?

"I'll have to think about it," I finally said slowly. "We really need to talk."

"Christina, this is your dream," said Buck. He sounded annoyed. "Don't blow it."

Anna had come back into the kitchen and was giving me a strange look. That gave me an idea.

"I'll need to send my assistant," I said. "I'm busy that day."

"That won't do," he barked.

"She helps run things," I said. "She's good."

"Only you have the background, the reputation, and the charisma to pull this off." Buck sounded hurt.

It made me feel fearful.

"The donor will close his checkbook if you don't show. Just like that," he added.

"I'll see what I can do to clear my schedule," I said.

Buck sighed. "Look, if you don't show, the ballet company is dead. It's all over."

He kept going, but I couldn't quite make out what he said. I gently put the phone back in its cradle and started to weep.

"Hey there," Anna said, taking me by the arm and pushing me gently onto a chair. "What's going on?"

"I can't work with him," I said. "This is wrong. We have to get rid of him."

"Girl, have you lost your mind?" said Anna. "Because that man is hotter than a house on fire, and he's rolling in dough."

I started to laugh at that. I knew it was hysterical laughter, but I couldn't help myself.

"The man is a menace," I was finally able to choke out.

Anna looked confused. "Come again?"

"A menace. He forced himself on me. Yesterday. He forced me to have sex with him."

I got up and started pacing around the kitchen and opening cupboard doors. Apparently we didn't have any booze in the house. My being pregnant and nursing had certainly depleted our liquor stores. I couldn't find anything, so I started slamming the doors. Hard.

"Holy crap, Christina," said Anna. She stood there, watching me and rubbing her own arms, her eyes wide. "Are you serious?"

I swung one of the cupboard doors closed so hard that it made the dishes rattle.

"No. Late April Fools' Day," I said. "That's one of my better ones, don't you think?"

"Oh my God," said Anna. She sat down, still watching me. "Adam doesn't know, does he?"

"Oh, of course. I told him first thing," I said. "What do you think I am—an idiot?"

"Well," she said.

"He'll think it's all my fault," I started sobbing again. "It was all my fault, in fact. I am so stupid. I shouldn't have gone up to the room with him."

"Well damn," she said.

"And now he wants me to meet him and a donor, some Frank Wichman, for a press conference this Friday to announce his big coup."

Anna's eyebrows shot up. "Oh, girl! *The* Frank Wichman? He's the one that lives in that huge mansion out on Lakeview." She paused and looked thoughtful. "He's kinda old, though. And married."

"God, Anna," I groaned. "Can you focus?"

Her eyes narrowed. "What were you doing with that smooth-talking guy in a hotel room anyway?"

"It's a long story," I said. "We were drinking wine at lunch. He made it seem like we were going to do some work upstairs. I assumed we were meeting in a conference room. Turns out he has a permanent suite there."

"Oh, I hear it's fancy up in those rooms," she said.

"Anna, you aren't helping," I said.

"Well, did he really force himself on you?"

I knew I should have been angry with Anna, but I simply felt sad and angry with myself. "Why would you ask?"

"I know things haven't been so hot between you and Adam lately," she said. Then she stopped. "What? I'm just stating the facts. You two have hit a dry spell. No one would blame you if you wanted a bit of fun on the side."

"I didn't want it," I said. But then I remembered how I had stood up on my tiptoes and kissed him on the cheek. I'd hugged him.

"What?" said Anna.

"I might have given him mixed signals," I admitted before sighing and telling her the whole story.

She brightened. "Well, there you go. It doesn't need to happen again," she said. "Unless you want it to."

"It was terrible, Anna," I said. "I feel so terrible."

"There, there," she said. "You don't need to feel so bad about it. Your meeting was like a couch-casting session; sex happens all the time at castings. Don't worry about it."

"Oh, God. Adam is going to leave me," I said.

"No, he's not," said Anna. "Because Adam's not going to find out. You're going to get your fanny to that press conference, accept the money that the ballet has coming to it, and tell Buck Johnson in no uncertain terms that you are not part of the package."

I fished a tissue out of my pajama pocket and blew my nose. "You sure?"

"Sure, honey," she said. "And you can send me in your place if he's still looking for action. I'd take one for the team."

"God, Anna, you're rotten," I said. But in spite of how worried I felt, I had to smile. Buck Johnson wouldn't know what had hit him. Anna was the scrappiest person I knew.

"That's why we're friends," she said. "Now why don't I make you some of Auntie Anna's world famous silver-dollar pancakes?"

"I'd like that," I said. "Thank you." I gave her a quick hug, walked into the living room, and sat down on the floor with Chris.

"You gonna watch *Sesame Street* with me?" he said brightly.

"Yes, I am," I said. "What's Big Bird up to this morning?"

While Chris talked to me about the cast of characters, I realized that I needed to set some boundaries with Buck Johnson.

Adam was tentatively scheduled to arrive from his trip late in the evening. I needed to put some distance between me and what had happened with Buck Johnson. I wasn't sure I could handle being too close to Adam until I sorted out what had happened and what I was going to do about it. I felt raw and emotionally vulnerable.

When he did come home, he looked at me and offered to cook supper and take care of Chris while I went for a walk. He seemed tender and concerned. I felt like garbage. What had I done to my marriage?

Adam put Chris to bed, and I went and sat out on the porch swing. It was a warm spring afternoon, and the tulips were emerging in the flower beds along the sidewalk. I felt excited about the possibility of the ballet being funded and about being able to move forward with the company, yet I was guilt ridden because of how things had gone down.

I heard the screen door open, and my husband appeared carrying two glasses of wine. "Hey, darling," he said. "I thought you could use this."

He settled himself on the porch swing beside me, set his wine down on the table, and put his arm around me. I tried not to flinch. I wondered miserably if my icky feeling of filth would ever go away. I'd taken another shower that morning, but it hadn't helped.

We were silent for a few moments as Adam gently rocked the swing back and forth. Then he cleared his throat and turned to me, looking me in the eyes.

"Listen, I see that you're feeling pretty sad these days," he said. "And I'm really sorry that I've been traveling for work so much and haven't been around for you and Chris."

I felt tears rising up in my eyes and started to sniff.

"Aw, honey, what is it?" he said, dabbing at my tears with his thumbs.

But I just couldn't tell him what had happened. He'd never forgive me. And part of me wondered if I had just been so lonely in my marriage that I'd wanted it to happen on a subconscious level.

I hated myself.

"It's this press conference," I blurted out to my surprise. "It's making me so nervous."

Adam looked mystified. "What are you talking about?"

So I told him about Buck getting some funding and about how the new donor wanted to announce it in a press conference on Friday.

"That's great news!" said Adam. "You'll knock them dead. No need to be nervous."

The audacity of what I was doing made me feel stretched thin. I was beyond nervous. "No," I said flatly as I dried my eyes. "You're right. This is a wonderful opportunity."

"That's my girl," he said, raising his glass. "To new partnerships and the success of your company."

My wine glass met his a little too hard and tipped his over. Wine rained down on both of us, though mostly on Adam.

"Oh, crap," he said. "There goes this shirt."

"I got this," I said, jumping up and running into the house for a glass of water and a towel. "No worries."

As I ran the tap in the kitchen, I hoped that the spilling of the wine wasn't some sort of a sign.

I decided I needed to nail that press conference on Friday and get things back under control with Buck Johnson.

Ten

THE PRESS

Christina

ON THE MORNING OF THE PRESS CONFERENCE, it took me the longest time to figure out what to wear. I wanted to wear something that befit the artistic director of a successful ballet company, but I didn't want to wear something that would suggest to Buck Johnson that I was his plaything.

I couldn't decide between my cream, black, or green dress. I put on the cream dress and was looking at myself in the bedroom mirror with a critical eye when my husband stepped out of the bathroom, toweling his hair dry. "Sexy lady," he growled, snapping me with his towel.

"Ouch," I said. "Not the look I was going for."

I waited until he went back into the bathroom before I stripped off my dress and stood there, holding up the other two dresses. The black one looked too dowdy and stereotypical, I thought. I was trying to differentiate our company, to put it on the map, and black said "just another New York artist" to me. It was practically a uniform. The green one, which had a scoop neck, was just a perfect emerald color. It was risky with most skin tones, but I had just enough Irish in me to pull it off, I thought. I accented it with an elegant silver belt and a pearl necklace that had been my grandmother's. I found some hose that, by some miracle, didn't have runs in them and slipped on my silver pumps.

"That's perfect," said Adam. "The press will love you, and so will the new donor."

"That's the plan," I said. I knew my smile was a bit forced, but I was pretty sure no one else could have seen how much turmoil I was feeling. Not even my husband. Part of being a professional performer is becoming practiced at pushing aside your personal feelings, and I was very good at that.

In the back of my mind, I thought that if I could really impress the new owner, perhaps that would be enough to dislodge Buck. I could work with him, but I needed to bring him back into line. I couldn't risk being in a compromising position with him.

Thinking of him made my hands tremble.

"No need for nerves," said Adam.

"No, indeed," I said. I reached up to give him a peck on the cheek. "You need to get going so you aren't late."

Chris and I walked to the garage to see Adam out. Everything seemed perfect. I allowed myself a brief moment of happiness, seeing my family all together like that. I waved to Adam and waited until his car drove out of sight, and then Chris and I went into the house. I took off my dress and hung it up so it would be perfect for the press conference that afternoon.

The street in front of my parents' house was lined with cars, which made my stomach tighten just a bit. My mother felt obligated to take her turn as hostess for a women's luncheon at least twice a year. She always joked that it gave her an occasion to break out her candlewick plates and punch glasses and to serve canapés and perfectly petite sandwiches garnished with olives on tiny swords. I frantically wondered if she had forgotten she was babysitting that afternoon. I parked and swung out of the car, and Chris clambered out obediently behind me.

I smoothed my dress and took Chris in hand to inspect him. He had some jelly on his face from breakfast, and his hair was sticking up. I licked my finger and wet down his cowlick, and then I scrubbed the jelly off his face. He protested the whole time. "I hate spit baths," he said.

"Grandmother has company," I said soothingly. "We want to be presentable for her friends."

That done, we marched up the drive to the house. I was gritting my teeth and hoping I could get away with simply handing Chris over, but knew I might be delayed. Mom always likes to show off her daughter, the dancer, even though most of her friends have known me for years.

I rang the doorbell, and my mother opened it with an exclamation that made it seem as though she had not been expecting me, such a celebrity, to drop by. She had on a fancy dress and even pearls. I sighed. She looks like Elizabeth Taylor, with the same curvy figure, raven hair and eyebrows, and pale skin, though her eyes are more blue than violet.

She looked me up and down, gleefully taking in the outfit I had carefully chosen for the press conference. I glanced at my watch pointedly; I had an hour before I needed to be at the civic center. She simply gave me a wicked grin.

"Girls, my Christina is here with my only grandson," she sang out. "Do come in, darling, and say hi to everyone."

"Mother, I have someplace I need to be," I said as she picked up Chris and grabbed me by the arm, pulling me into the house. She was deceptively strong.

The girls glanced up from the card tables set up in the living room. It was ladies bridge day. Each table was perfectly appointed with nuts and the little rose-shaped mints my mother had fussed over herself.

I walked around, greeting my mother's friends. My mother beckoned me over to a table at which a few women my age were sitting. "My dear, I would like to introduce Olive, Jane, and Cynthia. They're the newest members of our bridge club." Behind her hand, my mother whispered to me, "That one is a divorcee."

I murmured my greetings and shook their hands politely. My mother pulled out a chair and said, "Sit, please."

I resisted my mother's request. "I am so sorry, but I have someplace I need to be today."

"But you don't have a rehearsal," she said. "Surely you can stay."

"There's something important going on with the company today," I said. She wrinkled her forehead. "But what could that be?"

"We've received some funding," I said. "And the new business manager and the donor want me to be there when they announce it to the press."

My mother gave me a spontaneous hug. "Well, dear, who is this mystery donor? And since when do you have a business manager? I had thought that Anna person was handling all that." She sniffed; she didn't much care for Anna, and the feeling was mutual.

Discussing money might be gauche, but my mother was new money enough to appreciate the notoriety. "A Mr. Frank Wichman is the donor," I said.

"Oh, I know the Wichmans," said my mother. "His wife, Nancy, is lovely. We are in La Coterie together."

I could always trust my mother to know everybody who was anybody.

"He was solicited by Mr. Buck Johnson, who has been appointed as our business manager."

I flushed as I said that. I tried to say his name with as much neutrality as possible, but my poise had been trampled by the passion with which he had accosted me.

Another woman laughed. "Oh, isn't that the cat's pajamas," she said. "You're getting the five-star treatment."

My mother frowned at her. "Why, Jane, whatever do you mean by that?"

"Your daughter is running with a fast crowd," she said. "I'm sure the ballet is going to take off with that sort of investment."

She smiled at me, but I felt myself grow hot and uncomfortable, and my mother finally pulled me away to the kitchen.

"Really," said my mother, fanning herself. "This women's lib stuff is for the birds if people cannot act with decorum and not talk business all the time." My mother put her finger to her forehead as if she were going to pass out. "Christina, you must swear to me that you will never make a spectacle out of yourself."

"Of course not, Mother," I said.

"All right," she said, smiling sweetly and giving me a kiss on the cheek. "You'd better go, or you will be late for that press conference of yours. Make us proud."

I let myself quietly out of the house

I tried to put my entanglement with Buck Johnson out of my mind; I had to assume the role of artistic director of the Lockville Ballet Company. I hoped that Mr. Johnson would keep his hands to himself. I decided to treat him as if nothing had happened, but I certainly would remain distant. And I would not hug him or peck him on the cheek.

When I walked into the huge lobby of the civic center, I stopped short. Rows of folding chairs had been placed facing a stage and a podium and were flanked by ferns that hadn't been there when we'd had rehearsals. A huge banner behind the proclaimed, "Lockville's Ballet Company Dances Forward."

Holy cow, I thought.

In the middle of it stood a throng of gentlemen in suits. There weren't many women in the press corps, and the few there were wrote recipes or covered social events. I had mixed feelings about the fact that my venture was not going to be thrown in on the ladies' pages. At least the company was being taken seriously. Mr. Johnson greeted me eagerly, which made me very uncomfortable. Beside him stood Mr. Wichman, and then there was Mr. Turner. I gave them a big smile.

"Gentlemen," I said, walking up the aisle between the chairs. "This is amazing. Thank you so much!"

Buck walked up to me and whispered, "I am so glad you could make it." I didn't answer; my heart was racing with nerves from just being around him. He took me by the elbow, steering me around the group and making introductions. Mr. Wichman, our donor, appeared to have an affinity for strong drinks, judging by the bulbous appearance of his nose, but he beamed when I mentioned that my mother and his wife were in the same club. He kept shaking my hand, squeezing it tightly in his sweaty palms, and saying just how proud he was of me for doing this ballet.

"I am so happy to be able to invest in a smart young businesswoman like yourself," he said, and then he leaned over and whispered, "I'm a fan of Jackie Kennedy's, you realize."

"She's very gracious," I said solemnly.

"She sometimes vacations at the Cape without her husband. We—Nancy and I—travel in the same circles."

I didn't know what to say to his attempts to impress me. He had won my loyalty already by saving the ballet company, and I began to wonder if he also came with strings attached.

"Save the celebratory parties until after our debut," said Buck, coming to my rescue. He then steered me toward Mitch Carter, who introduced himself as the business manager of the Lockville Symphony Orchestra. "I'm very happy to be part of the program," he said. "Intersecting with another company like this will add a lot to our offerings."

Since money had become involved, Mark Turner had not shown any of his previous animosity or doubts about the company. It was clear from the way he had inched closer to Mr. Johnson and was laughing at his jokes that he admired the man. For a minute I was struck with how similar those men were to the ladies in my mother's various clubs, and I was struck with an image of them all standing around in tea dresses and hats, waving fans. I had to hide a laugh, but the men were so engrossed in impressing each other that they didn't notice.

"It looks like all the newspaper fellows are here," Buck said as some men in suits carrying cameras and pads came trickling in the door. "We'll give it a few more minutes before we get started."

He turned to me and said, "Christina, could I have a word with you before we get started?"

I saw no way to avoid speaking with him about business, but I wondered if I should make it clear that I would welcome no more advances.

He turned to the group and said, "Gentlemen, I need to have a private conference with my artistic director before we get started."

The way he said "private conference" made my lips go dry.

"I believe we can find some privacy in your office," he said.

I nodded, but my mind was racing, and I was wondering how to head him off at the pass when we got to my office.

I didn't need to. When we got to my office, he stood there looking at me with an intense expression of longing on his face. He kept clenching and unclenching his fists.

It was at that moment that I realized that Buck Johnson was interested in more than sex.

"Mr. Johnson, please," I murmured. "When you look at me that way, it makes me feel peculiar."

His ears turned pink. "I haven't been able to take my mind off of you," he said. "That was the most magical afternoon ever. There's not a woman who compares to you."

I felt myself flush, and I was trying to think of what to say when a knock came on my office door. I looked up to see Mr. Turner standing in the doorway. "There you two are," he said. "They're ready to start."

Buck smiled and said, "Then let's get started." He gestured to the doorway, and I walked ahead of both men.

"This is Christina's first press conference," said Buck. "I was just giving her a pep talk."

"Oh, you'll do just fine—just fine," Mark, said enthusiastically.

Then Buck walked out of the door, turning Mark around and wrapping his arm around his shoulder as though they were old buddies.

I stopped at the entrance to the ladies' room. I needed a few moments to steel myself. Buck's continued interest in me had rattled my composure.

"Do you mind?" I said.

Both men shook their heads. "Of course not," said Mark. "We'll meet you there. Don't be too long."

I went into the bathroom and resisted the impulse to just lock myself in and not come out. In the mirror, I looked pale and worried. I wet a paper towel and dabbed it under my eyes so they wouldn't appear to be so puffy. I then took out my compact and carefully powdered my lips. Next, I refreshed my lipstick, making an O with my lips and dabbing them with Maybelline red. I took a small vial of Chanel Number 5 out and dabbed it on my temples, hoping to cool myself off. My hair needed a little hairspray, but I managed to repin it so I at least looked the part, or so I told myself.

The part of what?

Mark Turner had seen Buck and me together just then, and I wondered if he had overheard our conversation. I wanted to impress him. I didn't want him to think I didn't have any dance talent or wasn't able to run a company.

And if he had heard Buck, would he say anything? Suppose he happened to say something in passing to Mr. Wichman, whose wife, Nancy, was my mother's bosom buddy—then what?

I groaned. I wanted to save the company, and yet it appeared that I was the person who needed saving. How much more could go wrong before things went right? I wondered.

As it turns out, plenty. But I didn't know it at the time.

As it was, I gave myself a pep talk. No need to keep the press waiting. I opened the door to return to the press conference and walked down the hall and back out into the cavernous world.

The festivities had just started. I recognized exactly none of the reporters, and it felt like I was the only woman in the room. I felt like the men were watching me, waiting for me to fail, and I felt like I had nothing left to give.

The rest of the press conference was a blur. Buck got up and gave a big speech about how it was an "exciting gathering" for the city and the surrounding communities. Then all the men had to get up and give a little ditty. I wanted to be excited, and I was excited, but somehow all the troubles with the ballet company and then this incident with Buck were weighing on me. I remembered how Anna had said that men in the art world were full of themselves and realized, for the first time, what she had meant. I would have given anything to have her with me at that moment. I knew that she had to take care of her mom and that she had a day job.

Then I had a wicked thought. She probably would have jumped on Buck right there in the dressing room. I had to stifle a laugh. I felt that the circumstances weren't really that funny, yet there I was, laughing. *I must be going crazy*, I thought.

Buck Johnson frowned at me. Mark Turner, who had just finished speaking about what a wonderful opportunity it was to be working with the company, looked at me with open curiosity. I wondered uneasily about how my relationship with him would change.

Buck stood up and returned to the podium. "You know all these gentlemen quite well, but not so well known, at least not yet, is Mrs. Christina Cramer." Buck waved me up to the podium. "I want to take this opportunity to introduce Mrs. Cramer. We are indeed fortunate to have an individual who has unrivaled experience, training, and talent in the ballet." He went on to give a detailed summary of my training and experiences at the New York

Metropolitan Ballet Company. I wondered uneasily how he had gotten his hands on such a detailed dossier.

I felt as though I were in a fog. I found myself walking up to the podium, bending over the microphone, and giving a pretty little speech about the ballet and our goals.

I started to leave the podium to sit down, but Buck shook his head, so I stood there while Mr. Wichman took to the microphone to express his desire to support the cultural aspects of the ballet and his admiration for Mr. Johnson, Mr. Carter, and Mr. Turner. "I have a long-held admiration for the ballet," he said, turning to me and smiling. "I have completed some research on Mrs. Cramer's accomplishments, and based on my findings, I'm confident that this endeavor will be successful. Accordingly, I am here to announce my contribution of one hundred fifty thousand dollars to the start-up fund for the Lockville Ballet Company. And I am asking my fellow citizens to join me in a campaign to support this unique opportunity."

His impassioned plea was met with a smattering of applause from the journalists assembled, though I noticed, for the first time, a few of the members of the ballet company, some members of the chamber of commerce, and a few other prominent people in the arts.

At that, Mark Turner's assistant brought out a supersized check, and the principal players all stood behind it for photos.

Then a string quartet that I had not noticed earlier, so rattled had I been by Buck's proclamation of ardor, began to play, and we broke for a small reception. I talked politely with a few reporters while they took notes, and I posed for more photos.

At one point Buck pulled me close to him and told the photographer from the *Times* to take a photo of "just the two of us." His hand around my waist unnerved me, and when it looked like things were slowing down, I told Buck and Mark I needed to leave.

Buck looked disappointed. "I was hoping we could grab a celebratory drink together," he said.

"I need to pick up Chris," I said quickly. "He's teething and not feeling so well."

I couldn't tell him "no more" in front of Mark. I didn't want to bruise his ego; who knew what would happen if I did? His actions made it seem like he wasn't going to be stopped quite that easily.

I thought I saw displeasure and disappointment flash across his face, but he quickly got himself under control.

When I got to my parents' house, the bridge goers had cleared out, and I found my father and Chris puttering around in the backyard, pulling weeds. My father loved his flowers and his fresh tomatoes. My father told me that my mother had a headache and was lying down, resting. My mother put stock in being social, but she also got worn out. I wondered if she had chased everyone out.

"How did the press conference go, my famous daughter?" he asked.

"It was okay," I said.

"Just okay?" he asked, looking concerned.

Sometimes he knew me better than my mother did. He certainly understood better than she did how much I missed being in the ballet. To her, there were no greater roles than those of wife and mother, and I often felt suffocated by her domestic ambitions.

I sighed. "I think I might be in over my head," I said.

"But now you have the support of men who have done this before and who are very experienced in what they're doing, all for free," he said. "I know you'll follow their advice and be fine."

It appeared to me that I was being asked to pay and that it wasn't free at all.

But my training in finishing school kicked in—a refined gentlewoman does not complain or fuss—so I merely smiled at him and said, "Thank you, Daddy!"

That seemed to placate him. I picked up my fussy child, said my good-byes, headed home, and spent the rest of the afternoon scrubbing the house until it shone.

That night, when I saw myself on the local evening news, I was surprised by how poised I appeared.

Eleven

The Obsession

Buck

THE GOOD TIMES CLUB WAS IN FULL SWING THAT NIGHT
when I hit the doors. A band occupied the stage in front of the dance floor,
covering a Mancini piece, and the dance floor was packed. I found a spot at
the bar, and Zack acknowledge me with a nod and placed a Manhattan in
front of me. I sipped on my drink and turned and was watching the band
when Zack tapped me on the shoulder. I turned around, and he leaned over
and cupped his hands around his mouth.

"Hey, you're notorious," said Zack.

"How so?" I said.

"You made the news," he said. "It's coming on now."

He motioned at the television behind the bar. A commercial for the dry
look, which I personally despised, was airing.

"You should try that," I said.

"Shut up. Here it comes!"

I went around the bar so I could see it better. Zack merely nodded at me.
"Can you get it to come in better?"

"Nah," said Zack. "Do you want a smoke?"

"No, thanks," I said.

Zack shrugged and lit up.

I watched with interest as the anchors gave the ballet a thumbs-up. When the footage of the conference ran, I was impressed with how gorgeous Christina looked, standing there beside me smiling. Then I frowned. She hadn't wanted to go with me to get a drink afterward. Of course, she had said her kid was sick or something, but it felt to me like Buck Johnson had been given the cold shoulder.

"That your lady friend?" said Zack, whistling appreciatively. "She's a looker."

"She is," I said.

"So what's happening now? The other evening you were professing guilt and remorse for your coerced encounter with that magnificent woman. What's the story now?"

I chuckled. "Guilt is a useless emotion," I said. "It's hard to feel guilty around someone that desirable."

I didn't tell him that I felt out of control—a little obsessed. I prided myself on being a rational man, and my obsession overwhelmed me. I found myself tongue-tied around her, and yet I felt the desire to do impulsive, crazy things.

"Well, I can understand that," said Zack. "She is a sight to behold. Even on a crappy television."

"They make colored televisions these days," I said.

"Too rich for me," sighed Zack. "So are you still sleeping with her?"

"We'll be working together and planning for the ballet, if that's what you mean," I said. For some reason, his question irked me.

"That's not what I meant," Zack said, finishing his cigarette and crushing it in a glass ashtray.

"Well, I think she's going to come around with the other thing," I said.

"Tell her to get on the pill," he said. "She'll come around. It's no big deal these days. Everybody is having sex with everybody else. She'll see that."

"I think she's concerned about cheating," I said.

"Well, just assure her that you're discreet."

"I wouldn't be unhappy about it getting out," I said. I made the statement impulsively, but the moment it was out, I knew it to be true. If she and her husband got a divorce, I would be happy. "She's a keeper—someone to take home to good old mom."

"Isn't your mom dead?" he asked.

I laughed grimly. That was pain I did not want to resurrect. Zack did not know my mom was dead, and my stepmom—well, let's just say my old man had robbed the cradle on that one.

Just then, one of the cute cocktail waitresses walked up to the bar. "Hey, Zack, you on break? I got a line of drink orders coming out my ass and no bartender in sight."

"Yeah, be there in a moment," Zack said. He stood up and said, "Next drink's on me."

"Thanks, Zack," I said. "I owe you."

"You bet your sweet ass you owe me," he said. When he smiled, it didn't look too innocent, but I ignored any sort of warning bells that went off. I had bigger fish to fry. I needed to lock Christina in. I had some photos I needed to develop.

I returned to my regular seat and sipped on the Manhattan that Zack, wearing that cocky grin of his, had slid my way. I was watching the band and enjoying the music before I needed to go back to my apartment. While I enjoyed my solitude, the thought of going home made me feel a pang of loneliness. I again thought about Christina, savoring the memory of her lips under mine.

"Well, hello, Mr. Big Shot."

Despite my best intentions, I flinched, and then I turned to see my ex-wife standing there, smirking at me.

"Hello, Marilyn," I said stiffly.

She pursed her lips, waiting for me to continue talking and perhaps for me to ask her why she was there, but I had no desire to do that. She looked a little loose, in my opinion, wearing some shiny white boots, mint-green eye shadow, and fake eyelashes. She put her hand on my knee flirtatiously, but the way she kept peering around made me think she was expecting someone. Since our divorce, I had heard she was running with a pretty wild bunch, but she'd already started in with that crowd when we were married.

"Aren't you going to buy me a drink, Buck?" she asked.

"I've bought you enough drinks," I said.

"I heard you're spending your money on dancing these days," she said. She had an amused look in her eyes that I didn't like.

"Do you always listen to rumors?" I said.

She scowled. "You can't even buy me a drink, then. Is that it?"

"What happened to Robert? Isn't he making the big money?"

She sniffed. "Robert's doing okay, but a girl has needs."

"Robert should uphold his responsibilities," I said.

She dabbed at her eyes. "I feel like you never loved me."

I drained my drink and stood up. "Marilyn, it's been lovely to see you," I said.

At that point, Robert himself walked up and put his arm around Marilyn. She shot me a haughty grin. He looked quite dapper in his Nehru jacket, and he had taken to wearing little wire-rimmed glasses. I wanted to punch him. "Hey there, old man," he said.

I gave him what I hoped was a nonplussed look. I wouldn't let myself be bothered by the way those two had carried on before the divorce had been final. After all, I had Christina. She was a classier lady by far than Marilyn could ever hope to be.

I nodded at Robert and walked away through the growing crowd and out the door. I could feel that fake smile of my ex-wife's paramour long after I left the building. He was as phony as a two-dollar bill, all right. The way I saw it, he and Marilyn were perfect for each other.

It was a lovely night for a walk, the run-in with my ex-wife notwithstanding, so I took one. I wanted to iron out my plan for the coming week, mostly about the ballet and Christina, and a walk would clear my head. But seeing Marilyn had brought up old wounds, and the more I tried to rationalize our end and tell myself that it didn't matter, the more pain I felt.

The only cure, I decided, was Christina. I most definitely needed to see her again.

I busied myself at work, but as the week went by, I still felt a certain sense of dread. I found myself in the dark most nights, my head filled involuntarily with memories of Marilyn: Marilyn flirting with me at a dive café in Harlem, where we had both gone to see the famous Savoy dancers give a performance. Marilyn taking a drag on a cigarette she had bummed from a friend of mine. Marilyn going topless at the beach on the Hamptons late one moonless night—the night we'd first made love. Marilyn charming the socks off my old man and pissing off his too-young wife, my stepmom, at his obligatory birthday dinner at the Four Seasons. Marilyn picking out the pattern of china she wanted for our registry. Marilyn walking down the aisle of the church at our wedding, her face dark and inscrutable, only lighting up with a smile when the ceremony was over. Marilyn in the bathroom late one night, cramping from her second miscarriage and refusing to let me take her to the hospital. Marilyn telling me she had never wanted children, anyway. Marilyn putting on a new shade of lipstick, a bright poppy red, before we went out to the Sondheim musical the evening I dropped the news I was leaving her. Marilyn's absence in our apartment the day I moved out.

I found out later that she had moved to New York after I had left. Our relationship was sad and empty. I wanted a family; she refused to try again. After the divorce, I went to see a psychologist. My father insisted on it and said I was crazy for leaving such a wonderful woman. His relationship with her was stronger than ever; I ran into the three of them once at the Four Seasons in New York. After a few months, I realized that I had married Marilyn precisely because she pleased my father. She vied with my stepmother in the looks department. But she wasn't the kind of woman who could make me feel happy and fulfilled.

I began to doubt myself during the aftermath of our divorce. I had spent months rebuilding my sense of self, my trust in the world.

I tried not to drink but found myself filled with regret over Marilyn and spending each evening under the tender ministrations of Zack and his steady supply of alcohol. Then I went home and drank myself into a stupor.

I worked, but I wasn't present.

Finally, after a week, I picked up the phone and dialed Christina's number. I knew it by heart.

After several agonizing rings, she picked up.

I paused. I felt myself suddenly too shy to talk.

"Hello?" she said again, her voice sounding both assertive and fearful. "Who's calling?"

"It's me," I said finally.

"Mr. Johnson," she asked. Her voice was cool and remote. My heart hurt.

"How are you?" I asked.

"I'm okay," she said. "I'm fine."

We both knew she wasn't—that I'd thrown her into a series of inexplicable events and that I'd altered the emotional and sexual tone of her world. And I wasn't sure how much I could pretend otherwise or avoid demanding that she go with me—that she leave her husband.

But I'd had plenty of practice in deceit, starting with my life with my father and continuing, most recently, during my life with Marilyn. My life alone since then was another story.

I took a deep breath and stated what I needed. "I need to set up a meeting," I said. "There's a lot of planning work to do to get the company up and running. An important topic is when we'll be ready for the first performance."

There was silence on the other end of the phone, which unnerved me.

"We can't just guess at it," I said. "We need to create an itemized listing of all the activities that must be accomplished between now and the actual performance. We must project realistic dates for each item. That will allow us to fix a date for our first performance. Can you meet with me tomorrow at noon at The Classic?"

My heartbeat was unaccountably rapid as though I were running a fever. I felt unmoored, and a little voice in the back of my head said, "This isn't right. This will be your undoing."

But I'd already been undone.

Finally she spoke. "Why at the hotel, and why at noon?" she asked. "You should know that I'm not going to go to anymore of your parties."

"Well, I have a busy work schedule aside from the ballet company." I managed to make my voice sound frosty and distant to convey the possibility that I was not available—that her relationship to me and my ability to help were breakable, unreliable. That was a lesson I had learned that from my father:

keeping someone interested means doling out love in bits and pieces but never being predictable. "If we can meet over my lunch period at the hotel restaurant, it would save time."

My suggestion was met with silence.

"Look, I would appreciate it. And it's only for this next meeting."

My words were like birds flying out of my mouth. They beat the air like dead things.

"Okay," she said. "I'll be there this time. But no more parties."

I agreed, though I knew I would not honor her request. I needed our relationship to take another step further so that she could see that she needed me as much as I needed her. It would just take some time and planning.

I was waiting in the restaurant when she arrived and had ordered a glass of cabernet already. I noted that she was dressed demurely in a yellow dress and a white cardigan with her hair pulled back in a ponytail, but it would have been impossible to hide her perfect body. I could see her pulse beating rapidly in her neck.

She looked at me coolly, and, not for the first time, I admired the greenish tint to her eyes and the slight sprinkling of freckles across the bridge of her nose.

I poured us each a glass of wine as she sat and then held mine up. "To our venture together," I said.

She raised her eyebrows slightly, but she then murmured in assent. "To our venture." I did not like the way she had omitted "together," but I didn't want to quibble.

I engaged her in conversation about the company, steering her away from any talk about her son or her damned husband because I assumed doing so would cause her more anxiety. I plied her with questions about the details of rehearsal and some of the issues she'd been having with the other members of the company, and then I engaged her in a discussion of possible performance dates and of what the company needed to pull together for that to become a reality. She opened slowly and reluctantly, but after another glass of wine, she became a little more relaxed, and her eyes dilated slightly. At one point, I caught her looking at me with bemusement, and I smiled inwardly at that small triumph and knew I needed to act quickly.

I picked up the briefcase that had been sitting by my feet and stood up. "I have some papers in here for you to sign," I said, patting it. "I've reserved a room, and it would be more convenient to work upstairs so I can spread them out on the desk again."

It was a flimsy ploy, and I knew it. She turned pale.

"Please don't ask me to do that again," she said. "I don't want to offend you, but I'm married, and it's not fair to my husband."

I didn't answer her. I just kept my expression blank.

"Don't you understand?" she said. She smoothed her napkin out nervously. I could see her fingers trembling. "Adam might find out and divorce me. He'd take my son away from me."

In the face of my silence, she stammered on. "He would probably kill you."

I loved how her skin was so translucent, yet her ears had reddened and a mottled flush had crept up from her breasts, which were apparent in the fetching dress she had worn. I wondered if the dress was so stunning on purpose.

I stepped closer to her, brushed her hair away from her cheek, and spoke softly as one might to a scared child. "As I have said before, extramarital sex is common. It will improve your marriage, and Adam will never know."

She refused to meet my gaze.

"I know how to handle things like this so the 'old man' will never know. So relax, and live a little. You should lighten up."

She seemed unmoved by my confidence, so I sighed and sat back down. I realized that she might be a tougher nut to crack than I had anticipated.

"Let's get the ballet thing going and have some fun while we're doing it."

She stiffened and looked straight ahead, her eyes filling with tears. I couldn't stand to see her that way and wanted to sweep her up in my arms in that instant, but I restrained myself.

"I know you enjoyed our lovemaking. Also, you should know that you are so beautiful and so irresistible that I will do anything and everything that's necessary to have you." At that moment I realized that what I was saying was the truth. I'd never felt like that about anybody before. I needed to make her understand—to believe me. I impulsively reached across the table and grabbed her hands in mind.

"Mr. Johnson," she said. "You can't possibly think that I'm available."

I couldn't let my heart break. "I can't go on. I'm obsessed."

She frowned slightly and tried to take her hands from mine. I let her. I looked around the restaurant and saw everything with remarkable clarity: the sun streaming through the stained-glass window in the corner and the dust motes dancing in its light. I heard the crooning of Frank Sinatra coming from the radio playing in the lobby.

"I'm not proud of my conduct. I know that it's not right, and it's not who I am as a person. I admit that my conduct and my actions are not right. I am really out of control. I can't help myself."

I stopped speaking at that moment, giving her a second to let what I had said sink in and waiting for her to rush to fill the moment. But her eyes did not meet mine, and she sat stiff and straight as though she would run at the first chance. I felt again the old sadness, the shame that I'd felt when my father had left my mother and had come home with this slip of a college girl only a few years older than I was. The girl had laughed at me when my father hadn't been looking.

Something in me hardened.

That day in the restaurant would become another moment in time that I look back at with regret, but not for the obvious reasons. My undoing was deeper than I had imagined.

My voice felt like it would crack in sorrow, but I knew how to modulate myself. "From the first time I met you I knew I wanted you." I kept my voice even, and I looked at her, willing her to meet my gaze—to see what I was offering her. "I had hoped that we could get something going—that I could win you over without the unfortunate use of pressure."

And then I was babbling, talking again about my goals for the company, which I knew were her goals. I knew she would be impressed if she knew how much I cared about what she cared about. I assured her that we could achieve our goals and spend time together. "No one will get hurt. I am a master of discretion."

She began to sniff as she sat there. I was beginning to feel desperate. "However this all turns out, I hope that someday, when things are in perspective, you will not think of me as evil." I reached across the table and lifted her chin so I could look into her eyes. "I hope you'll try to understand that old

Buck was a decent man who fell under the spell of a very beautiful and charming woman."

Time was of the essence. I could feel my life draining away—I could feel myself growing old and irrelevant. After Marilyn and I had parted, I had gone down to the draft office to volunteer my services. They could ship me to 'Nam, for all I cared. I was plenty fit, but that damned psychologist had flunked me. He had offered me a cigarette, which I had declined, and he had asked me if I was a Kennedy supporter, if I went to church, and if I had grown up with guns and hunting. I told him that I wasn't any sort of a supporter and that my family members weren't regular churchgoers but that I had gone hunting with my cousins once or twice and, while I had no love for hunting, I didn't hate it either and could appreciate the feel of a gun in my hands. It had felt like I had been giving him all the right answers until he began probing all too much into my history with Marilyn and my father and his wife; all the while this loud clock in the corner was ticking. I must have been in there for hours, and it was the middle of the summer, and I was all sweaty and sad. Then I had to take some sort of a test with dark, inky pictures and had to tell him what I thought they meant. And in the end they told me I hadn't made it in.

I had told my old man I was going, and then I hadn't gotten in. Marilyn and I went up to dinner with them once or twice after that, then we'd broken up, and I hadn't talked to him since.

When Christina finally spoke, her voice was soft and halting. "Buck, I can't make love with you again. Please don't ask me."

I know I must have made a small strangled noise in my throat. Or I thought I did, because she looked up at me, startled.

"I did enjoy our sex, but it's not right," she said. "I won't do it again."

She ran her fingers through her hair, and her eyes looked wild for a moment. "Following our recent party, I felt so bad, so guilty, and so embarrassed."

She was practically whispering at that point.

"You must know that it is so unfair to my husband."

The sounds of the restaurant, the music from the radio, and the conversations of the other diners fell away until I could only hear my own blood rushing in my ears. I felt cold and faraway.

"You are really making things difficult for me. I can only hope that some-day we can laugh together and enjoy ourselves with a single purpose in our minds."

With that, I put my briefcase on the table, opened it, and removed a stamped business envelope that I had left unsealed whose contents I had care-fully prepared the evening before.

I handed it to Christina, and her eyes widened when she saw the name written on its front. Her hands trembled as she removed its contests: three black-and-white photographs and a typewritten note.

I kept my expression neutral as I said, "These are the great pictures that were taken during our party. Look them over, and let me know what you think."

Her face and her skin betrayed her emotions. She turned a deep red and sunk down into her seat. She thumbed through the photos while I studied her. I did not need to see the photos to know them. In one, we are naked, arm in arm, leaning against the side of the bed. In another, we are kissing.

In my favorite, she is smiling at me.

There were more, of course, but those were sufficient.

She looked pale and beautiful. I wondered, for a moment, what she would look like dancing, and I wished I could have seen her.

Then there was the note. I wanted to kiss her fingers while she read it, but I sat there silently, half-afraid she would get up and walk off.

Dear Adam,

I want to thank you for letting me spend some time with Christina. She said that because you were so busy with work and all, it was okay with you that we spend some time together and that you understood that she needs more attention than you are able to provide.

I thought you would enjoy these pictures. As you can see from her smile, she has been having a good time. I coached her on some new love-making techniques, and I understand she is going to share them with you. I have told her I would love to continue to be with her as long as she wants to and as long as it is okay with you.

She is a beautiful lady and is great in bed. You are a very lucky man.
Thank you,
Buck Johnson

Christina looked stunned. "I must have these pictures. No one can ever see them."

I was enjoying myself then. I had passed through my moment of worry. She was still there. I was in control of the situation. "Aren't they great? I knew you would want to have them."

The waiter appeared with our bill, and Christina quickly turned the photos upside down. He looked at her curiously, but I gave him a hard stare that dissuaded him from lingering.

She sat there for about five minutes, staring off in the distance. Her eyes were filling with tears, and I hated myself for hurting her. I let her take her time.

"Will you send them to Adam if I don't do as you say?"

I hesitated. "Please don't put me in that position."

"But will you?" she said. "Is that what you're saying? This is…blackmail?"

I felt agitated at the accusation. "I wouldn't put it in those terms."

"But that's what it is, isn't it?"

"I have nothing to lose."

The waiter came again and filled our water glasses. We sat in silence. She seemed to be holding back tears. I was doing my best to maintain my composure. Finally, I had to move things ahead. "Now, after we go upstairs, the envelope is yours," I said firmly. "You can do with the letter and the pictures what you'd like."

She looked at me, stricken. She was forcing me to play hardball.

"Or if you would rather not, that's okay, too. I'll drop the envelope in the hotel mailbox on the way out."

She looked defeated, but I pressed on. Lord help me.

"So, what do you want to do? What will it be?"

I saw the gears in her brain working, and I could see her turning over her options in her mind. Would her husband divorce her? Would I keep my word? I longed to press my lips against hers. I wanted her to know she could trust me.

"So these pictures and the note will be all mine."

"Yes, of course," I said.

She paused, and I took my time, taking another few sips of my wine. She left hers untouched.

"I will do anything to keep these photos from seeing the light of day," she said. She paused and then spoke without looking at me. "I guess one more time won't hurt. Let's go upstairs."

I exhaled. "Good girl. Great decision," I said. "I will do everything possible to make sure you enjoy yourself."

I stood up and extended my hand to her to help her up. She shook her head and sat there a moment longer, dabbing at her mouth daintily with her napkin, until I shrugged and stepped aside. She finally stood, so graceful in even her most mundane movement that I was once again struck by a sense of overpowering desire.

Yet even as she walked beside me, she would not look at me.

I pressed the button for the elevator and touched her shoulder while we waited. "And Christina, please drop the guilt and embarrassment stuff. Everything is really going to be okay."

She simply sighed.

"There is nothing wrong with this. We're just two people who enjoy each other."

"I have a son," she said.

She had appeared to stop talking to me, and I felt a twinge of anguish, though I was confident I could win her over if she would allow me to.

I had made sure the room, number 812, which I rented on a monthly basis, was impeccably set up again. I had wine chilling and snacks. I had had my secretary at work buy a little sheer silk robe for her to wear after she showered.

Christina stood awkwardly by the door for a moment before I instructed her to sit on the love seat. I took off my jacket and tie and poured us some wine. I saw that she was fixated on the painting above the mantle.

"I see you're an art admirer," I remarked, sitting down beside her. "Do you know about that particular painting?"

She nodded, but I could tell she found it both repulsive and fascinating.

"It is an odd piece, isn't it?" I said. I proceeded to tell her how I had found it in a little antique shop in upstate New York during one of my forays for items. I love collecting things, and I grow passionate when I talk about finding artists whose works have languished in attics and family houses, largely unappreciated. The topic made me passionate, and Christina seemed to warm up to the topic. I stroked her on the shoulder and gave her small kisses in her hair, on her ears, and on her neck, though she felt altogether too stiff and tense for my taste.

Finally, I thought that I had to break her of her forced modesty. I was sure it prevented a satisfying sexual experience for her.

"I just saw a production of *Hair* on Broadway the other day," I remarked. "Have you seen it?"

She shook her head "no." *Of course she hasn't,* I thought. I'm sure the immodesty of the players running about nude would offend her husband. It seemed like her husband treated her like she was a medieval princess and had locked her up in some musty attic so she couldn't see the sun. She planned to liberate the ballet. I planned to liberate her.

I started to unbutton her shirt. She stiffened again, and then she laughed nervously.

"What are you doing?"

"You know," I said. "Don't fight me on this."

She looked solemn again, a cloud on her face, but I slowly removed all of her clothes with her protesting the whole time until she was entirely disrobed.

She attempted to turn off the light next to the lamp.

I grabbed her wrist. "Stop it," I said gruffly. "I want to see you."

"You can see me," she said.

"No, put on this robe," I commanded. I handed her the package that I had slipped under the chair earlier.

She looked subdued, and I poured her another glass. "Salut," I said.

She raised it to toast me and wrinkled her nose, but she drank more. Her breathing was becoming more relaxed, and she swayed a bit; I could tell the alcohol was beginning to have its way with her.

I leaned her back on the couch and kissed her then, all over her body, trying to determine all the places in which she craved to be touched without realizing it. As I worked my way down and she protested, I realized that she was married but vastly inexperienced. Did she and her husband even regularly have sex? I imagined he was not as gentle or as patient as me.

I let her sit up and urged her to finish her glass, and then she crawled obediently into bed to wait for me.

At last, I turned out the lights, and at several points during our lovemaking, I heard her whisper, "We should not be doing this."

When it was over, her deep breathing made it seem like she was asleep.

I got up and let her lie there for a few moments while I got dressed. I tossed her bra and panties on the bed, and in a bit, she stirred and put them on. I sat down and took her in my arms and petted her back. Her skin felt like silk, and she shivered despite the warmth in the room. I thought for a moment about presenting her with the burgundy robe, but I could not bear the thought of covering even another inch of her beautiful body.

"Before I go, I need to talk to you," I said.

She looked at me expectantly.

"The pictures."

"Yes," I said. I stood up and retrieved the envelope from the hall table, where she had set it down when she had first come in. "Here's the envelope with the pictures and the letter that I said I would give you."

She looked, for a moment, relieved, and I knew with utter certainty that she was not yet mine; I had not managed to win her over. Our relationship was still tentative—still fragile.

I stood there for a moment, regarding her steadily. She flushed under my scrutiny. When I was sure I had her full attention, I spoke. "You and I have an obligation to the city to continue our effort to get the ballet company going. It would be a feather in the cap of the community if it happened. We must continue to work together to make that happen. We will both be recognized for this accomplishment. We will become successful in what we love to do."

"I see," she said.

"At the same time, we must continue to spend some time together. Sex is a normal thing between two people who admire each other."

I sat back down on the bed and took her hands in mind. They felt warm. "It is no more harmful than a kiss on the cheek. The puritan norms about sex between consenting adults are outdated. Nobody believes them anymore."

She colored at that, but it seemed like she was not going to dispute me.

"I know that you enjoy our time together, and after a short time, you will look forward to our meetings."

She grabbed her hands from mine and put them in her lap. She looked a little angry at my last statement.

"Hey, come on, Christina. You enjoyed our lovemaking, didn't you?"

She stood up and walked over to the window and looked out of it. Anybody on the street would have been able to see her standing there in her bra and panties, but she seemed not to notice. I felt satisfied knowing that she had grown a little even during the afternoon's brief encounter.

I wanted to confront her with that fact but did not want to push her too fast. Perhaps that had been one of the problems with Marilyn. Women are not creatures who take on adventure that readily, I mused. My ex-wife had grown bitter and ugly in her outlook toward men and was materialistic.

"In time, I believe that you will call me for special arrangements. Maybe when your husband is out of town."

"So that's it, then?" Christina turned to face me. "You think this is our deal?"

"Listen to me," I said sharply. "I have a made a decision. When I call, there will be no more discussion about if we will meet. We will only talk about when and where."

Christina walked over to the love seat and started picking up her clothes. She hugged them in front of her and said, "I don't think so. Can you please turn around while I get dressed?"

I felt myself grow cold, and though I felt sorry, I couldn't seem to help myself. "I'm sorry if I did not make things clear. I still have the negatives and the original copy of the letter, and I will send them to Adam if I am forced to do so."

She had such a beautifully shocked look on her face that I regretted not bringing Zack's camera to our meeting.

"You can't do that," she said. "I already did what you asked."

"After I become convinced that you are committed to this arrangement—and I am sure that you will be—I will give you the original copy of the letter and the negatives."

"You'll ruin my marriage." Her voice sounded like a little girl's.

I grimaced. Her accusation showed that she thought less of me than I would have liked. She did not understand that my attention was merely to clear a path for our relationship. "Just a few more times, and then I will give them to you regardless."

She looked at me in disbelief.

"Clearly neither of us want those things hanging out there," I said. "I don't like them anymore than you do."

She swayed there for a moment as though she might faint. I started to walk over to her to steady her, but she stepped back.

"I am sure you misunderstood, but the greater good must prevail." She said nothing, but a small sob came out of her. It broke my heart. "Look me in the eyes, please," I said.

I touched her gently, pulling her face up so she could see the sincerity in my own.

"Do you understand the arrangement? When I call there will not be any more discussion about if we will get together. We will no longer have unpleasant talks about the photos. We will only talk about where and when we will meet."

She nodded. The tears in her eyes made them look large.

"If you quibble in any manner, I will hang up and immediately mail the pictures and letter to Adam. That is a promise. I have nothing to lose and everything—you—to gain."

The tears ran down her cheek, and I wiped them away with my fingers.

"Do you understand?"

"Won't you give them to me now?

I said nothing.

"Yes, I understand," she replied in a voice that sounded faraway and like glass.

I took her in my arms and kissed her warmly; she did not protest.

I stood up, then, to take my leave. I felt happy and yet not happy all at the same time. I wanted her to be more fully on board with this. Why was she dragging her feet?

"One last thing. To ensure that our arrangement remains discreet, future meetings will be located in an outlying community. Not in our hometown."

She nodded dully.

I looked at her for a moment. There was so much in my heart, so much to say, but it was clear she was not ready to love me in the way that I loved her.

So I said nothing and merely let myself out.

I felt happier once I got out of the hotel room. Perhaps the oppressiveness of all those antiques had been weighing me down and making me feel uneasy. I made a mental note to see if there were any quiet, out-of-the-way parks that I could take Christina to. I could pack a little picnic, and we could take a loaf of bread to feed some ducks. I liked that plan and knew she would like it, too. She seemed like a picnic sort of gal.

The Good Times Club was a little quiet when I stopped by for my daily cocktail. Zack was wiping out glasses but looked up and grinned when he saw me settling in at the bar.

"So, tell me all about it," he said. "With that big smile on your face, it's got to be interesting."

"Yes, yes," I said. "Plan B was a smashing success. She enjoys the sex, and I have her trapped."

"Piece of cake, then?" Zack asked as he handed me a gin and tonic.

"She has agreed to an ongoing arrangement, but only because of the photos." I frowned slightly at that. "I would be happier without the coercive aspect. But I think it will pass."

I sighed and added, "What a woman." It was best to accentuate the positive. She wasn't Marilyn. She had a more positive outlook. This would work for us.

"Good for you, Buck," said Zack. He looked around, even though the people at the other end of the bar couldn't have possibly heard him when he dropped his voice down to practically a whisper. "So when and where is the payback? Remember our deal. You owe me."

I felt a little sour at that. Some of those young Turks were so impatient. With so many guys off at war, you'd think there'd be plenty of babes around for the picking, but guys like Zack were always looking for the next big thing. Nobody was getting married and settling down anymore. "Oh, Zack, don't get in a hurry. Just give me some time to figure things out," I said.

His face darkened. "Okay, just don't forget me. I won't wait forever. If you don't come up with a plan, I will."

I shifted in my chair. I loved Zack like a brother, but there were some things you just didn't mess with. I didn't want him to think that he had a shot with Christina, for God's sake. She was mine.

"What kind of a plan?" I asked, keeping my tone neutral, though he must have read some menace in my expression.

He held his hands up and gave me a big grin. "Hey, man, I wasn't trying to hone in on your dance partner," he said. "I just wanted you to remember that you owe me a favor. Okay, bro?" This should be deleted right?

"It's cool, Zack," I said. I raised my glass to him. "Here's to paying what we owe."

"Thanks, Buck," he said, relief on his face.

I swiveled the stool so I could look out over the bar and out the window. I wondered idly how cool things were. I was still uneasy over Christina's bouts of defiance and over the limp way she had returned my feelings, even though she had responded aggressively during our lovemaking. I needed to button that up. I didn't like leaving anything to chance. I was already exploiting her weak points, and I wondered, as I went through my mind, what else there was. I remembered her very pretty dancer friend who had been with her at the ballet. I had seen her at events before. I needed to figure out who she was and see if she could help me in my quest to woo the lovely Christina.

I heard Zack saying something, and I turned to face him. "Sorry," I said.

"Would you like another one?" he asked.

I regarded my glass. Was it half-full or half-empty? I decided that whatever it was, the drink was becoming too cloying. "No, thank you," I said. "I need to get to work."

Twelve

The Spiral

Christina

I SAT IN THE PARK SHELTER, SHIVERING IN THE THIN JACKET that I had thrown on that morning. My canvas tennis shoes and slacks were soaking wet. I'd put boots and a thick raincoat on little Chris and had decided to chance it, but it had started raining on the walk over., Chris was splashing around in the puddles, flapping his elbows and quacking like a duck. "Where's Auntie Anna?" he asked me.

I looked around and felt relieved to see Anna walking up the street in the opposite direction. Unlike me, she had an umbrella. I wondered who was more organized. "There she is," I told Chris.

"Fine day for a walk, don't you think?" said Anna, sitting down on the park bench beside me. "You look like a drowned rat."

"Thanks," I said. "I knew I could count on you for support."

"Anytime," she said. "What's so urgent that it couldn't wait until our normal tête-á-tête over tea after rehearsals?"

I sighed and watched Chris for a moment. He had plopped himself down in the sandbox and was driving his toy car around, making *vroom* noises.

"Spill," commanded Anna.

"Well, it's a long story," I said. "I need your help. And advice."

"Of course you do," said Anna, smiling and patting me on the arm. "I give the best advice."

I pursed my lips. I felt very glum about the whole thing. "Buck is blackmailing me."

"What?" said Anna.

"The last time we met, I made it very clear that we weren't going to…well, you know. No parties."

Anna nodded solemnly.

"But Anna, he had pictures of the two of us from the first time. We were both nude. They are so awful, so mortifying, so compromising."

I felt tears spill over my cheeks. "No one must ever see them."

"That rat," said Anna.

"It gets worse. He had them, along with a letter, in an envelope addressed to Adam. He said that if I had sex with him again, he'd give me the photos and the letter. If I didn't, well…" I started sobbing in earnest. "He said he would mail the envelope to Adam immediately."

"Oh, honey," said Anna, putting her arm around me. "He didn't mean it. He was just jerking you around."

I sat up and wiped my face. "Oh, Anna, he meant it. I'm convinced he did. And I would do anything to keep the photos hidden away, especially from Adam."

"And what did you do?" she asked.

"What could I do? I had sex with him again."

"You have the photos, though. That's what counts."

I stood up and started pacing around. I was so upset. "He double-crossed me. He said that he still had the negatives and that if I didn't continue to have sex with him, he would still send the photos to Adam."

"Good God," she said.

"I know. He said that in time, if I cooperate, he will give the negatives to me. But I have no idea what he means by 'cooperate.'"

"We need to think," she said. "It's not time to panic."

"Anna, this is going to destroy my marriage. This will destroy me."

Anna regarded me for a moment. Chris stopped playing for a moment and said, "Hi, Momma. Do you see what I'm building?"

"Yes, dear! You are such a great builder!" I said.

Anna stood up and tugged me along with her until we stood a little ways away from Chris. "Get a hold of yourself, Christina," she said. "What are your choices?"

"I could just kill myself," I moaned.

"Stop that," she said. "You could tell Adam, for starters."

"No," I said. "I can't do that. That will be the end."

"Okay, then," she said. "How about the police? Blackmail is illegal."

The thought of the police getting involved frightened me. I could see two problems with that. The first was that I would have to explain what I had been doing drinking wine in Buck's hotel room in the first place. Anna echoed my thoughts. "It would be hard to prove that you were raped," she said slowly, looking at me carefully. "A court of law would never convict him."

I hugged myself, but I was so shocked that I could no longer cry.

"Then there's the publicity," said Anna.

I shook my head. "Scandal! The business manager and the artistic director of the Lockville Ballet Company caught in an illicit affair."

Anna looked at me with a stern expression on her face.

"No one would believe he raped me," I whispered.

The rain started again, and my little guy whirled around in it, laughing. I watched him tilt his face to the sky and open his mouth, trying to catch the drops.

"You got yourself into this," she said.

"What do you mean?"

"By going to a hotel room with another man." Anna looked at me with pity in her eyes, but her arms were crossed in front of her.

"You encouraged me," I said.

"I did," she said evenly. "Get a grip. It's 1962. Live a little. Have a good time. Adam's not going to find out. I didn't think that sleeping with another man would freak you out the way it has. You really should just learn to enjoy yourself." She paused. "I guess I am on Buck's side in this matter. You have two men after you, and you don't appreciate either one."

I felt angry and stood up. "Well of course it does. I betrayed my husband."

She frowned. "If you go public, you'll kill the company. The investors, the customers, and our audience will be gone. Don't you get that?"

I stood there for a moment, rubbing my temple. Chris had wandered over to the swing set and was trying to clamber into it.

"Yes, I have thought of all of that," I said, feeling heavy. "I was hoping you could help me find a way out. What do you think I should do?"

"I've given you my opinion. You can't back out; you have to move forward."

I walked over to Chris, wiped off the swing, lifted him onto it, and gave him a small push. "There you go, buddy," I said.

Anna followed me. "Just go along with his plans," she said. Then she regarded me carefully. "For now."

"I don't think I can do that," I said evenly.

She rolled her eyes. "Don't be such a square, Christina. It's like couch casting…It's not uncommon."

"For you, maybe," I said, gritting my teeth.

"Yeah, I had a thing going with Dimitry at the Metropolitan. He was a lot of fun."

I was silent and seething.

"Oh, come on, Christina," she said. "There's not going to be a problem unless you make a problem."

I didn't know what to say. And she rushed to fill my silence.

"So what about the sex?" she asked.

"Anna!" I said, nodding toward Chris.

"Oh, for Christ's sake," she said. "You are paranoid. I mean, does he treat you okay?"

I thought awhile. He did, to a certain extent, but admitting that to Anna would encourage her. "Aside from the feelings of guilt, remorse, and shame he's inducing in me, yeah, he treats me just fine."

"You are a hard nut," she said. "Look, just enjoy it for now. Do whatever he wants until you can charm the negatives out of his hot little hands."

I nodded, though I felt glum.

"Anyway, you might enjoy it. A little fun wouldn't kill you. Sometimes you act like one of those Victorian women, all laced up in corsets until they couldn't breathe."

"It's not like that at all," I said.

"Really?" She cocked her head to the side, regarding me with those big green eyes of hers. "Don't tell me you aren't getting a little bored with Adam."

I pushed Chris a little harder on the swing, and he squealed in joy. For a minute, his butt left contact with the seat, and I was afraid he was going to go flying off, so I stopped pushing for a few moments to let him slow down. It felt like I was always just on the verge of losing control of things.

"No, not at all," I finally said. "I like being married and being a mom."

"But you want to be a career woman, too," she said.

She gave me a hug, and I stood stiffly, my hands at my side. Anna hadn't exactly helped, and I was then feeling even more trapped than ever.

"Don't pout," she said.

"I'm not," I said.

"You are," she said. "It doesn't suit you. See you at rehearsal?"

"Sure," I said, giving her a fake smile. She stuck out her tongue at me.

"Good-bye, kiddo," she said, waving to Chris.

"Bye, Anna!" he called. "Come see me again!"

Anna leaned in and gave me a kiss full on my mouth. "I'm so happy for you, Christina," she said. "You are finally breaking out of your prison."

Then she whispered fully and fiercely into my ears. "I'll go party with Buck if you don't want to. Tell him I'm available. It sounds like a good time to me."

Then she turned on her heels and was gone.

At about that time, the sun broke out of the clouds, and I felt a little more warmth to the day. I held the chains on Chris's swing until it slowly came to a stop and he hopped out.

"Ready to go, little darling?" I said.

"No, Mommy," he said. But he didn't resist when I pulled on his hand and tugged him along toward the car.

My meeting with Anna had not quite gone as planned. I regretted following her advice earlier, and it had gotten me into a pickle, but it sounded like she had a sound plan at the moment. Well, it seemed like the only plan. She was right that going public would just blow up in my face. But charming Buck out of the negatives? Well, that seemed like something I might be able to do. I resolved that the next time he called, I would throw myself into our liaison instead of resisting. Maybe my enthusiasm would throw him off guard enough to give up the negatives.

The real challenge, I realized with a start, would be getting him to give me up altogether, to cut things off, and to do so without a fuss. I realized that Buck Johnson wasn't the kind of man who gave up easily. I wondered if I could match him.

Equally, I resolved that Adam must never know. I had agreed to meet with Buck the next day. Adam was out of town again. That was one thing I insisted on, I wouldn't agree to any get-togethers unless Adam was out of town. We were meeting at the Hideaway Inn, which was in Westlake, a suburb of Lockville. Buck was good at being discreet so that our affair seemed to go unnoticed. At least so far.

I was concerned that I had developed a level of comfort with our parties, almost a level of excitement. Buck was such a great lover and always found a way to make me feel really special. The lovemaking was so exciting. But then when it was over, it was the guilt, the remorse. I felt so bad, so dirty. I was resolved to go out of the way to respond to his lovemaking. I had to totally respond and show him the maximum passion to convince him that I did want to continue our affair. It was the only way to get possession of the picture negatives.

It took me a while, but I finally found the inn - it really was out of the way! I knocked softly on the door of room 312.

Buck was there immediately, as he opened the door he took me in his arms and kissed me tenderly on the lips. Wow, look at the candles. Buck had festooned every inch of the hotel room with candles, I paused involuntarily at the threshold and caught my breath. Candles adorned the mantle, the tables, the chairs, and the headboard of the bed that we would soon occupy, creating a mantle of light like little stars. I started to cry despite myself—despite my resolve to fake my pleasure and our intimacies so I could get what I wanted in return.

My freedom.

But I realized, as my sobs turned into little hiccups, that I did not want my freedom—none of it. That I liked being encumbered with a son and domestic duties, that they were not incompatible with my soul's desire to dance, and that I needed to figure out how to intertwine the two.

And I realized, as Buck put his arms around me, kissed me on the temple, and whispered "shush," that I was lonely in my marriage.

We were separate, my husband and I, and every day that he went to his office and disappeared into his world of men, I felt adrift. Certainly, Chris satisfied me as much as a baby could have, but he was only a child. I needed my husband to notice me—to really understand me.

I wanted to be recognized.

I realized that in some perverse way, Buck saw me. Really saw me.

Through my tears, the flames from the candles blurred into one big glow. I blinked, trying to clear my sight. I could not succumb to this feeling. It wasn't right.

But Buck kissed me, at first gently and then insistently. My resistance quavered and then fell. I responded to the thrill of his lovemaking.

Afterward, I felt slick with sweat and slightly dizzy from my conflicting feelings. I hadn't felt such sweet highs and despairing lows for a long time. I grew fearful that I was falling for Buck, even though I despised him.

Was it possible to entertain two different feelings about someone?

I idly traced the veins that stood out on his forearms. He was such a contrast to Adam, who was thin but not particularly athletic; he was more of an intellect and such a professor compared to Buck.

My heart ached, and I pushed the feelings aside.

Buck must have seen something float over my face, because he looked pensive.

"I think I love you," he finally said slowly.

"Buck, I don't..." I gasped and forced myself to smile, though I knew it didn't reach my eyes. I needed to do as Anna had indicated—to pretend that I was enjoying my time with him, even though the more I pretended, the more I was afraid it would come true. I felt like I was losing my soul. "Buck, I don't think we need to talk about our feelings," I said. "Let's just enjoy ourselves. Let things be."

He kissed me at that, though I could see from the pain in his eyes that he didn't totally believe me. Who could have blamed him? I didn't believe myself half the time those days.

He leaned on his elbows, peering at me intensely. "I know it's not fair, since you're married," he said. "But tell me: If I give the negatives to you, will you stop seeing me?"

I had not expected such a direct question, and I could feel my mouth go dry. Of course I would break things off with him.

Wouldn't I?

Nervous energy hit me. I needed to move, and I sat up and swung my legs over the edge of the bed. Moving made me brave. It always did.

I decided to channel Anna. I would sound like a liberated girl. The kind who would go on the pill, smoke pot, and easily sleep around on her husband.

"You are such a cool guy. You make me laugh!" I said.

He looked startled, but I continued to lay it on thick. "Making love with you is like going to another planet." I caught his hand and playfully pulled it up to my lips before kissing it sweetly.

"Now, if we could get rid of those awful negatives, I think that we would enjoy making love even more." I paused for effect, reached over, and let my fingers run down his chest. He shivered. "You aren't the only one with some ideas; I have a few kinky ones of my own."

He laughed at that and grabbed me, pulling me close to him until my face was nestled against his broad chest. And then it began again until the two of us lay together, totally exhausted.

"Oh, aren't you a vixen, Christina," he said. "Aren't you a girl full of surprises?"

"Well?" I said.

"Not yet," he said. "I'm not willing to give them to you yet."

Later that night, after I had gone home to an empty house, fed Chris supper, and put him to bed, the phone rang. I knew it was Adam, who was off on a business trip, but I couldn't answer it right away. The ringing stopped and then resumed after a few seconds.

"Where were you?" said Adam. "I was worried when you didn't pick up."

"I was taking a bath," I lied. It was amazing how easily the lies slipped off my tongue those days. "How was your day?"

He told me about the contract he was pursuing and the guys he was meeting with out in California. "These are real go-getters," he said. "If I get this contract, I'm in the running for a promotion."

"You'll get it, dear," I murmured.

He must have noticed the distance in my voice. "Everything okay?" he asked.

"Yes," I said. Another lie. I thought my nose would grow longer than Pinocchio's. I wondered if I would still be able to dance with all that counterweight.

"Are you sure?" His voice sounded genuinely concerned, and I felt a stab of guilt run through me. I wasn't sure I was going to be able to go on like that for much longer.

"I'm tired," I said, hesitating. Then I added, "And I miss you." I sighed as I realized that that much was not even true. He was gone so often—at work, off on business trips, or even golfing or at card night with his buddies—that I had stopped missing him.

I had fallen into dangerous waters.

"Hang in there," he said. He sounded slightly annoyed. "You'll be fine. I'll see you in a few days," he said.

"Sure," I said. "You'll be home soon enough."

"Go have dinner with your folks," he said. "Or go out with Anna. Have some fun."

Oh, if he had known how much fun I was having, he would have been livid. He would have murdered me.

"Sounds like a great idea," I said. "I'll do that."

We said our good-byes, and I found myself torn between wanting to get off the phone and wanting to pour out my soul to him—to beg him to come home and save us. To save me.

After I hung up the phone, I wondered how long it would take before I drowned. I couldn't sleep for most of the night, and as the birds started singing in the early hours before dawn, I got up, made myself some coffee, and sat in the backyard to watch the sun come up.

I needed to get a hold of myself. I needed more sleep.

I decided to ask Anna if she had any Valium that I could have. She had said it had helped her.

If I had some more sleep, I thought, maybe I could be more assertive with Buck. It was going to be tricky, getting the negatives without tipping him off or making him feel too rejected immediately. I needed to string him along until I got the evidence.

But first I needed to get cracking on the choreography and score for our performance.

Thirteen

THE REBELLION

Christina

EVEN THOUGH I HAD HIRED A CONSULTANT AT BUCK'S INSIS-
TENCE (he could be oddly kind), I wanted to do the bulk of the work myself.
I spent a week choreographing the production by spreading large sheets of paper
on the dining room table, scribbling drawings, and jotting down notes. It was
backbreaking work, really. The difference between being a dancer and designing
the dance is the difference between being a model and being the painter, but it's
magnified by a cast of dancers and amplified over each scene. In fact, choreographing the dance was like painting on the stage—like creating individual moving tableaux in such a way that highlighted the dancers' individual personalities.

I had learned a little bit of that perspective—of building the scene on stage
and taking into account both technique and artistry—when I had studied at
school. I had been able to watch over the process under the tutelage of my
professors. But it was the first time I was handling the complex task on my
own, and the terror absorbed me, warding off the overwhelming emotions I
felt whenever I contemplated the entanglement with Buck and the peril I was
putting my relationship with Adam in.

Looking back on that time, I realize that the danger I was in spilled
into my work. *Swan Lake* has long been regarded with reverence, and it was

undoubtedly foolish to have chosen the work for a modern treatment. I was risking everything with that undertaking.

I had put together something that was more expressive, a little more physical, and even more sensual than had been seen before in the ballet. I had created a stark distinction between the lovely Odette and her treacherous rival, the Black Swan. The movements I had created for the Black Swan Pas De Deux were inspired: all seduction and entrapment. When I showed Anna some of the choreography I had designed, her eyes had gleamed, and she had said, "Illicit sex is good for your creativity." I had dismissed her comment with irritation—it wasn't the kind of support that I wanted from my second in command. But the guilt that my work might indeed reveal my recent activities, my shadow side, or my need spurred me on harder. I needed to inspire the dancers—to make them engage with what I was doing. I was in the studio, listening to the music for what I swear must have been the hundredth thousandth time and making some revisions to the plans I would share with the company that day, when Buck came in. I was so absorbed by the music that I was startled. He looked pleased to see me, but I immediately disengaged with him, standing up to turn off the music. I didn't want to be abrupt with him, but the studio was my space, and he had already invaded me so entirely that I didn't want him there. We had continued to conduct our business together at the hotel but had not ventured into the studio since that first day.

I had to remain friendly. The negatives were still at large, and I did not want to alienate him.

"What a pleasant surprise," I said brightly. "Are you here to see if I'm upholding my end of the bargain?" I had increasingly begun to think of our business relationship as a mirror of our personal one—as a deal with the devil. A very handsome devil at that, but a devil nevertheless.

He did not seem to be in the mood for pleasantries. He frowned. "Why aren't you dancing anymore?" he asked abruptly. "Why only directing?"

"What do you mean?"

He gestured to the drawings I had spread out on the floor. "Why are you only directing? I am not under the impression that you're working yourself into the show. You're not practicing, for one thing."

I felt dumfounded and then annoyed. "How do you know?"

He looked at me, amused. "Christina, I know every inch of your beautiful body. I can tell that you're not working out at the level of a professional dancer. "

"Oh?"

He looked at me appreciatively, but his words made me feel upset. "You are a little more…soft and curvy than you might be."

"Oh," I said, feeling heat rise in my face. I touched my tummy self-consciously. It was true that I was not working out in the studio anymore. Worse yet was the fact that he had been perceptive enough to notice. My own husband was not keen enough to appreciate the demands of being the artistic director of the company and hadn't noticed that I had gotten soft.

"You're still beautiful," he said hastily. "I didn't mean to offend you."

"You didn't," I said stiffly. Then, because of his chagrined and genuinely guilty look, I added, "Truly."

"A dancer's career is very brief," he said softly.

I nodded.

"Let's not think about distressing things," he said. That was Buck's answer to everything. "I wanted to talk with you about some marketing plans."

"Does it have to be now?" I asked helplessly.

He looked puzzled. "Don't you have a little time to talk before rehearsal starts? When I rang your house earlier, your babysitter said you had left for work already."

I frowned. Buck had talked to my mother. The fact that he was crossing paths with so many aspects of my life, again, made me feel uneasy.

"What's wrong?" he asked. "Should I not have called your house?" He hesitated, searching my face with his gaze. "Is your relationship with me… embarrassing?"

"No, no," I said, noting the distress in his voice. I didn't want to jeopardize my chances of putting my hands on the negatives. I felt that I was very close to getting him to trust me and to having him believe that I was as smitten with him as he was with me, and I would not lose him. "It's just that you talked to my mother and…" I searched for a rational explanation—one that would cover up my true feelings and would not wound him. "She's a bit of a worrier. She'll ask me if everything is okay with the ballet."

"I talked with your mother?" The amused look had returned to his face.

"Yes," I said.

"Well, she's a very lovely woman," he said. "I cannot wait to meet her."

I felt stricken and must have looked it, because he hurried to add, "When the time is right, my dear."

I smiled. The smiles were coming easily, but so were the heartbreak and the feeling of sliding on ice. "Of course, darling," I said, taking his hand in mind. "It's just that I need to get these plans finished up before rehearsal."

My distraction had worked. When I talked of love or business, Buck was all ears. He brightened. "Then I mustn't distract you."

That time, he let his hand rest on my cheek for a moment, but he didn't try to kiss me before he said good-bye and left the studio.

I looked at my watch. I had twenty minutes before the dancers would start showing up.

I needed to be ready.

Swan Lake epitomizes romantic tension that is tragic. The scenes of celebration in the first and third acts bracket the torrential tragedy that plays out in the second act. The whole thing rises to a full-blown tempest in act four. I had rearranged the score in my mind to highlight the nuances of the story and to bring them more into focus.

Throughout it all, I felt Tchaikovsky was standing behind me, muttering over my shoulder. I couldn't tell if he approved or disagreed with me; his gray-bearded presence ran together with all the instructors of my youth, with my father, and even with my grandfather. Sometimes, I would wake from a dream in which he was chiding me for not understanding what the story was trying to convey. He stood in the middle of the stage with a blue light on him and with swan feathers falling all about him like snow. "It's about transformation, Christina," he said, his tone elevated. "It's not about *your* transformation."

And it wasn't. But it was. But before I could speak to him, I woke up.

The dream occurred almost every night. I awoke tired and edgy. I found myself unable to be patient with Chris. Anna got on my nerves, my mother kept trying to feed me, and the encounters with Buck were beginning to take on an unreal, dreamlike quality. I stopped asking for the negatives altogether; I was beginning to lose hope and with it, my mind.

Adam and I were unfailingly polite to each other, but I did not feel the intimacy and closeness with him that I longed for.

Swan Lake was about high tragedy, but my life quickly started to feel like personal tragedy. The company members were spread throughout the room, clustered in little knots that I realized, belatedly, signified allegiance, while I stood at the front and presented my vision. Anna had come in a little bit late and was standing off to the side, giving me encouraging smiles and nods, but it didn't offset the hostility I could feel rising from the dancers. For the first time, I became acutely aware of a divide between me and them, director and dancers.

Jill, who was playing the double heroine, Odile/Odette, and would alternate between swan and human form, was the most resistant to my treatment. I could tell by the way she was fixing me an icy, unblinking stare before she spoke.

"So there's dialogue?" she asked.

"Yes," I said briskly. "That and the acting will make the storyline more obvious and easier for a broader audience to follow."

This wasn't the Bolshoi. And they wanted the Bolshoi.

"At least you get to neck onstage," quipped Emily. Emily was a pale redhead with a full, expressive dancing style and an equally expressive mouth.

The other dancers tittered, and Jill looked unhappy. The lead male, Michael, crossed his arms.

"I think it's going to work just fine," said Anna. "It's going to be marvelous, in fact. Groundbreaking."

"You aren't dancing in it," one of the other female dancers muttered.

Jill looked at me pointedly, and I thought I saw Michal hiding a smirk.

"Oh, for pity's sake. Take some creative risks," said Anna. "Get empowered."

There was more muttering from the members of the company. I appreciated Anna's help, but hers was not a light touch. I needed to exert some control, but I needed to get them on board willingly, and insults weren't going to help matters any.

I cleared my throat. "I'm sure that you all have some questions about the direction we're taking, but I want to reassure you that our backers tell us that we need to be innovative in order to keep a company going successfully in Lockville."

At that, some of the expressions on the faces of the dancers looked more open and eager. I knew that the idea of an ongoing company in Lockville interested them as much as it did me. We all had a vested interest in the venture, and I simply needed to remind them of it.

"The times, they are a-changin'," I said, singing a little Bob Dylan, hoping to get a laugh. Nobody did laugh, and Anna gave me a peculiar look. I realized my singing might have been a little off. I continued. "We need to start building an audience here that is unaccustomed to attending cultural events and draw them into the performance with an exciting and modern concept."

A few people nodded. I did some math and figured that about 70 percent of the group was excited, but there were still a few members who looked opposed to the idea. I realized, with a sinking heart, that my principal dancers were in that group.

I needed a way to reach out to them.

"Well, why don't we get started with a few of the additions I've talked about," I said. "Emily, could you take charge of rehearsals for us?" She looked surprised, but she and her big mouth were influential members in the company, and I needed to press every advantage. Putting her in charge while I did some damage control would benefit me. "I have full confidence in you!" I said, smiling

"All right then," she said, jumping up and clapping her hands. "You heard the lady. Let's get started. We have some work to do."

Jill and Michael were looking at me expectantly. "I guess we have some work of our own to do," I said to them. "Let's meet in my office, shall we?"

I walked ahead of them with Anna by my side. "I hope you know what you're doing," she said to me out of the corner of her mouth.

I didn't know if I knew what I was doing, but I needed to fake it. I wanted to slink away with my metaphorical tail between my legs, but instead, I straightened up and said, "I have a plan."

In my office, I gestured to the chairs, asked Jill and Michael to sit down, and closed the door. Anna sat on the corner of my desk, and I stood. I hoped that doing so would make me look more confident than I felt.

Perhaps I should have asked Buck to stay.

I felt a sob work its way up my throat, but I pushed it down. I desperately needed my principals for our opening performance. I thought the best bet would be to level with them. If they could see what we needed to do, what we were up against, and how close we had come to losing the company, they would have to throw themselves into it.

"We have to change to survive. To survive, we must expand our audience to include the general audience," I said. "I'm asking you to join with me… with us to give this new direction a chance."

Jill still looked dubious. "I just think this is going to ruin my career," she sniffed.

"It's going to help your career," said Anna. "It will set you apart from all the other wannabes."

Jill looked even angrier, and I tapped Anna on the arm and shook my head "no." When I glanced at Michael, it appeared he was greatly enjoying the show.

"I'm going to level with you," I said. I leaned forward and lowered my voice. "No one in the company must know, because I don't want them to lose confidence, but we are in danger of being shut down."

Jill straightened up at that, and Michael looked somber. "Shut down? As in closed completely?" he asked.

I nodded. "But we had someone go to bat for us and get us some funding. We have a stay of execution, so to speak, but we need to pull together and nail opening night, or there's not going to be a Lockville Ballet."

"Okay, okay," Jill said. "But who's our guardian angel?"

I laughed at the thought of Buck being an angel, though I saw that he had good intentions.

"I'll let you know at a later date," I said. "Just, please, please help us keep things on course."

"It's going to be a disaster," opined Jill.

"Please, let's just give it a try," I said. But my stomach was twisted in nausea. How sure was I about my new choreography? "Let's see how it feels. Okay?"

"Well, okay. We'll try it, even though we all know it's not going to work," said Michael.

Jill was looking stonily out the window, and I wondered if she was going to sabotage things. Without her help, it wouldn't work.

But I knew that that was the most I was going to get out of my principal dancers. I had to keep pushing ahead anyway. I didn't know what else to do. I hoped that after they became immersed in the new format, they would come around. The choreography, the style of dancing, and the costumes were all liberating. I wondered, not for the first time, if the forces of tradition could be moved, even just a little.

Didn't they want to breathe?

I dismissed them, and after they had filed out, Anna turned to me and said, "Do you think they're on board now?"

"I hope so," I said tiredly. "I did the best I could do."

The confrontation with the two dancers made me feel spent. I was beginning to feel more and more out of sorts, like everything around me was spiraling out of control.

"Why don't you take a walk while I finish up the marketing paper work Buck Johnson left for us to fill out," she said. "I can help get a jump on that."

"No, I must fill out these papers for Buck," I snapped. "I have to get these just right."

"Well, okay then," said Anna, withdrawing. "I guess I'll just go to lunch then."

"Fine," I snapped. I sat there staring stonily at the papers until the office door closed behind her, but it was hard for me to concentrate.

Fourteen

The Breakdown

Christina

I WENT TO REHEARSAL EARLY THE NEXT DAY because Adam was still out of town and my mother and father wanted to take Chris to the zoo in Central Park. "You look tired," my mother had said. "Why don't you take a little break?"

But I had anxious feelings about showing the consultant some of my ideas. I was meeting with him the next day and really wanted him to understand my vision for our performance. The character of Odile haunted me. I understood how she felt ashamed of her swan aspect and how deeply she had fallen in love. I felt like the characters related to my own life, but I wasn't sure who was playing which part.

I had just tucked into the marketing papers, which I'd been putting off, when a stylishly dressed woman I had never seen before walked into my office, closing the door behind her.

"You're Christina," she said, beaming broadly and reaching out her hand to shake mine.

"I'm sorry," I said, startled. "If we've met already, I've don't recall it."

"No problem," she said. "I know all about you and your work with the ballet. Can I have a word with you?"

"Who are you?" I asked.

"Marilyn," she said. She leaned over the desk, and I could smell her perfume. It was sweet to the point of cloying. "Marilyn Johnson."

It took me a moment, but the floor felt like it was falling up to meet my face, and I blurted out, "Oh my dear God, I didn't know that Buck was…"

"Married?" she said, letting out a little laugh. "Don't worry your pretty little head about that. I kept Buck's last name, but we are no longer legally entangled. At least not in that way."

"Oh," I said, feeling rattled and ashamed for simply having blurted out the first thing that had popped into my head. It didn't bode well for my being able to keep a lid on things while I figured out how to disentangle myself from Buck, to protect my marriage, and to still save the company.

And yet, this was the woman that Buck had been attracted to before he had pursued me. Despite myself, I was curious about her and gave her a sidelong glance. She had a great figure and was curvy in a way that dancers typically weren't. She was tall, much taller than I was, a tall that Balanchine would have approved of, and her long red hair fell in soft waves over the paisley shift she was wearing.

She saw me studying her and laughed again. "I see you've fallen for him, then."

I felt myself flush. "It's not like that at all."

"Don't worry, dear. I'm not judging you. Buck has that effect on women."

"I'm happily married," I said. "Look, what do you want?"

"If you were happily married, you wouldn't be fooling around with him, now would you," she said. Her voice sounded friendly, but she regarded me coolly.

I drew in a deep breath and tried to keep my voice calm. "That's a rather severe accusation," I said.

"Oh, don't get yourself all in a lather, pet," she said. "Do you want to hear what I want or not?"

I thought for a moment. Did this woman, Buck's ex-wife, know about him and me, or was she just bluffing? For a moment, I listened to the music coming from the studio—the rousing sounds of Tchaikovsky's score.

I decided that I didn't want to find out.

"I don't see what business we would have," I said, gritting my teeth.

"Oh, that's not true!" she laughed again, waving her hand at me. I noticed that she wore a profusion of amber bracelets almost in the Bohemian style that clanked against one another as she moved her arm. "It's just that Buck owes me some money. From our divorce."

"I'm so sorry," I said. "But what's that got to do with me?"

She leaned forward, and for the first time, I realized that she was truly dangerous. Beautiful, but without remorse. And she was standing in my office at the heart of my work.

"I know about your little tête-à-têtes with Buck, and I also know how much you will lose if word gets out about your affair." She waved her hand around casually as if the civic center were mine and it was up on the auction block. "If you want me to go away, you need to ask Buck to pay me twenty thousand dollars."

My throat closed up. "I can't possibly do that," I said.

"If I don't see that money right away, your hanky-panky is going to see the light of day."

For a moment, I thought I might faint.

"I know who to talk to at the Lockville *Courier*," she said sweetly. "And wouldn't Adam like to read about that in the paper."

She leaned in closer. Her perfume smelled exquisite. Everything about her was perfect, and I knew she would make good on her promise if I didn't comply.

"You can and you will," she said. She sauntered to the door as if she were going to a party. "I'm not going to wait long."

She gave me a cool smile and walked out of my office, leaving the door open behind her.

I walked over to it and closed it halfway, and then I leaned against the wall as if I could keep the world out if I just remained where I was.

I heard a voice. "Hey, are you okay?"

It was Anna, looking concerned. I hadn't even noticed her approach, and I wondered how much she had heard. I closed my eyes. I felt a massive headache coming on, and my chest felt so tight that I could hardly breathe.

"Christina, can I get you anything? You don't look well," said Anna, her eyebrows furrowed. "I think we can work everything out with the dancers if we just talk some more. Perhaps the new consultant can help sort things out. "

I didn't respond to her suggestion; she didn't know about Marilyn and her threat. That was taking things to a whole new level. I didn't intend to tell Anna either, because it was all my fault, and I had to fix it myself. I didn't need anybody's help.

I forced myself to keep my voice even and calm sounding, but from the look Anna gave me, I probably hadn't succeeded. "I have some issues to take care of, and I plan to take the rest of the day off."

"Well, at least that's a plan," said Anna drily.

"I need to sort things out," I said a little more emotionally. "I need some time alone."

If she didn't leave soon, I would cry. And I didn't want her to see that happen.

Anna hesitated at the door; she looked like she was going to refuse to leave, but the pleading look I let myself give her was convincing. "Okay, dear," she said, looking resigned. "Let's talk tomorrow. You take care of yourself."

"I will," I said. But by that time, Anna had left, and I was talking to myself.

So I couldn't stand the silence—couldn't stand being alone with myself and my guilt. I wondered if Marilyn would hold to her word or if she was going to be like Buck and perpetually keep me on the hook. I wondered how I would be able to tell Buck that I had spoken to her and that she wanted him to give her all that money.

Would he refuse me? Could he be so heartless?

I walked into my office, picked up the phone, and fumbled it, dropping it. I started dialing, my hands trembling so badly that I couldn't pick out the numbers. It rang a few times, and then an unfamiliar woman answered. I felt confused. Maybe one of mom's friends was there and had answered the phone for her?

"Hello? Hello?" said the woman.

"Is my mommy there?" I whispered, barely able to speak.

"Hello?" said the voice. "Speak up. Did you say 'mommy'?"

"Yes," I said. My voice felt dry, and I felt as though I was floating above myself and that if I wasn't careful, I might float out of my own body and into the wind, where I would be blown away and lost.

"I'm afraid you have the wrong number," said the woman. Her voice sounded kind but distant. I had to try again, and with shaking hands, I dialed the number. "Hi, Mommy," I said, my voice trembling slightly. "I have a favor to ask."

"Yes, dear, of course," she said.

I cradled my head in my hands on my desk. I felt feverish. "I have so much to do with the new costuming and choreography, plus the set designer needs to meet with me to go over some specs. Would you be able to keep Chris for the night?" I paused and took a deep breath. "I could pick him up after lunch tomorrow."

My mom's voice sounded warm. How I wished I could have confided in her. "Why, yes, we would love to keep the little darling."

"Thanks," I breathed a sigh of relief.

"Is everything okay?"

I hesitated. *Now is my chance to tell her—to have her make everything okay,* I thought. But then I thought no, it's my problem to bear. She couldn't fix it anyway. What could she do? "Yes, of course I'm okay," I said.

"Are you sure?" she asked, a worried tone replacing her warm one. "You sound like you're down."

"Yes, I'm okay," I said. But as soon as I said it, a wave of emotion hit me, and I started crying, just like that. Not just crying but sobbing. I held the receiver away from my head and took a couple of deep breaths, trying to get myself under control. What was happening to me?

I could hear my mom's distant voice. "Christina? Christina? Are you there?"

I blew my nose and wiped my eyes. "Yes, Mom."

"Maybe you should come by and talk. We can talk, and maybe I can help."

"No, no, I'll be okay," I said. "I just need some time alone to think. I have problems to figure out."

"What kind of problems? With the ballet?"

I began to cry again, and I needed to get off the phone.

"Remember, honey, that we're here if you need us."

"Thanks. Bye."

I barely registered the drive to the house—it was a blur. Once I got home, it took me a few moments to figure out how to put the key into the door and open it. *Stupid, stupid,* I told myself.

I walked inside and sat at the family-room dining table in stunned silence for I don't know how long. Part of me wanted to go drive back to my mother's house and to take her up on her offer. Another part of me just wanted to go down to the airport, get a ticket, and join my husband in California, where he was off doing business again.

The image of Marilyn, her threatening posture, and the gleeful look in her eye frightened me. I could not shake that picture.

What was I to do?

What could I have done?

I came to the inevitable conclusion: my beloved Adam would divorce me. It was that simple.

I might lose Chris in the divorce. Would Adam do that? I tried to think, but I was feeling a bit of a headache coming on. More like a massive migraine.

The affair with Buck would be exposed in the papers. My reputation would be ruined. I had cheated on my husband. Everyone would know. Those awful photographs would be passed around to whomever. My thoughts ran wild. The principal dancers were destroying my ballet company. My life was not worth living.

I hated Buck.

I hated Marilyn.

I hated Jill and Michael.

"Dammit," I swore, but the sound hung perfectly still in the silent house. No one was around to hear me, dispute me, or comfort me.

I'm not sure how long I was there, alone with my thoughts and my stupidity whirling about me. I know that I wept and wept, eventually throwing myself on the bed in my self-pity. I contemplated taking my life, as I was sure it was not worth much. I even dragged myself up at one point to see what tools I could use for my own destruction. I had no sleeping pills; I'd given the bottle to Anna after her last breakup. I had no razor blades, and the knives we had gotten for our wedding seemed too beautiful to sully and not nearly sharp enough. Eventually I wore myself out pacing, and I dragged myself back to bed, feeling sharp pains of regret over my life and the decisions I had made.

I was aware that the room grew dark.

Frequent flashes of lightning filled the room. The wind blew the tree branches. A storm approached.

I tossed and turned as if in sync with the storm. I eventually fell asleep. When the storm passed sometime in the night, I did not notice. But I must have felt it.

Fifteen

The Transformation

Christina

IF I DREAMED ANYTHING THE PREVIOUS NIGHT, I didn't remember it. It was the first nightmare-free night I had had in months, and when I woke, it was light out, and the clock said 7:30 a.m.

I jumped out of bed and walked to the window. The world look freshly scrubbed by the rain, the birds sounded more beautiful, and the sky even appeared to be a special shade of blue.

I realized that I felt rested. I felt better. What had happened?

A barrage of thoughts washed through my mind: I'm going to be okay. I must take action. I will not be pushed around. I will be in charge. I will be in charge. I will fix what I can fix and not worry about things that are out of my hands.

The storm seemed to have cleansed me. The threat of Marilyn Johnson had somehow pushed me over the edge. But I realized I needed to be rid of the bad people in my life. I would start small and then deal with Buck Johnson.

I walked downstairs and called one of my father's old friends, a lawyer, and made an appointment with his secretary to see him. I tried not to think about meeting with him too much. I had to forge ahead. Then I called Scott Pierce. He seemed surprised to hear from me, since he hadn't gotten the job of principal dancer in the first place, but I told him that I wanted him and Meg

Cameron to come in. When I told him the roles were available, he seemed overjoyed.

After I had had something to eat, had showered, and had gotten ready, I was still running on a feeling of serenity, which I hadn't felt for a long time. It felt good to have made a decision and to be moving forward in a new direction, even though I didn't know what the consequences were going to be. It was easier to get ready without Chris around, so I headed in to work earlier with a feeling of determination. As I drove, I noticed that even the streets of Lockville looked different that morning. Maybe it was the morning sun, or maybe it was the feeling of summer, but everything had a beautiful glow about it. I felt different. I felt confident. *What is it?* I wondered. Maybe it was simply the fact that I saw such a blue sky. It was beautiful. I took it as an omen of blue skies ahead.

I knew it wasn't the weather, and it wasn't the fact that it was summer; it was more than that. I had a feeling that I would be okay. Even though I didn't know how Adam, the dancers, Marilyn, Buck, and even my parents were going to react, I knew what I needed to do. I knew I had to move forward. I was determined to face my problems and to try to fix them for good.

I hoped that Adam would understand. But I pushed the worry that he might leave me out of my mind for the day and tried to focus on the blue sky.

I needed all the energy I could get, especially because when I parked my car and walked into the civic center, Scott and Meg were already waiting in the lobby. The first hurdle would be convincing them to sign on as lead roles in the performance in the middle of the season. They would have a lot of work to do to catch up, and it would be challenging and risky for them. I was confident they could pull it off, but I needed them to share that confidence.

We shook hands, and I gave them a stellar smile. "Oh, hello. I'm so happy to see you both. Thanks for coming in on such short notice."

They both smiled and seemed energized. "Oh, we're excited to be here," said Scott. "Meg was so thrilled when I told her that you had called."

I felt a sense of relief. It didn't seem like it was going to be a hard sell. I invited them back into my office, and along the way, we talked a little bit about how the publicity was going for the performance of *Swan Lake*.

I asked them to sit down and brought them up to speed about where we were. I was blunt about the fact that we were doing some innovative choreography. "Some might even say it is edgy," I said. "It certainly pushes the boundaries of what would be considered classical ballet."

I watched them with interest, gauging their reactions. If they weren't going to be on board, or if they were resistant, I didn't have a fallback plan. That, and the fact that they hadn't made the company the first time around, meant that I needed to be diplomatic.

They looked at each other for a moment as if they were coming to some sort of unspoken agreement. Scott spoke. "Yes, we do want to be part of your company and are excited about what you're doing," he said. Meg nodded.

I felt a sense of relief, but I needed to level with them. There was, after all, some dissension in the company. That wouldn't escape their notice, and they needed to be able to lead the other dancers in order to make the performance click. "May I be frank with you?"

They looked curious but nodded.

"Michael and Jill never really accepted the concept of modernized choreography. Their hearts are just not in it. They're great dancers, but the rehearsals are going nowhere without a commitment to change on their part."

They looked at each other with quizzical expressions. "Well," Meg said. "Is this a problem company-wide or just with Michael and Jill?"

"Most of the dancers seem to understand and are working in a modern direction, but without that work coming from the two lead members, the rehearsals are not productive. There are maybe one or two more who are resistant, so we're going to deal with that. We want a cohesive unit."

"I could tell by the way you acted in the tryouts that you're on board with this. And I am hoping you still feel that way."

Scott leaned forward. "Yes, and I think I speak for Meg. We like this idea very much."

"Good," I said.

"We agree that a midsized town has to provide a product that attracts a broad audience."

It made me feel relieved that at least Scott was a visionary and not stuck in the mud. Sometimes it's hard for dancers to think about the entrepreneurial aspects of the ballet, but that's something that the arts need to deal with better.

Meg danced a little on her seat. "Oh, yes," she chimed in. "I like the new concept. A lot. I think it'll appeal to a wider audience, and it'll be more fun to dance."

At that, Meg got up and started doing an improvisational Charleston right there in my office. I couldn't help but burst into laughter at that.

"Okay, so I'm offering you the lead roles in our upcoming modified performance of *Swan Lake*."

Meg did a little bow, and Scott clapped and whooped. "We accept," said Scott. "Thank you," said Meg.

"Thank you," I said. "I'm glad you'll be on board. We are now well funded, and we're planning for a performance in October."

I asked them to fill out some employment papers and to stick around in the conference room while I took care of business.

Scott's eyebrow shot up, and Meg looked a little uncomfortable. "We'll just stay put in the conference room, then," she said. "No screaming and hollering, I hope."

"I hope not," I said.

"Good luck," Scott said brightly, though he didn't look too sad about my upcoming task. Who could have blamed him? He benefited from it.

Scott and Meg had just gone to the conference room when in huffed Anna, toting several shopping bags and looking frazzled. "Hi, Chrissy. Sorry I'm late," she said. "Did I miss all the fun?"

"Some of it," I said. "But I'll save some for you."

Something in the tone of my voice must have been different, because she gave me a sharp look. "Are you feeling better?"

"Oh yes, I'm fine," I said. "I feel great."

Anna plopped down in the chair and gave me the once-over. "Really, what is going on?" she asked. "What brought on the quick recovery?"

I smirked at her. "There will be plenty of time to talk over tea later. I have a busy schedule this morning. We have important business to take care of."

"Well, just keep me in the dark, why don't you?"

"I think you can handle it. Anyway, I have a task for you. I would like you to order Michael and Jill to come to my office immediately."

"Order?" Anna said, an amused look on her face. "That sounds strong. What if they refuse? As you know, they usually do what they want to do." She didn't need to say it, but I could tell by the look on her face that she was also surprised at the new me. I was a little surprised myself, to be honest.

Anna wasn't the type to be put off too easily, though. "So what's going on that's got you so busy? Do you have another Buck Johnson meeting?"

I felt aggravated with Anna for slowing things down and for accusing me of being in thrall to Buck Johnson. "Anna, do what I say—now!"

She looked at me impishly.

"Before I have to fire you too."

"You wouldn't," she said. "Who would you have to go for coffee and tea with if you fired me?"

"Oh, just do it," I said. "Before I lose my temper."

"Yes, boss," she said. But before she left, she came around my desk and gave me a quick hug. "I don't know what happened, but I like the new Christina."

"Go," I said.

After Anna left, I had one more task in front of me. I called down to the front desk and asked for Officer Cook. That morning, when my plan had become clear, I had called him and prepped him for backing me up. I didn't know how ugly things would get with Jill and Michael, and I didn't want to take any chances. I told him that I needed him right away. "It's time to come to my office. Michael and Jill will be here any minute."

"Yes, ma'am. I've been waiting for your call," he said. "I will be right up."

From the unprofessional glee in his voice, I got the feeling that he didn't much like Jill and Michael either. I sighed. How had I let things go for so long?

Officer Cook was in the office ready and waiting by the time Anna managed to convince Jill and Michael that they needed to leave practice and meet with me. When they walked into the room, they seemed surprised to see him there. Anna merely looked amused. She was the kind of person who liked her soap operas, and I could tell by the expression on her face that she was really satisfied with the way the morning drama was unfolding.

You'd think they would have seen the handwriting on the wall, but Michael merely looked annoyed. "Now what do you want?" he said, his tone disrespectful.

Beside me, I could see Officer Cook's eyebrows shoot up. I could tell he was going to enjoy escorting them out, and it looked like he was going to need to.

I sighed. No need to draw this out.

"No need to sit down," I said. "You are both fired."

For once, Michael was speechless, and Jill looked shocked.

"You are no longer members of the Lockville Ballet," I added. "I will have Anna go with you while you collect your personal belongings. You can change in the dressing room, but you will not return to the rehearsal area."

Michael looked, for a moment, angry and like he was going to hit me. "Wait, what is this? You can't fire us," he said. "Without Jill and me, you have nothing."

Jill's face was red and splotchy as though she was going to cry; her eyes were dry as she glared at me. "You don't have the authority to fire us," she said, a faint smile flickering over her face. "You aren't the business manager."

I had practiced that moment in my head, and I knew that if I acknowledged their accusations or argued with them in any way, I would be done with. I slightly nodded to Anna, who was frowning at the two of them as though she meant to lambast them. But I wanted to get them out of the office as quickly as possible. My mind was quite made up.

A flicker of disbelief washed over Michael's face when I turned to the officer and nodded. "Can you escort these two out of the building?"

"With pleasure," Officer Cook said, taking a few steps toward Michael and taking him by the elbow.

Michael withdrew his arm from the officer's with a huff. "You are absolutely crazy!" He slammed his hand on the desk, and Anna and Jill both jumped, but I had experienced so much stress by that time that I actually laughed.

"Go ahead and hit me," I said. "You'll be leaving here in handcuffs."

"You're a sanctimonious little bitch," said Michael.

"Be careful," said Officer Cook. "One more insult and you'll be arrested."

Michael looked frustrated and shot an angry look at Jill, who was standing there with that slight smile frozen on her face as if she didn't know what else to do. I felt a little sorry for her, but not enough to change my mind. When he stormed out the door, he looked back and gave me the finger, and then he was gone.

"Well, that was charming," I said out loud. Anna let out her breath as though she'd been holding it. Jill was still standing there, and I looked at her and nodded toward the door. "I really need you to be on your way," I said. "Why don't you catch up with your colleague?"

She looked at me thoughtfully. "Honestly, I didn't think you had any backbone," she said. "You surprised me."

"Well, you didn't surprise me," I said. "In fact, you were so predictable that I don't think you could possibly dance the new choreography." I watched with delicious satisfaction as her eyes widened at my comment. "It takes someone with a bit more creative imagination to dance in our company." Where I had developed such a sharp, spiteful tongue was beyond me, but what surprised me even more was how enjoyable it felt to talk so freely. I realized I had frequently spoken in a guarded matter.

"Well, I'll be happy to see you fail," she said. "Then you'll see that we were right."

"Don't count on it," I said. "I think you'd better be on your way."

"Gladly," she said, and then she stormed out of the office in the most ungraceful way possible.

The office fairly buzzed with energy after they left. I exhaled and sat down in my chair, and then I spun around in joy. "That felt great!" I exclaimed.

I smiled at Anna and noted that she was giving me a steady curious look. I realized she hadn't spoken the whole time Jill and Michael had been in the office.

Finally, she said, "Wow, what has gotten into you?"

"What do you mean?" I asked coyly, even though I knew darn well what she was talking about.

"I have never seen you so in charge."

I considered her comment. It was true that I was in charge. I needed to be in charge if I was going to take back my life and rescue my family's happiness from the clutches of Buck Johnson and his frightening ex-wife.

"Well, get used to it," I said, a feeling of satisfaction washing over me and drowning out the tiny voice that said I still had to worry about how my husband was going to respond to all of this.

"Yes, ma'am," said Anna, looking pleased. "I'm really proud of you."

"Well, save it," I said. "We've still got some work to do."

"Yes, I suppose we do," she said. "We still have to talk to the company. And what are we going to do for the lead dancers?"

I felt a little bit giddy from how well my plan was falling into place. "I already have dancers in mind," I said.

Then Anna looked even more impressed. "You do?"

"Yes, I do. Do you remember Scott and Meg from the tryouts?"

"Yes, I do," she said. "It was a hard decision."

"Well, not anymore," I said. "They're waiting in the conference room to be introduced to the company."

Anna looked like she was about to fall over. "Christina, you are so fired up. I am so amazed." She laughed. "Well, *shocked* is more accurate. But it's all wonderful.

I walked around the desk and hugged her. "Thanks for hanging in there with me," I said. "I know it's been tough."

"Well, that's when we get going, right?"

"Right!" I laughed.

Everything else that morning felt like it was happening to somebody else; it was as though I was a ghost floating over myself or as though I had been possessed by some better version of me. I saw myself walking with Anna down to the conference room, where we met with Meg and Scott, who were waiting patiently. I led them to the rehearsal area, which, admittedly, had slowed down considerably since Michael and Jill had been summoned not a half an hour earlier. The dancers looked a little disorganized. A few of them were working on the bar when I entered, but the majority of them were standing around and talking. All eyes flicked curiously to Meg and Scott and then back to me. I could see the questioning looks on their faces, though some of the more seasoned veterans were obviously putting two and two together and realizing that their leaders had been fired.

This was a moment that needed to be handled delicately, or I could destroy the faith of the company. I took a deep breath, willing that floaty feeling away. I had never felt so euphoric, and I didn't want to let that feeling jeopardize a smooth transition between company leaders.

"Good morning, everybody," I said. "Could you please give me your attention?"

A buzz of conversation permeated the room, but I held up my hand in warning. "Give me your attention, please; I have an important announcement to make."

The talking died down, and I waded into the fray. "I want to introduce our dancers for the lead parts in our upcoming ballet performance, though many of you may have worked with them in the past. I am pleased to give you Meg Cameron and Scott Pierce."

At that point, the dancers exchanged looks with each other. A few of them muttered in surprise.

"Yes, this means that Michael and Jill have left the company," I said. "They were unable to work as part of a team." I looked around the room challengingly. A few of the dancers looked down at the floor or otherwise avoided my gaze, but I hoped that with the ringleaders gone, the dissent that had divided our company would also be eliminated.

Was I right?

After a few moments of what seemed like confusion, a scattered round of applause broke out with a few cheers. Scott took a mock bow, and Meg looked a little dazed but happy. The company wasn't totally pulling together yet, but I figured it would take a little time.

Of course, all we had was a very little amount of time in which to get the show together.

After the milling about and congratulations were done, I asked the company for a few more moments of their time and attention. I told them that we had our funding in place and that costuming and set design were going to be underway.

"As you know, there has been some concern about the choice to adopt new choreography." I wanted to pace around the floor, so nervous was I to be talking about it, but I was determined to stay the course and to hold with my new "amazing" personality. So I stood there, elongating my spine, standing still and confident. No fidgeting there.

There was some restlessness again. I waited while I mentally ran through the lists of the dancers who would be loyal and work hard and those who were questionable. Judging by a few of the sullen looks, mostly from the younger members—mostly from women—there were still a few remaining dancers in the ranks who might resist the new direction.

"I want to address those concerns, and if there is anyone who is still concerned, I would like for you to come to my office so we can discuss this."

The members of the company stirred a bit and looked at each other.

I looked at Anna and gave her an imperceptible smile. I knew we were in the homestretch, but I also knew we needed to give the dancers a moment to sort themselves out.

"Thanks again for your attention, and I appreciate your giving Meg and Scott your full support," I said.

"You know where to find us," Anna said with a cheerful tone in her voice.

We left the room while they were all talking and walked down the hallway to my office. I'd been spending a lot of time there lately, and I wondered what Chris was doing. I missed him like mad that morning. I wanted to cut the morning short and go pick up my baby boy. I was starting to feel a little more grounded and wanted to keep pushing forward. I had some big conversations ahead of me—ones that I was trying to push out of my mind.

I was giving Anna some instructions on working with the seamstress who would be making the costumes when there was a knock on the door, and then one of the dancers, Debra, poked her head in.

"You two ladies have a moment?" she said.

"Hello, Debra! Come on in," I said.

"What can we do for you?" Anna added.

Debra walked into the office and sat down in the chair. I studied her carefully. She was a petite redhead with freckles who had a lot of strength and agility. She was a hard worker but didn't have the best attitude; she often hesitated before trying something new or difficult. I assumed that she was not there for a social visit.

"Well, you said to see you if we were concerned about the new choreography," she said, sticking her chin up with defiance.

I smiled at her to encourage her to go on, though inwardly I groaned. "What's your concern?"

"Well, Angie and me—we talk a lot. And we think it's a mistake."

I wondered why Angie was not there with Debra as she lodged her complaint, but I kept that thought to myself. Angie seemed to be one of those people who talks a good game, but she always held back in practice as though she were seeing which way the wind was going to blow before she attempted something. I figured, with amusement, that Angie had put Debra up to this and that Debra believed that she would be coming in to support her at any minute.

As if to confirm my belief, Debra shifted in her chair and looked behind her.

"Waiting for somebody?" I asked.

"I was just seeing where Angie was," she said.

"Why don't you just go on? Why do you say that the choreography is a mistake?"

"Well, it's heresy," she blurted out. Then she blushed slightly. "It's not really ballet," she stammered.

For a moment, I almost felt sorry for Debra. But then I thought of the face of my little boy and how devastated he would be if his father and I divorced. My resolve once again hardened. I didn't have time for any more nonsense.

"I respect you for speaking up and for being honest," I said. Debra beamed at that, but her happiness was fleeting. I continued, "I'm going to let you go. You're terminated."

"What?" she said. Shock spread over her face.

"Immediately," I added.

"But you said…"

"I must have one hundred percent commitment to this company and its direction.

Anything less than that is unacceptable."

Debra started to tear up. "We didn't say we wouldn't dance the program. We just think it's a mistake."

"I'm sorry, but you are obviously resistant to change. And those who resist change in this world become roadkill." I felt myself getting inexplicably riled up as though the pent-up fear of the last past few months was seeping out as anger. "Now please leave at once, or I will call security."

Debra looked horrified, but she complied, muttering, "Okay, okay," as she left the room.

I figured I could get used to the new me, but Anna gave me a sharp look, and in a tone of disbelief, she said, "Christina, that was a little too strong."

I must admit that I felt a little crazy at that moment, but I felt strong, too. I felt like I could tackle anything that I needed to. I felt like Anna, because she didn't have a child and a husband, wouldn't really understand. Ever since Buck had come on the scene, a gap had been growing between the two of us, I realized. Would I have noticed our growing distance if not for him?

It didn't matter. I had to persevere. I stood up to go and very gently said, "In this world, you must be strong. You cannot accept the unacceptable."

Anna sat there with a pained expression on her face. "Would you ever fire me too? If I disagreed with you?"

"Don't be silly," I said. "You're my very best friend."

"Okay," she said, though she didn't look convinced.

After we'd wrapped up our morning and I was driving away in the car to pick up my son, I realized I didn't feel convinced either. But it didn't matter anymore. I was determined to be free.

Attorney Bill Wenzlick and my father went way back. Both of them had gone to college together at NYU, and then they had served in Korea. He was my godfather and had attended every birthday party without missing a beat. He had convinced my parents to let him dress up as Santa Claus every year, though they had thought I would be spoiled. He was kind and good, a friend to all in the Parker family, and always "Uncle Bill" to me.

I sat in the lobby, sinking down into the orange davenport and wishing I could disappear. I imagined that the secretary was looking at me disapprovingly and searched her face to see if she was a frequent diner at the hotel dining room and had seen Buck and me together. I took a deep breath, trying to quell the knot that was building in my stomach. I needed someone to help me, and though I was ashamed of my behavior, I didn't know who else I could possibly trust.

The thought that Bill might not be on my side and might even turn against me made my mind sharp and keen. I was happy about that, at least. I'd snapped out of that fog I had wandered in for the past few months.

At a few minutes after eleven o'clock, the office door opened, and out stepped Uncle Bill. He smiled broadly and greeted me with a hug and a kiss. I remember that at one time, I had had to stand on my tiptoes just to reach his cheek, which was always smoothly shaved. Now I merely had to crane my neck. He was not a tall man, but what he lacked in height he made up for in width, and I regarded his girth as comforting. He was the one who had always reminded me to eat and had said that I didn't need to be skin and bones to be a principal dancer. If only he had been right.

"To what do I owe this grand treat—a visit from my dear Christina?" he asked. "It's been a long time since you just dropped by my office." He gave me a searching look. "Adam hasn't cut off your candy supply, has he?"

"Uncle Bill," I said, flushing. "It's not like that. Though I am grateful for your seeing me." There had been a time when I'd drop by after school with a pack of giggling girls in tow just to see what sweets he had in his office. He liked to keep jars of licorice and tins of chocolates on hand. He said it was a great way to tame the criminal lot that he worked with.

"Then what is it? Can I presume this is simply a social call?"

I shook my head slightly and glanced involuntarily at the secretary, who, to her credit, appeared to be engrossed in filing papers.

Bill frowned. "I see. Well, let's go into the office and talk."

His dark-paneled office was a private reserve for him, with dark paneling on the walls behind the stacks of barrister bookcases. I sat down in one of the leather club chairs while he took a seat opposite mine. I wasn't sure if the fact that he had not sat on his desk should make me nervous or not. I smiled at him nervously.

"Christina, surely you don't have need of an attorney."

I cleared my throat. "I'm afraid I do."

"What's this about? Are you and Adam changing your will?" He seemed to have a sudden thought and smiled. "Are you two expecting another baby?"

I looked at the floor, studying the oriental carpeting. "No, nothing like that."

"Then what?"

I looked at him in his eyes, trying to measure the man. I felt like since I had encountered Buck Johnson, my friends had fallen by the wayside. Anna was peeved with me, my parents suspected something was awry with my marriage, and the dancers were rebelling. I realized that I didn't even have time to go to my mom's group anymore, and at that, fresh tears sprang to my eyes.

"Christina," he said, concerned, leaning forward to take my hand. "What's so terrible that you need to talk to me?"

I dabbed at my eyes, willing myself not to cry. "Will you promise to keep things confidential?" I asked. "Especially don't tell Daddy. Or Adam."

Bill didn't say anything for a moment, but his eyes went to the ceiling, and he appeared to be praying. I hadn't known him to be the religious type, though.

Finally, after several long seconds had ticked by, he answered. "Yes, I promise. But please don't make me regret this." He rubbed his forehead. "I owe your father a great deal, you know."

"Yes, I know," I said, more shame filling my heart. "Also, I don't have a lot of money, and I don't want my husband…to know."

Bill's eyebrows shot up, but he said nothing.

"I will pay you, but I need some time," I added hastily.

He let out a sigh and wiped his hand through his hair, a gesture that indicated both worry and resignation. "Of course, there is always the matter of attorney-client confidentiality," he said. "And don't worry about the money."

"Thank you," I said. I blinked away my tears. There was no more time for crying, although those were tears of relief.

"You're welcome," he said. "Now tell me what's going on. Were any laws broken? Have any crimes been committed by you or anyone else who might have been involved in this matter?"

I drew in a deep breath.

"Also, if a crime has been committed by someone other than you, it is standard procedure for your comments to be recorded under oath."

I sat up straight and nodded. "Yes, a crime has been committed by someone else," I said.

Bill looked at me intently for a moment. He didn't look the least bit jovial at that moment, and instead he looked rather upset.

"Much as I hate to wait, I'm afraid that I'm going to have to call in our criminal lawyer."

Telling someone else my story seemed to be too much. "No, please," I said. "I don't think I can talk to anybody else."

My dear Bill came and kneeled on the floor next to my chair, taking my hands and rubbing my hair as though I were still a little girl. "Uncle Bill's got you," he said simply. "You don't have to be afraid."

We sat there for a moment longer, and I'm afraid I cried, just a little bit, despite my resolve not to. I had started things in motion, and I had to finish them, but I wondered what the price would be.

"Thank you," I said, my voice sounding muffled. "I'm ready."

Bill gave me a kiss on the forehead and struggled to his feet. "I'm not a young man anymore," he said.

"Oh, gosh, I'm so sorry," I said. "Let me help."

"I've got it," he said, raising the palms of his hands to me. "You worry about yourself and keeping your story straight." He straightened his tie. "You ready?"

I nodded.

He picked up the telephone and pushed a button. I heard him say "hello" to somebody named Art—the criminal lawyer, I presumed. "I have a young lady here, and we might need your help," he added.

Bill hung up the phone and turned to me. "Art should be here momentarily; he's just downstairs. Do you want some tea or a soda?"

The intercom buzzed, and Bill's secretary said, "Art is here."

"Please send him in," said Bill. He grinned at me.

A tall pleasant-looking man with sandy hair walked in. "Hey, Bill," he said. "What do you have going this morning?"

Bill came around his desk. "Christina, I'd like to introduce Mr. Arthur Ashmore, one of our best criminal lawyers. Art, this is Christina Cramer."

Art grinned and extended his hand to me to shake. "I'm pleased to meet you, Ms. Cramer," he said. "Don't listen to Bill; he always exaggerates."

"Bill and I go way back," I said, smiling despite how horrible I felt. The energy of the two of them made me feel somewhat safe and as though it were possible to rewind time and get a piece of my old self back.

"It's a special treat to meet you. I've heard a lot about you and am looking forward to your ballet performances."

I looked at Bill and laughed. My parents must have been bragging to Bill a lot, though around me they would have been a little more restrained. They were always careful to not let me get a big head. "Thanks, Mr. Ashmore," I said.

"Please," he said. "Call me Art. All my friends do."

Then he nodded toward the table and said, "So why are you here?"

Once I started talking, it seemed as though I couldn't stop. It took me about an hour to tell them everything, though it seemed as though the world had turned fully on its axis by the time I was finished, so drained was I from the telling. Uncle Bill and his colleague were discreet and sensitive, and they didn't press me for all the sordid details but instead extracted just enough of Buck's intentions and motives to paint the full picture. As it came spilling out of me, from the first encounter in the hotel room to the last encounter, I realized that I had developed feelings for this man that were totally inappropriate.

At one point, I actually said, "It's not his fault. I shouldn't have been there."

My Bill touched me gently on the shoulder and said, "Christina, I want you to put that out of your mind totally."

I looked at him tearfully. "I'm not sure why I feel like this," I said.

"It's common," he said curtly. I must have looked stricken, because he smiled at me. "It's not your fault at all, dear. He's a predator, and he used and manipulated you. But you must stay strong for your child, your folks, and your husband."

At that, I crumpled. "I'm afraid he's going to mail the pictures to my husband since I don't want to see him again."

Art pursed his lips, and Bill shook his head. "No, Christina, that's not going to happen. We're going to make sure of it."

I was sobbing in earnest then. "And then Adam will kill Buck and then divorce me. And the ballet company will fall into scandal and collapse."

Bill handed me a tissue.

I took it, but the tears kept falling. "As you can see, there's no good outcome for the mess I got myself into. Especially with Buck's ex-wife trying to blackmail me, too."

In the silence that fell over the two men, I heard the gentle chimes of the clock on Bill's shelf. It seemed to break the ice, and Mr. Ashmore spoke first. "Well, my dear, don't be so sure. I think that we can help."

I exhaled. "I'm afraid I'm not that hopeful. I'm ruined."

"We have our ways," he clowned, waggling his eyebrows in a pretty fair Groucho Marx imitation.

I had to laugh at that, and Bill looked relieved.

"There's my Christina," he said.

"So based on your statement, there are a number of crimes that Mr. Johnson has committed," said Art. He stood up and began pacing around the room. "These include kidnapping, entrapment, rape, blackmail, and extortion."

"That's a long enough list," added Bill. "If a conviction could be achieved, it would put Mr. Johnson away for a very long time."

"Yes, but the rape charge would be hard to stick," said Art. He turned to me. "Because you went to the hotel room with him on numerous occasions, he could claim consent. And a jury would probably give him the benefit of the doubt."

I blinked fresh tears. This would be even harder than impossible. I thought glumly about moving in with my parents. Would they even have me?

"Yes, rape charges are always tough nuts," said Bill.

Art slammed his hand on the table. "What we need here is evidence. We need proof that the pictures are being used to blackmail you. You said you have copies—is that correct?"

I hesitated. "Yes, I do. But I don't want anyone to see them." I didn't need to say "especially an old friend of my father's." But I'm sure the thought hung in the air.

Bill looked away from me, clearly embarrassed, but Art merely fixed me a stare.

"Is there anyway to get through this without everyone looking at those pictures? I just can't stand the thought of it." I buried my face in my hands. "It's almost worse than continuing to go to Buck Johnson's parties."

Art patted me on the shoulder. "Look at me, Christina. I have a plan that, if successful, will limit those who need to see the pictures to your attorney, the district attorney, and a judge."

I looked at him, though my eyes were blurred with tears. "Really?" I sniffed.

"No one else will see them," said Art. "But they are the evidence that is key to the resolution of the case."

"I don't think we have any choice, Christina," added Bill. "I know this is hard for you, but you have to see this through. You were strong by calling me. Now stay strong."

Art then proceeded to provide a brief outline of the plan, which, as I understood it, entailed getting the judge and the district attorney to agree that my case would not be made public until after the end of our company's first performance. "After that, I assume that the company will succeed or fail on its own merits," he added.

I wanted to ask about my marriage succeeding or failing on its own merits, but I merely nodded. I hoped Adam would forgive me. It was too late then.

"We need the pictures to take to the DA and the judge," said Art. "We will ask for a wiretap on this Johnson fella's phone. It's urgent, so we'll need the photos right away."

I sighed. In for a penny, in for a pound. "Okay."

"When he calls to set up another encounter, you will, at first, refuse," said Art. "Do you think you can do that?"

My hands were trembling then, but I nodded.

"Presumably, he will then threaten you as he's done in the past. You will then agree to meet with him, except you must make up an excuse to delay the meeting until we can get the wire and initiate the plan." Art looked at me with concern in his eyes. "Can you do that, Christina? It's very important that you delay him. We might even need a week."

I took a deep, shaky breath and said, "I can handle the situation."

"Tell him it's that time of the month or something like that. Make up an excuse." He winked and added, "You're a woman—you already know how to handle that."

I smiled wanly.

"How you handle this with your family, your parents, and your husband is up to you," said Art. "In the short run, there is no way to keep this from them."

I shot Bill a look. Would he help me with that?

"We might decide to have them meet here with Bill and me," said Art, catching my look. "We could explain the details of this case and the rationale that drove your actions. All of that in a nonemotional rendition."

I blew out some breath and raised my hands above my head. I needed to think.

"You need to think about how to handle that issue," said Bill. "I'll help you as best I can."

"Well," I said, pulling myself up from the table. I needed to move. "Thank you so much. I think you have an excellent plan." I paused and tried to joke a little. "Why didn't I come to you sooner?

Bill stood up then and pulled me into him for a hug. "You should have come to me sooner, little girl," he said. "Remember that your parents will always love and support you, no matter what."

I wanted to scream, and what about my husband? Will he love and support me? But the fierce look on Bill's face frightened me, and I didn't want to even contemplate losing Adam.

Art put his hand on the door. "I'll leave you two, then," he said. "It was a pleasure to meet you, Christina. And by the way, do not discuss this case or provide any details to anybody, even friends."

"Yes, I understand," I said, even though it would be tough to hide things from Anna.

At that, Art walked out, and I stood there in the room with Bill, with the problem of my husband hanging heavily, unspoken between us.

After a moment, he gently said to me, "You're going to have to tell your husband sometime, Christina."

"I know," I said.

"Better to do it sooner than later," he added.

I smiled at him, trying to muster up more enthusiasm for the task than I actually felt. It wasn't going to be easy, and I wasn't sure of the outcome.

"Thanks," I said. "I'll keep you updated with my progress."

"This isn't going to be easy, but it has to be done."

"I'm on board," I said. "I've got this."

He gave me a hug, and I resisted the urge to cry all over his shirt as though I were a little kid. I had to deal with this myself. The ball was set in action. I would wait for the right time.

Sixteen

The Setup

Christina

THE NEXT DAY WENT BY AS IF IT WERE a dream, with me waiting to hear from Bill about what our next step would be.

My husband was back in town again and spent the day at home with Chris and me. I hoped he didn't notice that I was preoccupied. I watched him closely for signs that he still loved me, that he would always love me, and that he would be true to me and to our marriage even if I had not been true to him. I leaned up against him every chance I could get, feeling his solid warmth in passing and reaching for his hands. My husband would get a puzzled look on his face, but he made no comment.

Although things between my Adam and me seemed uncertain, I felt better than I had in months, in an odd way simply because I was so relieved to be passing everything off to Bill, who I trusted as one of my parents' dearest friends. I knew that what was coming up was going to be hard, and I worried that the DA wouldn't cooperate with a warrant and a wiretap. I hadn't ever been involved in anything like this operation before, and on impulse, I dug out a couple of John le Carré novels that were my husband's, selected his most recent, and buried myself in reading about spies. Adam found me reading on the front porch swing and seemed amused by my reading selection. If only he had known.

That afternoon, the phone rang, and I was lucky that I answered it instead of Adam. I felt jumpy those days, of course. It was Bill.

"Christina, the DA is on board," he said. "He agreed to a search warrant and authorized a wiretap on Buck Johnson's telephone."

Adam walked into the kitchen and looked at me quizzically. "Who is it?" he asked.

I covered the receiver. "It's Bill," I said.

"Oh, what does he want?" asked Adam. He knew Bill, of course, but it was strange that he would call the house.

"Wants to talk to me about the ballet," I said. "He's interested."

I waved him off with my hand.

"Adam's in town, then," said Bill. "Have you told him?"

I eyed my husband, who was poking around in the refrigerator.

"No, but I will," I said.

He sighed. "I won't tell you how to run your personal life, but it's show time."

"What do you mean?" I asked, my stomach sinking.

"The wire is already on place on his telephone. Step one is already in place."

"Okay," I said. "What's next?"

Bill told me the necessary response to Buck's next phone call while I listened nervously, wishing my husband wouldn't linger in the kitchen. I had questions, but I would have to wait until Adam was gone to ask them.

"Okay," I finally said, forcing a fake cheerful tone to my voice. "I think I have all of that. Thanks for your input."

Bill chuckled. "You could have gone into acting, too," he said. "Let me know if you need anything else. And call me the minute he calls you."

I hung up the receiver, and Adam walked over to me and tousled my hair. "I'm so glad you have something to occupy yourself with while I'm working so many hours," he said. "I sure appreciate how you've kept everything going, and you're getting all your family and friends involved. I'm proud of you."

It was the praise from him that I had longed for all along—the recognition that I was capable of pulling this off. And yet I stood there, a big fake smile plastered on my face while inside my heart was breaking. When Buck Johnson had walked into my professional life in the spring, his expertise and money had seemed like the answer to my prayers. Then I prayed that everything wasn't going to blow up in my face.

"Thank you, Adam," I said. "That means a lot to me."

"My pleasure," he said absently. I could tell his mind was already on going out to the garage and getting a few things done. He started to walk away, and I couldn't help myself.

"Adam?" I called.

He turned. "Yes, dear?"

"Are we okay?"

He laughed. "Of course we are. We are wonderful."

As if to prove it, he did all his chores and yard work, and then he made supper for Chris and me. We sat in the back at our picnic table, eating hamburgers he had grilled and drinking strawberry soda. Chris was in heaven, and for a few hours, so was I.

Over the next few months, I would remember it as the last happy day we had had together that summer.

In the wake of the firings, the next few days of practice at the ballet went exceedingly well. We did interviews for the new principals, but I already had a couple of people in mind and was able to bring them on board right away.

I hadn't sorted things out with Marilyn, but she hadn't called, and I sincerely hoped that Buck would be out of the way before she realized that I wasn't going to be party to her plan to blackmail Buck. I was getting out, not further in. Timing was essential, though, and I wondered how long she would wait.

It didn't take long to hear from Buck again. I was making lunch for Chris and me when he called. I knew when I heard the phone ringing that it would be him. I put down the carrots I was cutting up and went to answer the phone. My hands were shaking just a bit, and after I said "hello," I had to clear my throat.

"Hello, Christina," purred Buck. A little bit of my heart leaped to hear his voice, and I hated myself for that. I felt torn; I didn't want to hurt him. I considered the possibility that maybe I could reason with him—maybe I could make him go away without having to go so far as to put him in jail. For all his faults, he had been kind to me, and he had treated me well. I had to admit I had some feelings for him.

Then I thought about Marilyn and the threat she had made, and I realized that I couldn't have it both ways. Buck helped the ballet, but he threatened my marriage and my status as a mother. I had to make the ballet work without Buck. He had taught me a thing or two, and I could do it on my own. I had to.

I straightened my spine and lifted my chin. I could soar through this. This was a stage. The curtains were open. It was time.

"Hey, I miss you," he was saying. "I want to get together sometime this week. Which day is best for you?"

I had rehearsed my lines, the ones Bill had given me, and I knew what to say.

"Buck, I'm not going to get together with you anymore. It's over."

There was a pause on the other end. I could imagine the look of disbelief on his face. I heard him exhale. I heard his voice, which was calm. "Now, baby, I'm sorry if I've made you unhappy. But I'll pretend I didn't hear you just say that."

I played with the cord of the phone nervously. "No, it's over," I squeaked. Then I took a deep breath and spoke more forcefully. "I won't see you again."

I held my breath. Buck was getting angry and agitated, which is just what Bill had been banking on. He walked right into the trap.

"I think that you're forgetting something," he said, his voice sounding a little desperate. "Remember the pictures. We have a deal."

I said nothing. I let him squirm on the end of the line.

"The stamped envelope with the pictures, the one addressed to Adam, is right here in my desk. And it's going into the mailbox as soon as I hang up."

I forced myself not to respond. I counted backward from ten.

"I'm going to do that right away unless we can dispense with this unpleasant conversation." His voice sounded a little hurt. "Christina? Are you there? Did you just hear me?"

"Oh, Buck. Oh no," I said, letting emotion flood my voice. I needed to convince him that I was truly contrite. "I'm sorry, dear. I haven't been thinking clearly lately. We have so much going on with the company."

I took a deep breath and let him wait a little bit more before I added, "Of course I'll meet with you."

"That's what I was hoping to hear," he said, the relief evident in his voice. "You are as intelligent as you are beautiful."

"The things you say," I murmured.

"Will tomorrow work for you?"

"Oh, Buck, darling, I'm sorry to make you wait, but…it's that time of the month."

"Oh," he laughed. "That explains your moodiness."

I let it pass. "We'll have to wait for next Wednesday. Is that okay?"

"Okay, my darling girl. Next Wednesday it is. I'll call you with the name and the address of the hotel."

"I'll wait for your call," I said firmly. And then, before he could regale me with a long, drawn-out good-bye, I hung up. I hadn't said good-bye. I didn't think I had needed to.

I leaned against the wall for a moment, taking deep breaths. That was done. There was no going back.

I got a call the next day from Bill, letting me know that the contents of the wire were exactly what they had been looking for. They were able to get a meeting right away with the DA and the judge to present their proposed plan of action. Bill and his partner had made the plea that this was a special case that needed to be handled delicately to avoid the publicity of a scandal involving the business manager and the artistic director of the newly formed Lockville Ballet Company. The judge had been reluctant, Bill told me, but had eventually agreed, and both men had signed the written document that defined the terms of the plan.

Buck was going to be called into Bill's office the very next day. The game was in play.

I tried not to worry, but worry was all I did.

That night, I tried to call my husband, who was away on another one of his ever-loving business trips, but the hotel number he had given me rang and rang, and nobody picked up.

Seventeen

The Trap

Buck

SOME MORNINGS JUST AREN'T WORTH THE TIME OR ENERGY, and it appeared to me that this was going to be that type of morning. I normally would have been very excited about a business proposition, but there was something about the vagueness of this particular proposal that bothered me. The fellow, an attorney in Lockville who I had met on a few occasions at the chamber of commerce and the Elks Club, had called the day before, requesting to set up a business meeting for the very next day. My secretary had given me the message and had said it was an urgent proposition; the man had wanted me to get back with an answer immediately.

I had wondered what was so urgent but had resisted the urge to pick up the phone and call Bill Wenzlick himself. It didn't do to look to eager in these types of situations in case it was a particularly lucrative deal.

I went into the office earlier than normal. I felt worried, but I couldn't put my finger on what was bothering me. I wanted to call Christina just to hear her voice, but I figured that I would see her in a few days and that that had to be enough. I was certain that our future would be together, and I didn't want to demean myself by looking too desperate and obvious. As far as I was concerned, our relationship was moving in the right direction. I was sure she had fallen in love with me as much as I had her. I no longer felt as though the photos and the threat of exposure were the only things holding us together.

Still, I couldn't settle into my morning's work.

I paced a bit, looking through the window at the downtown area. The day looked like it was going to be hot. *Good day for a deal*, I thought. Then I thought of all the times I had run into Bill Wenzlick at meetings of the chamber of commerce or the Elks club. It bothered me that I couldn't remember how we had first met, but I finally shook it off.

At 9:30, my secretary knocked on my door, and when I opened it, I saw that Bill Wenzlick was with two other men who I recognized from various events. One of them was the district attorney. They looked somber, and a sick feeling knotted the pit of my stomach for the briefest of moments. I told myself not to worry. Everything was an opportunity.

"Hey, Bill," I said, extending my arm "You didn't say you were bringing an army. What's this about? Do I need my own attorney?"

The men laughed, but it clearly felt as though there was tension permeating the room. "No, no, we just want to talk," said Wenzlick. "Do you have time?"

I asked my secretary to hold my calls and shut the door. We all sat down at the conference table. I offered them tea and coffee, and they declined. When I was formally introduced to Counselor Ashmore and District Attorney Chuck Voglar, I made myself show evident pleasure in reacquainting myself with them. But the way one was fidgeting in his chair and the expression on the other one's face made me feel as though something was afoot.

"Gentleman, what's your pleasure this morning?" I asked.

The DA spoke first. "Buck, all of us here have known you for a long time, and we consider you a friend."

"Lockville takes care of its own," I said, smiling fiercely.

He and the two other gentlemen exchanged meaningful glances. I felt a tightening in my stomach.

"But we are sorry to say that you are in big trouble."

"Trouble?" The smile on my face felt frozen.

Bill Wenzlick frowned. "I think you know what we're talking about."

My mind raced, looking for explanations. Then I remembered the photographs and Christina, and I felt faint. Would she be so callous as to turn me in?

The room was silent while I pondered my options. It was a seminal moment for me. My life did not quite flash before my eyes, but I wondered, in that instant, how I must have looked to those men. I must have raised my eyebrows, because Wenzlick regarded me with a clear, cool gaze. I saw contempt in his expression. "Christina's father and I served in the war together," he said, leaning forward. "She's my godchild."

I felt the menace in his voice, and I nodded reflexively, trying to figure out a way to deal with the accusation that hung in the air. Would I admit fault when there was none? I supposed that legalities were one thing, but the truth was that Christina herself had made a choice. Christina had chosen me. Christina was in love with me. I had merely professed my feelings for her and wooed her.

"I may need my lawyer after all," I said, forcing myself to keep smiling. When wolves are on you, it's best to bare your teeth.

"You don't need an attorney for this meeting," said the DA smoothly. "We will not ask you for your testimony."

"Oh?" I said, cocking my head.

"At this time, and for the near future, there have not been, nor will there be, any charges filed in the Christina Cramer case."

I feigned disinterest, but my heart was beating wildly. What was afoot? I suddenly thought of the photos filed neatly in my desk, which was locked. Not even my secretary had access to my desk. I took a deep breath, thought about what to say, and, coming up with nothing, exhaled.

"There is a squad car outside, and if you end this meeting or ask us to leave, you will be arrested and charged."

I laughed at that—what charges were they going to draw up against me?— but Bill Wenzlick gave me a look that stayed me. I needed to keep my cool until I could talk to Christina to ascertain from her what was going on.

"We want to offer you a deal," said the DA. "A deal that you can accept now. Or you can have you attorney look at it and give us an answer later."

I nodded. Listening to a deal was not an admission of guilt.

"I'll listen," I said.

Bill Wenzlick looked to the ceiling and muttered to himself. Ashmore, who hadn't said much yet, said, "Keep it together, Bill. We've come this far." Ashmore shot me a look that said "shut the hell up," and I obliged. I would have called my attorney into it, but I decided I was in no particular danger at the moment.

"Bill?" asked the attorney.

"Proceed," Bill said, giving me a look that could have killed. I shivered.

"Number one. You need to relinquish possession of the photographs. No one must see them except law enforcement and the judge. If they are disclosed to anyone other than those entities, the deal will be considered broken."

I was beginning to feel agitated. I could lose Christina.

"Do I need to answer this now?"

"No," said the DA.

I was beginning to sweat. The heat was beginning to pour through the windows, and I got up and closed the shades. I paused by the bar, and with shaking hands, I poured myself a whiskey sour. "Would any of you gentleman like a drink?" I asked.

"No," said Bill. I noticed that his eyes looked bloodshot.

"Number two. You must accept the punishment terms of the plea bargain. You must sign the plea-bargain agreement before criminal charges are filed. Criminal charges will not be filed until after the close of the first performance series of the Lockville Ballet."

I downed my whiskey sour and poured myself another. "Go on," I said.

"That will protect the company until then," added Bill. "After that, it will sink or swim on its own merits."

I said nothing, but I nodded ever so slightly in the DA's direction.

"Number three. You must not have any further contact with Christina Cramer. You will delegate all further administrative activities to the symphony manager, Mitch Carter."

I felt a sense of panic overcome me, but one look at Bill Wenzlick's face told me I would have been a fool to challenge them at that point. I needed to wait and plot and plan. I did not believe this could be it for Christina and me.

The room was silent for a moment. "Is that it?" I asked. I wanted those sons of bitches out of my office.

"Number four. You must pay your ex-wife, Marilyn, the amount she has asked for."

That came out of the blue. "What the hell does *that woman* have to do with anything?" I had been able to keep my composure regarding Christina. Too much was at stake. But I should have figured my ex-wife was behind this somehow. She had never been able to let our relationship go. You would have thought she was my daddy's own daughter from the way she carried on so.

Bill Wenzlick regarded me coolly. "Didn't you know?"

"Know what?" I said, waving my hands wildly. I had to keep myself from punching his fat face.

"That your ex-wife was blackmailing Christina."

"Son of a bitch," I said.

He smiled at me, but it was more like he was baring his teeth. This was more serious than I had thought.

"What pictures?" I said gruffly. "I don't have any pictures."

Bill frowned, and I could see the DA was holding him in check. He must have really loved Christina, and her going out with me was going to be a hard sell for that old bastard.

"Well, I took some because she asked me to. And I gave them to her. I swear."

The DA cleared his throat and said, "Are you sure this is the road you want to go on, Mr. Johnson?"

I stood there awhile, a man trapped in his own office—in his own life. I had really erred when I had married Marilyn in an attempt to please my old man. There was no pleasing anybody then, I realized. I had a sudden thought that Christina herself might have been behind this; why else would her godfather have been involved? The thought made me ill. But these were reasonable men. They must have known how women behave, how they act, and how they can lie to save their own skins. *Christina must be on the run from Marilyn,* I thought. I would get that straightened out, get Marilyn off the track, and get Christina back in my arms, but I had to mollify these men first.

"Look, all of our sex has been consensual."

Bill coughed.

"She asked me to meet her in hotel rooms. It was her idea from the beginning. Just ask her."

The DA sighed and laid a hand on Bill Wenzlick's arm. "Mr. Johnson, you should know that the truth is out. It would be in your best interest to come clean at this time."

I studied them carefully. I had to be careful. I wondered if it was too late to call my lawyer in, but doing so would have been admitting guilt. I was pretty sure they had nothing on me.

The third attorney spoke. "We have a brief recording that will interest you."

Then he brought out the recorder he had sitting by his feet and set it up. My mouth was dry, but I vowed to reveal nothing. When the recording began, I heard my voice talking to Christina on the phone. It was from several days ago. *Son of a bitch*, I thought. My life was over.

When it was done, the silence hung there like a noose. The men stared at me. I was trapped. "What does the agreement say?" I asked evenly.

"Good question," responded the DA.

He articulated the list of all the possible criminal charges along with the possible jail time. I could barely listen, so enraged was I that this was happening

"Mr. Johnson, as you know, conviction on any of these charges would send you to jail for fifteen to twenty years," said the DA.

That's a lifetime, I thought.

"In addition to the four conditions, the agreement specifies criminal penalties." He went on to say that if the terms were violated, the state would pursue all charges and seek at least twenty years. "But if you accept the terms of the agreement, which means handling over all the photographs and negatives here and now, the DA and the judge have agreed to five years in prison with the possibility of parole in two and a half years."

A fist squeezed my heart. I pressed my trembling hand against my chest.

"Can you continue?" asked the DA.

I nodded mutely.

"Charges against you will not be filed until after the first performance series of the Lockville Ballet. The reason for that is to keep this thing away from the media. As you know, if this comes out now, it will take down the program."

How very civic-minded of you all to consider the ballet, I thought, but I kept that thought to myself.

I took a deep breath. "I am truly sorry for my actions. I realize I became obsessed."

Bill Wenzlick looked like he wanted to strangle me. I closed my eyes. "She hypnotized me," I murmured, talking more to myself than to them as if I was trying to clarify and understand what had happened. "Such an unbelievable lady."

I opened my eyes and looked around the room at the men who were there to accuse and judge me. I had lost everything. "I believe my attorney would tell me to wait. But I will give you the negatives—all of them."

I reached into my pocket, where I kept my key, unlocked the desk, and took out the file with the photos of my beautiful Christina. I hoped they wouldn't look at them. I never had intended them for anyone else but me. They were a souvenir of our love and our time together. I wanted to weep.

With shaking hands, I handed the folder to the DA. He then pushed a pile of paper in front of me and handed me a pen. I signed and dated all three copies.

Bill Wenzlick sighed and stood up. "I gotta get out of here," he said. He looked at me and took a step closer, and then in a low voice, he said, "If you ever go near her again, I swear…"

"Bill," said the DA. "Not now. We got what we came for."

"It's okay," I said to the DA. "I understand." Then to Bill Wenzlick, I said, "I love her."

He shook his head and stalked out of the room, slamming the door behind him.

The DA watched him go without comment and handed me one of the copies.

"You might want to review this with your attorney. You can contact me if there are questions," he said.

I leaned against the table, hiding my trembling hands, and nodded wearily.

"Let me be clear. The terms are not negotiable. Any noncompliance will bring down the full kubida."

"Yes," I said. "I understand."

Then the meeting ended, and the two remaining men shook my hand. I was left with my nightmare.

After the attorneys left, I sat in my office at my desk, trying to organize my spinning head. *What have I done?* I thought. I had thought it all made sense—I had had a plan. Why had she done this? The hum of the window air conditioner became an annoyance. I tried to file some of my paper work and realized I was misfiling it. I felt restless and scared. My head was about to split.

I decided pretending that everything was okay was a losing battle, so I poked my head out the door to talk to my secretary. She gave me a concerned look. "Mr. Johnson, is everything okay?"

"I might be in trouble," I said.

She looked shocked, but not as shocked as I would have figured. She must have seen the police car out front, recognized the DA, and put two and two together.

"Let me know how I can help," she said.

"Thank you so much. You are always so helpful." I thought to myself, why hadn't I decided to go out with her instead of the elusive, married Christina? I just hadn't been thinking straight recently. *It can't be age; I'm not that old,* I thought. "Could you cancel all my appointments this afternoon?"

"Certainly," she said. "Take care of yourself."

I ducked back in my office and surveyed my cluttered desk. My heart just wasn't in it. I decided I would duck out and go talk to Zack. I needed a drink or two—maybe then I could think straight.

I decided to walk the two blocks to the bar. The sun was shining, and when I walked past the park, I saw loads of moms out with their children, playing on the equipment. For a moment I thought I saw Christina, but I realized it was some other blonde with a little towheaded boy. My heart sank even deeper.

As I walked, I tried to think through everything rationally. I was torn. I had thought everything was okay, but the DA had a noose around my neck. And that Bill Wenzlick fellow—it looked as though he was going to show up in the middle of the night and slit my throat before the law had a chance to hang me. I felt desperate. My life was ruined.

Walking the two blocks to the bar seemed like it took forever. *She has to know that I love her*, I thought. *But she's married and has a kid, and I'm screwing up her family.* I wondered how she could have done this to me and if it had been her choice. Perhaps her husband had forced her hand. Or the ever-meddling Marilyn. As I walked, my agony became laced with anger. What was all that talk about my paying Marilyn some sort of money?

I walked into the Good Times Club feeling sorrier for myself and more confused than I had ever been in my entire life, even after the death of my mother, and I had thought I would never pop up from that loss.

It felt like a death. But I wasn't sure whose death.

Zack was washing glasses and gave me a concerned look as I approached the bar.

"Hey, Buck, what's cooking? Why the hangdog look? You look like you lost your best friend."

"Hi, Zack. Give me a double. Make it a martini." I sat at the bar.

"Coming right up, but I need to know what's happening."

He wiped his hands on a towel and poured my drink, garnished it with olives, and slid it down the bar. I fumbled the catch, watching in disbelief as the martini and olives went sliding across the top of the counter.

Zack looked at me carefully. "No worries, my friend. I got you covered. That one is on me." And then Zack wiped the counter down in seconds, made me another drink, and handed it to me, that time setting it right in front of me. "Here, now don't spill this one. It looks like you need it."

It had sure been a day. "Zack, I'm in big trouble," I said.

Zack's eyes widened for a just a second, but he quickly recovered, leaned in, and said, "So tell me about it. You know that I have all the answers. What's going on?"

I sighed. "Not this time, you don't."

"Try me," said Zack.

"This Christina thing has caught up with me. She turned me in." Even as I said it, I found it hard to believe that she would have done such a thing. I had thought she was becoming comfortable with our arrangement. She liked the sex. She liked me.

"She what?" said Zack.

"She ratted on me." I let out a little hysterical laugh.

"You can't be serious! What about the pictures? The publicity? The ballet company?"

"I'm not pulling your leg."

"Did she tell her old man?" asked Zack. Someone at the end of the bar was trying to get Zack's attention by waving his empty glass around, and Zack held up a finger to him. "Be with you in a moment, buddy," he called down.

"I don't know about her husband," I said, feeling bitter. "But she has an attorney who brought in the DA and the police."

Zack raised both his hands and paced toward the end of the bar and back. He looked a little shocked, which didn't help my mood any. He came back to stand in front of me and took a couple of deep breaths. "Wow, this is serious," he said. "So what're they going to do to you? Are they going to string you up?"

"Not helping," I said. "They set up a wiretap. They have a recording—a telephone call of me threatening Christina. I told her I'd send the pictures to Adam."

Zack gave me a stare of disbelief. "I thought she was breaking it off with me," I said. "It was stupid."

To his credit, Zack didn't kick me. I was already down.

"They came to my office," I continued. "The attorney and the DA. And they played the recording right there. The police were waiting outside in case I didn't cooperate. It was a really bad scene."

I still felt like my world had been turned upside down. I felt a pain in my chest, and my head throbbed. I took a sip of my martini, hoping it would settle my nerves. Zack made a drink for the fellow at the end of the bar and came back to me.

"And then what happened?"

"They laid out the charges—rape, blackmail, extortion, and kidnapping." My voice broke. "They threatened to go for twenty years to life."

"Wow, Buck, this sounds bad." Zack rubbed his face, looking thoughtful. Then he came around the bar and sat on the stool next to me. The guy down at the end of the bar indicated he wanted another, and Zack called down to him. "Taking a break, buddy! Be back in ten." To me, he said, "Tell me."

I sipped my drink. It hardly felt real to me, but I figured the telling the story might make it more realistic, and then I might figure out a way to wiggle out of it. "They offered a plea bargain that will send me up for five if I accept their terms." Then I laid the whole sorry deal—no trial, no contact, no nothing—on the table. A sure jail sentence.

"You're kidding," said Zack.

We sat in silence for a moment. Then he asked, "What are you going to do?"

"I'm going to take the plea bargain," I said. "I've no choice. You know the real kicker?"

"There's more?"

"I'm required to give my ex twenty thousand dollars."

"What?" said Zack.

"It seems that she went to Christina and threatened to blow the whistle if she didn't convince me to give her the money." I paused and stared darkly into my glass. "I think that's why Christina went to the lawyers."

"That's extortion," Zack said. "How could she do that?"

"If by 'she,' you mean Marilyn, I guess it doesn't surprise me," I said. "I should have seen that one coming."

"I thought you were through with her," Zack said.

"I guess she wasn't through with me." I was silent, trying to bury thoughts of Marilyn and how she had once again robbed me of happiness with her constant striving for material gain. I preferred to think of Christina, though the loss of her, which loomed large, pained me. I wondered, for a moment, if I should have gotten more hands on with the actual management of the rehearsals. But I had wanted to protect her privacy and to give her a real shot at making the show work. I had thought it would build confidence in her, which was something that I saw she was sorely lacking. "Plus, she can't seem to get things going with the ballet company," I added. "And I'm not supposed to have any further contact with her."

I realized I was repeating myself, but I wasn't sure how to get a grip. And then I felt a surge of peevishness with Zack for having encouraged me to take the photos in the first place. "So you always have all the answers," I said. "What do you say now? Should I go to Mexico or just disappear somewhere?"

I must have given him a murderous look, because he raised his hands and said, "I don't know, buddy. I'm with you. This is bad."

"If I run and they catch me, it's the big calaboose—twenty years to life."

Zack put his hand on my shoulder. "You don't want to do that, Buck. Not a lot of wiggle room. Now let me think. Trust me on this, okay. I've brought you this far."

"Sure thing," I said. I was tired and wanted to close my eyes, but that would have made things worse.

Zack got up from the chair and filled some more drink orders. Then he leaned over the bar and gave me a serious look.

"So, we do know the following: Christina did enjoy the sex. She lives and breathes the ballet."

I nodded to each one.

"You, my friend, are in love with her."

I couldn't deny that, but I'd sure messed things up.

"Her old man might split once he gets the story. Am I correct so far?"

"Yeah, but so what?" I said.

Zack looked pleased with himself. He obviously had a plan. I leaned forward, hopeful in spite of my dire predicament.

"So, what if you were to write a letter to her pledging your undying love and proposing to donate one hundred thousand dollars to the company? In return, she would have to go to the DA and request leniency," he said.

I must have looked stunned, because he continued on. "Hell, say that, to some degree, you're responsible for what happened."

"You think that would work?" I asked.

"Sure. You could add that if you get out in six months or so and Adam has left her, you would love to get together on a permanent basis."

I chewed on that awhile. The idea that this might be the final straw for her marriage—that her husband might just up and leave after all—had simply not occurred to me. I needed to start thinking more clearly and get my head on straight if I was going to navigate this storm with any certainty. My dad, a World War II vet, was a big fan of Churchill's and used to quote his saying, "When going through hell, keep going." If things played out the way I wanted them to, then this might just be a bump in the road to my eventual goal. I could imagine being married to Christina in a way that I had never been able to imagine with Marilyn. We were much more compatible. We both loved the arts. Except for this latest development, she was a loving, sweet woman and mother. She would make a spectacular wife. We could come through this stronger than ever.

"Why, Zack, that's brilliant," I said, reaching over and slapping him on the shoulder. "You are truly in the wrong business."

But then, my mind started buzzing with all that could go wrong with that plan. I was the kind of man who liked to have things buttoned up—who liked to make sure the outcomes were certain. I never liked to ask a question that I didn't know the answer to already, and that day had filled me with more unpleasant surprises than I generally allowed in my life.

And there was a clear fly in the ointment.

"But wait. The terms of the plea agreement stipulate that if I contact her, they'll put me away in the Big House." I realized I could not bear to use the term "jail." "Not sure if I should risk that," I added glumly.

Zack nodded. "Just add a note that explains all that."

I frowned.

"Do you think that she would want to see you go up for life?"

The pain that had been building all day washed clear through me. That was the big question that I didn't know the answer to. She clearly had been rattled by Marilyn, but would any of this have happened if my ex hadn't tried to blackmail her? Had the lawyers pushed her to ask for those terms?

Did she not have feelings for me?

I remembered her modesty, her gentleness, the way she talked about her son, and how she fiercely cared about her company. And, with a pang of guilt, how much she had resisted me…until I had held the photos over her head.

"No, I don't think so," I said. "She is such a nice, caring person." And I loved her even more for it. I felt my life was over, or, to be more accurate, that our time together had artificially elongated it. I had been essentially dead for the two years since Marilyn and I had divorced. I had been going through the motions but had had no joy in my life. And now that I had found joy, it was in danger of slipping beyond me.

It had been like that the night my mother had died. My father had told me my mother was sick, and I had learned through relatives that she had cancer, but at twelve, I hadn't really had a full recognition of what that meant. She'd gone downhill fast, and I'd seen her once in the hospital and had slipped in exactly once, for a few brief moments, when the nurse hadn't been watching. It wasn't my father who took me but my uncle, who stood in the hallway smoking cigars and watching out for the nurse. My mother hugged me and kissed me on the face and on my hair and told me that she loved me so much. The night she died, I was relegated to the lobby by myself, and I dozed off on the couch reading a book—it must have been *Treasure Island*, because I was in love with that book that summer—and I remember my father waking me up, and he was crying. And when I protested that I hadn't gotten to say good-bye, my father looked at me and said, "It's better this way. Don't ask for things you can't have."

My feelings almost overwhelmed me.

Zack was speaking to me and waving his hands in front of my face, trying to get my attention. When I gave him a nod, he launched into another one of his impassioned speeches: "Might turn out great. Think about it; she could be all yours. And I know you want her. This could turn out to be making lemonade out of lemons."

I sat there on the barstool, all the losses of my past and present swelling up and breaking over me like a big wave crashing down on a small boat, threatening to capsize it. I felt sick.

"You're right on, but still, I have to think about it."

Zack grinned, clearly believing he had won this battle. "Tell you what. You write the letter and give it to me. I'll hold it until you tell me 'yes' or 'no.'"

"And then?"

"If you tell me 'yes,' I'll intercept her out in the parking lot when she arrives for one of her ballet practices."

The thought of having Zack meet Christina in person made me feel a little jealous and sad. But I figured it might be worth a shot. Or it could put me away altogether.

"I'll let you know," I said. "I need to go think this through."

"Okay, Buck," he said. "It's going to turn out okay. Keep smiling."

I didn't feel like I had something to smile about, but I nevertheless gave Zack a thumbs-up and what I hoped wasn't too artificial of a smile.

"See you later, Zack," I said.

I didn't much feel like going to the office, and I found myself standing in front of the hotel where we had first had our assignations. I stood there looking at it, thinking about time layering over itself and how, not a few months before, I had practically skipped out of the lobby after bedding Christina for the first time.

I decided that if I was going to be haunted, I might as well embrace it. So I walked into the lobby and pressed the elevator to go to the top floor.

Eighteen

The News

Adam

BEFORE CHRISTINA AND I GOT MARRIED, I'D HAD A SCARE. I never told her about it, but it's why I proposed to her when I did. I'd been out with a friend, Erick, drinking beer at this little bowling alley tucked in the basement of a bar near my apartment—an alley that still had guys setting up the pins. We were celebrating. I'd been offered a position on the West Coast with better pay and more responsibility. It was a job for an adult man, a job my friends would envy, but the problem was that I was in love with a girl who was clearly not going to move, who was on a fast track in the ballet world herself. I was wondering if I was good enough for her to marry me, and if I was, if she would move with me to California. My buddy and I hashed it out all night, though in reality, the conversation was short. He told me that Christina was a catch, a smoking number who would make a beautiful wife and would make me feel like a king. In fact, he'd been trying to talk me into grabbing the job and cutting my losses. He'd had one too many beers, it seemed, and was feeling a little lonely and confessed that if I left her, he'd be happy to keep her company and to make her his wife. I stared at him a little bit, wondering if I should punch him in the nose or not. And he said to me, "Well, there's your answer."

I'd said, "What do you mean?"

He jabbed a finger in the middle of my chest and got in my face. "If you're too stupid to know when you're jealous, you don't deserve her."

I had to mull that over, but by the time we finished bowling several rounds, things were no clearer in my head.

It had gotten a little late, and it was after midnight when I started walking home. Erick offered to split a cab with me, but I waved him off. I was still a little sore at him, making a play for my girl, even though I was really at a crossroads. I wanted some fresh air—some time to clear my head. He shrugged and said, "Get some sleep," before turning the other way to look for his cab.

So I wasn't paying much attention and was lost in my thoughts when I saw, or rather sensed, somebody falling into step with me. I looked over, and it was a guy a little bit older than me with his hair a little on the longish side, and he was falling over his service jacket. It looked like he'd been in the navy or something. For a second, I thought about pulling away, but he asked me for a cigarette and seemed so congenial that I automatically went to my jacket pocket, where I kept my pack. I was a little clumsy, a little drunk, and I was taken off guard when he grabbed me by the shoulder and muscled me into an alley.

"What the hell?" I sputtered when he let go of me, but then he was standing there with a knife, which I could make out from the streetlights, and when I looked at his face, his weird smile made him appear a little insane. So I shut up and watched him warily, ready to move if he lunged at me.

"What can I do for you?" I finally asked.

He laughed and shook his head. "You college boys are all alike. You think you have the world by the tail."

I didn't know what to say to that, so I figured silence was the best option.

"What's the matter?" he said. "Am I not good enough for you to talk to?"

"It's not that," I said, watching him with care.

"Then what is it?" he asked.

"Girl problems."

"Girl problems!" he snorted. "That's just priceless. Girl problems."

He walked around in a little circle, muttering to himself, while I sweated despite the cold, feeling a sense of dread building inside of me. The city was quiet—not many cars or passersby that time of night—and I wished I hadn't been so bullheaded and that I'd taken the ride Erick had offered me.

He stopped and got in my face. "You got a photo?" he asked.

"What? No," I said. But I instantly regretted saying it, because it had agitated him even more.

"Waddya mean, you don't have a photo? What kinda crap you giving me?"

"I swear I don't," I said mulishly. I didn't want to share Christina with anybody, least of all this crazy.

"She ugly?" he asked. He jabbed at me with the knife, and I stood stock still. "Gimme your billfold."

"I lost it," I said, hoping he wasn't going to start pawing me to look for it, because it was right there in my jacket pocket, along with my apartment keys.

"What?" he said. "What kinda idiot are you? What kinda idiots they raising these days? Jesus Christ."

He started walking around, pulling his hair and muttering to himself. I couldn't quite make out what he was saying. I gave the sidewalk beyond the alley a furtive glance. I figured if I could take him off guard, I could bowl him over and run, even if I was drunk. But I wasn't sure. His mind was gone, but he looked pretty fit.

I must have twitched or taken a small step, because he came at me, and I started back, holding my hands up to protect myself. But he swiped at me, and I felt a burning in my hand and liquid running down my arm. It all happened so fast that I was surprised to see the gash in the palm of my hand. I swear I could see bone.

Then would have been the time to run, but I stood their dumbly, in shock, I guess, and just stared at him.

He started laughing. "You stupid college boys. You're all alike. Don't have a picture of your girlfriend. Probably don't have a girlfriend."

He came at me again, swinging his knife wildly, but that time something in the back of my brain screamed "move," and I kicked him hard in the shins, and I ran. I could hear him behind me, loud as a bear, loud as a train, swearing the whole time, but he must have been on something, or maybe I was just all jacked up on adrenaline and fear, because he couldn't catch me, and he gave up after a couple of blocks.

Then I was bleeding heavily; I was bewildered and a little woozy. I took my handkerchief out of my pocket and tied it around my palm, oriented myself, and realized I was a few blocks from the city hospital. That time I did hail a cab, and he stopped, though he might not have, considering it was the middle of the night and I had obviously been in a fight. But he was an angel, and he didn't charge me, even after I pulled out my billfold and tried to jam a twenty in his hand when we arrived in front of the emergency-room doors. He walked me inside and told me I ought to be more careful.

I was still holding the twenty when the nurse approached me.

It was the left hand. The nurse gave me some pain-killers, and the doctor said it wasn't as deep or as bad as it could have been. I was lucky that he hadn't cut any tendons. The bones I thought I saw must have been my own panic and imagination making things up.

"You're a lucky man," he said, working in small, slight stitches.

I started to silently weep at that. I couldn't talk.

Later, at home, after taking another cab, I pulled out the photo of Christina I kept in my billfold, the one of her dressed for the ballet in her black leotard with her hair pulled back in a bun. She looked beautiful, simple, and elegant. And I realized that I couldn't live without her.

When she asked me later what had happened to my hand, I lied to her. I said I had cut myself working on some shelves at Erick's house. She frowned and said, "He gets you in trouble, doesn't he?"

I told her that he didn't. That in fact, he had kept me out of the biggest trouble I could have ever landed in, but I could tell she didn't believe me.

I had the same sort of feeling of dread spilling up over me as I sat in Bill Wenzlick's paneled office. He'd called me that morning with some cock-and-bull story about needing to meet me to go over some financial stuff and had said that he needed my advice, but I had developed better instincts—at least I'd hoped I had—since that night I had gotten knifed in the alley. Had that been four, five years ago?

Bill was an old family friend, and regardless of the true reason for our meeting, it had sounded important over the phone. But then Bill was beating around the bush, making small talk about his golf game and his hobbies, all the while cleaning and loading his pipe. He refilled it with tobacco, patted it down with his fingers, and lit it. As he inhaled the first smoke of the sweet, cloying cherrywood—I could practically taste it myself—he looked ecstatic for a moment. Then the expression on his face changed, and he looked stern and even sad. I realized that we were about to get to the point of the meeting.

"There are both personal and legal issues that I want to discuss with you," he said.

"Sounds serious," I said, shifting uncomfortably. I could not tamp my feeling of dread.

"You are acquainted with a fellow named Buck Johnson?" he asked.

I thought for a moment, wondering at the odd turn the conversation had taken. I knew my wife had been working with him recently and that he'd taken on the role of the business adviser and the ad hoc fund raiser for the little ballet company she was trying to get going. But I realized with a pang of guilt that I hadn't had much to do with any of it. I hadn't formally met him since the arrangement had been hatched; I hadn't even insisted she invite him over to the house for a drink as a way of saying thanks. I'd been so busy traveling. I rubbed my jaw, trying to even think about what he looked like. It took me a moment to place him: cocky-looking fellow, always dressed to the nines, and a constant figure at the art events my wife loved to attend. He'd always had a mournful and slightly aggressive air about him that I'd found slightly unsettling, though I couldn't exactly say why. I'd put it aside when I had found out he was working with Christina, because I knew she needed help with her company.

"Yes, I've met him, but I wouldn't say I've had more than a few exchanges with him," I said. I was discomfited by the keen way that Bill was looking at me, so I added, "He's been working with Christina to get the Lockville Ballet Company up and running."

"Yes," said Bill. "That's exactly right."

The expression on his face was inscrutable, but I'd say he was bothered by something. He then picked up some papers and shuffled through them for a moment as though he was looking for something, but I got the feeling he was stalling.

He cleared his throat. "He's been involved with the Lockville Symphony for many years. This Buck Johnson knows how to organize and manage the business aspects of artistic organizations." He took a deep breath and sighed. "So Christina met with Buck for a business-planning lunch at the Classic Hotel."

"Swanky place," I said, laughing, but it was forced. I was beginning to feel my hackles rise. Christina hadn't told me about that. "What's your point here, Bill? I know that he's working with her. Have you called me in to warn me that I should be careful having him around my wife?"

It was a joke, but the steady way that Bill was regarding me with a look of what appeared to be…pity on his face made my stomach sour.

"Jesus," I said. "Is he that much of a player?"

Bill held his hands up. "Now simmer down, Adam. You want to hear the whole story."

"There's a story?" I said. I leaned forward. "I'm not sure I like stories, especially if they involve my wife."

Bill sighed. "Can we just do this, Adam? Hear me out, and then we'll talk."

I sat back, but I was feeling as wound up as a spring. "Go on," I nodded.

"Following lunch, Mr. Johnson insisted that they go upstairs to a conference room where they could spread out their papers and work in a quiet atmosphere."

I could feel the muscles of my jaw working.

"She trusted him," said Bill. "She knew him as a successful, respected businessman in this town who simply wanted to help out a struggling organization."

It felt like my world was falling apart.

"I didn't know that The Classic had conference rooms," I said.

"Exactly," said Bill. "It turned out to be his personal suite."

I didn't want to know more, but I felt a certain morbid curiosity.

"And?"

"They did have the meeting," said Bill.

"That's important?" I asked.

"You need to understand that Christina's part in this was unintentional."

"What are you telling me?" I asked, even though I already knew.

"He forced himself on her."

I said nothing, feeling my insides churn and an acidic taste appear in my mouth.

"He raped her," added Bill.

The room around us took on a funereal silence; the August air felt muggy. The box fan tried gamely, but the office still had the whiff of an earlier century.

My wife had been with another man.

"Adam," said Bill. "Are you still with me?"

"That's not possible," I said. My voice sounded oddly controlled. "She would not have let him."

"I'm sorry, Adam," said Bill. His voice was husky, and when I looked at him, I saw that his eyes were brimming with tears. "He locked the door."

"Son of a bitch."

"He's a strong man."

I stood up and paced around the office, feeling pent up anger roiling inside of me.

"This is unbelievable," I said. "Why would she go to a hotel room with a stranger?"

"Christina is a trusting person," he said. "Since she was a little girl, she has never seen the bad or wrong in anyone."

"I can't believe she did this," I said.

"She didn't do this on purpose," he said. "She didn't mean to hurt you. She's the one that got hurt... You've got to keep that in mind."

I stopped in front of his desk. "Why do I have to keep that in mind?"

"Because he was blackmailing her," he said. I noticed, then, that he had a large, overstuffed manila envelope in his hands.

"What are you saying?" I said. I felt wild with grief and anger.

"He secretly took photos of her in..."—he hesitated, clearly searching for the right words—"in compromising positions."

"You mean he took pictures of her naked?"

He sat in silence.

"Having sex?" I was shouting then, but I didn't care.

He nodded, but he looked at me with a pained expression. "Please keep things in perspective here, Adam. We don't want to go off half-cocked and do something we'll regret."

"There's no 'we' here!"

"Are you going to be able to continue with this?" Bill asked.

"There's more?"

"Yes," he said.

I deliberated for a moment. "Go on, then," I said. "Mind if I smoke?"

"Since when do you smoke?" asked Bill.

"Since now," I said hoarsely.

Bill rang his secretary for a box of cigarettes and some matches. I lit the cigarette and stood by the window. I turned the box fan around so it pointed out the window and blew into it. After a few drags, I felt a little less jangly.

"Do you want a drink?" Bill asked.

"That would be nice," I said. "Do you have bourbon?"

"The finest," he said, laughing, but it was without mirth. He poured it himself and handed it to me, and we stared at each other for a moment like two men in the heat of war.

He went back to his desk and sat down at it. For the first time, I realized that Bill was getting old. "Where were we?"

"Blackmail," I said.

"Mr. Johnson showed her an envelope of pictures that was addressed to you, along with a letter that would expose her. He convinced her that nobody would believe that the sex was hadn't been consensual."

I thought of my poor Christina and of how easily she became distraught over everything, but I could only bring up the barest ember of feelings. "And she fell for that?" I said. I sounded cold.

"Yes, she believed him. She was afraid to tell anyone."

"Hmm," I said, noncommittally.

"He used the letter and the pictures for extortion to force her into additional encounters."

The bourbon tasted strong, but it wasn't strong enough.

"He promised that he would give her the photos and the negatives back if she cooperated."

"She's very cooperative," I said. "But that's crazy." My voice sounded hollow and distant.

Bill had a wary look in his eyes. "The good news is that she came to me," his voice sounded brisk, almost jolly, but I wasn't going to fall in line with his everything-is-okay-now act. "I involved the legal system. We did a wiretap and recorded him threatening her."

I regarded him steadily. Said nothing.

"We, the police and I, have met with Mr. Johnson. He has confessed and has given up the material he was using to coerce her."

I blew some smoke out the window and downed the last of the bourbon.

"He has agreed to a plea-bargain deal and will go to jail."

I chewed on that awhile, lazily blowing smoke out the window and watching it pool on the other side, sucked through by the fan.

Bill walked over to me. "Adam, Christina is scared to death about this."

I gave him an impassive look.

"She basically had a nervous breakdown last week while you were out of town."

His hand was warm on my shoulder, and I wanted to hit him.

"She's afraid that you'll blame her—that you'll no longer want her."

Damn right, I thought.

"Her response to this was to avoid disclosure to avoid hurting you. She became ensnared. It was a big mistake."

The sound of the fan spinning out air was the only disturbance in the room. Finally, I said, "Does Christina know you're talking to me?"

He nodded. "Yes, I suggested doing so. Man to man."

I took out another cigarette and fumbled to light it.

"What about her parents? Do they know?"

He hesitated and said, "I think she should talk to her parents."

I suspected he was lying and that he'd talked to them himself, but I didn't want to be seen as interfering. I idly wondered how I would feel about his involvement in this a year later. It's amazing, the kind of peculiar details you seize upon when you realize that while you were out working to support your family, your life was kicked out from underneath you by some interloper. My breath caught in my chest. *And an unfaithful wife.*

"I hope you can put this behind you and move forward."

I drew away from Bill's hand—from his solicitude.

"So I don't get it," I said. "Why not call the police after the first encounter?"

Bill sighed and shook his head. "I don't know, Adam. I'm not a woman. He somehow convinced her that everyone would consider it consensual. That nobody would believe she had gone to a hotel room with a man for any purpose that didn't involve sex." He shook his head, and almost to himself, he muttered, "She is way too trusting." But the sidelong glance he gave me made me wonder if he wasn't also referring to her relationship with me.

The notion that her trust in me might also be misplaced made me feel hurt and angry.

"So, Adam," said Bill, clapping me on the shoulder again. "I believe that Christina is at home this afternoon. You may want to go see her. She's expecting you."

"I don't know," I said. "I may want to visit this Buck Johnson first. I may want to kill him."

I smiled when I said that, but it was more like I was baring my teeth, and I saw a look of concern wash over Bill's face. The bastard thought I was serious.

Maybe I was.

"He is no longer the business manager of the Lockville Ballet Company. He is under court order not to contact or see Christina."

I read between the lines. "You mean he's not in jail right now?"

Bill shook his head. "I couldn't button everything up that tightly. He's free pending formal charges and the implementation of his plea-bargain sentence."

"He should hang," I blurted out.

I felt so raw with emotion and so undone that I believe I could have killed him in that moment had he been standing right there in front of me.

"If you kill him, as you just threatened to do, you will only create a problem without a solution."

I wanted to say that I had been just kidding, that I was angry and had a right to say such things, but the threat hung there in the air, and I realized I had no desire to retract it.

"We have a solution for the situation as it stands today. The question for you is, are you going to make the most of it?"

I didn't answer—I just stood there with the lit cigarette dangling from my hand, dropping ash onto Bill's oriental carpet.

"Don't throw everything away because you feel betrayed," said Bill. "I know a thing or two, and I know that Christina is a marvelous woman, a faithful wife, and the mother of you child and that she loves you deeply. Don't act in haste."

The words "faithful wife" cut me to the core; I would mull over his words and this information about our marriage for the coming months without settling on a solution for the grief that had overtaken me.

"I'll leave you in peace for a while," said Bill. He moved about the office, packing his bag and grabbing a hat.

"Let me know if you need anything," he said. "I'm here to talk if you need me."

"Thanks, Bill," I said. "But I don't think that will be necessary."

My voice sounded cold and dead, and we both knew it. He was a gentleman, though, and left me in peace.

I don't know how long I stood in his office, looking absently out the window at the life below, because everything had taken on a certain, deathly pall. I had never felt more alone in my life. And I didn't know if I could go talk to Christina, or if I should go hunt down Buck Johnson and make him pay.

I thought about looking for Buck Johnson—I had a notion of a few places where that rat might have been hanging out, including his office—but I found myself driving home. I suppose habit takes over when there's a crisis. I drove, feeling stunned. I couldn't quite wrap my head around what he'd told me. I needed to see Christina to confirm it for myself. I felt sick and angry and hurt all at once.

When I pulled up in front of the house, I parked on the street. I don't know why, but I just couldn't bring myself to commit to pulling into the driveway, opening the garage door, and driving the car inside like nothing had happened.

I took a deep breath. I thought about what Bill had said about how troubled my wife was by the whole thing. I wanted to punch something,

In fact, I had noticed a subtle change in her—she had seemed more vibrant, more self-assured, and more in control. It wasn't that my wife was flaky or anything—I don't mean to imply that. She is—well, was up to that point—a really great mother and wife, and I had admired and supported her efforts to do something with the ballet company, even though it had seemed like the whole thing was a bit beyond her skill set. I figured she would get the support she needed.

I guess she did, I thought sourly.

I sat for a moment more and then realized that if I didn't get to it, it wasn't going to get done. My dad had always raised me to face trouble head on.

I found Christina in the kitchen. She was standing over the sink with a soapy cup in her left hand and a rag in the other, just staring out the window. I walked up to her without touching her, and she jumped and gave a little squeak. "Oh my goodness," she said, putting down the cup and the rag in the sink and wiping her hand on a towel. "I guess I'm a little jumpy."

I didn't say anything. I suddenly found myself without a good idea of what the right thing to say was.

She looked at me searchingly. I could see that there was pain and worry in her eyes. I noticed, for the first time, the dark circles under them and how pale and drawn she looked. Why hadn't I noticed that before?

She took a half step toward me and gave me a little hug. I stood stiffly for a few seconds, feeling a sense of aversion and anger that I tried to stifle. Then I hugged her back, but it was awkward, like hugging my ancient aunt, and I patted her on the back a few times before stepping away.

"So you talked to Bill, then? Today?" Her voice broke, and she started to cry, tears sliding down her face. She didn't bother to wipe them away.

"Yeah," I said. "I talked to Bill."

Her eyes scanned my face. I could see the need in them. "I so hope you understand."

"I'm trying," I said.

"Well, that's a good start," she said, sounding hopeful and smiling, just a little, through her tears.

I felt so torn up that I didn't know what to do or say. So I blurted out the first thing that popped into my mind. "I'm going to need a little space."

She looked even more stricken at that, and she put her fist up to her mouth and started sobbing in earnest. "I'm so sorry, Adam," she wailed. "I've ruined everything. I'm so sorry."

I loved her. I couldn't stand to see her cry, so without thinking, I drew her into my arms and pulled her close to me, kissing the top of her hair and saying, "Shhh, don't cry. Chris will hear you." I started to cry myself, then, the pain I had been holding at bay bubbling up and flooding over me.

We stood there for several long minutes, just holding each other as though we could make things go away.

Eventually, I felt small hands patting my legs. "Daddy, you're home," he said. "Why are you and mommy crying?"

"Hey there, buddy. Aren't you supposed to be napping now?"

I let go of Christina and bent down to pick up my son, who was then trying to haul himself up my legs. "You're getting big," I said. "Soon you're going to be too big for me to pick up."

Chris took my cheeks in his hand and scrutinized me carefully. "Did you make Mommy cry?" asked Chris.

"No, Mommy made Daddy cry," said Christina, backing away and wiping her eyes.

"Don't cry," Chris commanded.

"Okay, sport, we won't cry."

"Smile," said Chris.

"Why don't you take Chris and do something with him while I fix dinner?" Christina asked, patting me on the arm and giving me a quick but hopeful smile. "I'm fixing us something special."

To be honest, I didn't really feel hungry, but I figured that there's something to be said for going through the motions.

"That would be fine," I said.

Chris tugged at me, pulling me toward the hallway and his room. "I want you to read to me, Daddy," he said.

"Haven't we read all those books?" I said, stalling a little bit.

"Daddy, you're silly," he said.

Christina stood there in the kitchen, her back to me and her shoulders heaving up and down a little bit as though she was still crying. I was a little glad to be distracted by Chris. It would help me get my head around this.

It took Christina about twenty minutes to finish dinner, and we ate at the kitchen table in our usual places, but somehow it was clear, over the course of the meal, that things had changed. We had all changed—even Chris, who didn't know it. There were awkward periods of silence, and there was a lack of relevant subjects to talk about. The weather, what her folks were up to, my work—none of it seemed important compared to the big thing hanging over our heads, the proverbial elephant in the room: My wife had had an affair.

Christina was trying very, very hard. She kept touching me solicitously on the shoulder, and I helped her with clearing the table and doing the dishes just to prove I was still in the game. But I felt myself growing a little remote as I struggled to make sense of what had happened but found it made no sense to me.

I put Chris to bed, and then the gulf between us really bloomed. I had to fill it. So I sat myself down on the couch with the daily paper and read it from front to back, including the society section, which I had never much cared for. I saw Christina puttering around the house until finally she put her pajamas on and came to tell me she was going to bed. I gave her a perfunctory kiss on the cheek and put my nose in the paper until I fell asleep.

As the days passed, Christina and I kept to our routine—I went to work, and she continued to have practice at the Lockville Ballet and to drop Chris off at her parents' house. I had a few business trips out of town, but I cancelled them without explanation. I didn't tell Christina, but I felt uneasy about leaving town. I didn't think she'd see that Johnson creep again, but I wanted to make sure he didn't come sniffing around, even though he had the law hanging over his head.

We weren't the kind of people who fought. But we had plenty of silence and plenty of things unspoken until my accusations and questions started to spill out despite my best intentions. "Why didn't you call the police immediately following the first time?" I asked her one night while she was in the bathroom, running water for Chris's bath. The strained look on her face sent me out of the room, feeling guilty and dissatisfied at the same time. Another time, over breakfast, I snapped, "Why did you go to the room with him in the first place?" When she didn't immediately answer, I just sat there, frozen, and then threw down my paper. Then she defended herself, "Adam, I thought it was a conference room. I thought we were supposed to work on the business plan." She wrung her hands, looking agitated and sad. "He pushed me into the room. After the business planning, he...he locked the door...and..."

I snorted, pushing my chair from the table.

"I didn't tell anyone because I didn't think anyone would believe me. I thought it was just one mistake and that I would forget it and nobody would ever know."

I gave her a steady glare, surprised by how willing I was to go with my anger—by how my sense of betrayal fueled my stubbornness.

"And then there were the photos," she said, her voice small, like a child's. "He forced me to continue the relationship with him. He's a horrible man. He broke his promise to let me out of it."

I could see she was hurting, but I wanted to punish her. I wanted her to tell me in her own words—to confess.

The sad thing was that I wasn't sure anymore if confessing and apologizing and hashing it all through was going to be enough.

"Why didn't you tell me?" I felt my voice rise. "I'm your husband. I'm the one whose promises you should be worried about. I'm the one in a relationship with you."

She started crying and stood up. "Why didn't I tell you? Because I didn't want *this* to happen."

"Stop shouting," I said. "You're going to wake the baby."

Her eyes were red, and she was sobbing openly. Her voice had a hysterical edge. "I'm going to wake the baby? That's what you're worried about?"

I looked at her, feeling the muscles in my jaw work. "Yes," I said evenly. "We have to think about Chris."

She started to pace around the kitchen, holding her fingers in her hair. "Jeez, Adam, is that really the most important thing here? Because I think the important thing is figuring out how we're going to move past this. How you're going to forgive me."

At that point, I felt suddenly tired and deflated and sick of my own hot air. "I'm trying," I said. "I just need some time."

"Well, maybe we should try a therapist," she said softly.

"I'll think about it," I said.

I got up then and grabbed my briefcase, which had been sitting on the counter, gave her a kiss on the cheek, and ruffled her hair. She smelled good— like vanilla. I wanted so badly to put this nightmare behind us, but part of me refused.

"What are you doing?" she asked.

"I have to go to work."

"But it's early," she said, glancing at the clock and looking panicked.

"I have lots to do," I said.

I wanted to feel guilty, but I felt a sense of relief walking out that door and out into the morning light of the waning summer. For the first time in my life, I didn't have a plan.

Nineteen

THE CHILL

Christina

LIVING WITH ADAM WAS LIKE LIVING WITH A GHOST. Over the next few weeks, he came home from work late, and I suspected, by the smell of booze on his breath when he came in for a perfunctory kiss on the cheek, that he had started dropping by the bar. I hoped he was going out with one of his buddies from college or even with the guys from work, but I felt a pang of worry that he had taken up with some woman. And then I felt miserable and guilty for feeling jealous. How dare I?

I didn't dare ask him.

I kept the house super clean and tried not to neglect it or the baby in any way. I tried to act cheerful and welcoming and yet at the same time contrite, lest he think I was somehow happy about the situation.

We didn't talk about what had happened. I was afraid to bring it up.

I wanted to ask him for reassurances that he still loved me. But he had not moved out of the house or yelled at me or hit me or any number of things; he had simply withdrawn behind a wall that I could not hope to breach anytime soon. But he was still there, and he was still a good father to Chris.

That's what I kept telling myself.

I threw myself into getting the company ready for our performance. The opening was only weeks away. The summer had almost slipped past me, like a spirit in the night, and the evenings had taken on a slight chill. The dancers had, to their credit, become connected, and there was a new synergy to the program. Scott and Meg had become totally connected to the new format, and their enthusiasm had spread quickly to the rest of the company. It was building to new levels of excitement, and yet everything felt hollow to me, though I had a certain energy that mystified me. I felt as though I could run miles if I had to, as though I could keep up with Hannibal and his army of elephants, and as though I could slay Rothbart himself.

I also felt jittery and jumpy, and I wasn't able to sleep much. I dreamed of feathers and forests and of running through them in the night. Siegfried came to me, and I told him I could fix things myself. That I wasn't Odette. That I didn't need to kill myself. I passed my nightmares off as too much costuming work and the result of having real feathers clinging to my clothes, as I had taken some of the dancers' outfits home to help the seamstress sew some of the extra touches on them. We had funding, but I was unsure of how deep our pockets were, and with Buck Johnson gone, I was nervous about even approaching the subject with Mitch Carter, who had taken over everything. I was ashamed and didn't know how much he knew. I felt him look at me with curiosity, brimming with questions about what had happened to our fearless business manager. Rumors abounded, of course, but everyone cut a wide swath around me.

Except Anna.

Perhaps the undercurrent of rumors and the speculation about why Buck Johnson had a hangdog look on his face and had practically dropped out of sight fueled the fire. Or maybe it was the visits from national and international luminaries. But ticket sales were strong; the first night of the five-night run had already sold out.

It was ironic that just as I was launching my dream, I was living in a nightmare. I wondered how could I be so happy and so grief stricken at the same time.

Twenty

THE DISCUSSION

Adam

THE RAIN AND FOG THAT HAD COME ON MATCHED MY MOOD, and I welcomed the earlier sunsets. During those past few weeks, Erick and I had easily taken up where we had left off before I had gotten married. We had kept up golfing together, to be sure, but going out in the evenings had not been attractive once I had had family responsibilities. It's funny how those desires taper off. But there we were at the City Club, cloaking ourselves in whiskey and good spirits, hiding away in the dark-paneled room. Tonight we sat in the corner of the bar, watching the dancers on the floor. All we needed were a few cigars, and we would be set. He didn't ask me any questions. He was good about my crying on his shoulder incessantly, and he hadn't told me to piss off yet. He was my oldest buddy; we had been friends in high school, and I had stood up with him at his wedding. He had been married for five years when he had had a one-night stand, and his wife had found out. He had a daughter, but I don't think he saw her very often. Pity.

We'd been there only a half an hour when I spotted the trim blonde walking across the floor toward our booth. Erick straightened up expectantly; he was a bit of a ladies' man and liked to prowl. But the blonde gave him a cursory nod and smiled at me, holding out her hand. "Come on, big guy. Let's dance and have some fun!"

She did look nice in that tight blue dress, but I gave her a forced smile. "Not tonight. My dear friend and I are trying to solve the world's problems."

She frowned. "Aw, come on. Let's dance."

I shook my head and said, "Not tonight, sweetheart."

Tempting as it was to get on the slippery slope and to treat Christina in the same manner I had been treated, I didn't want any further complications at that time. I was still trying to sort through what to do about my marriage. Anyway, it just wouldn't have been right.

"Hey, that physical act means nothing. Unless there's an emotional component—a betrayal," said Erick. "My wife destroyed me. We had a great marriage and a great family, my wife, our three-year-old girl, and I. All because I made one mistake."

Erick took another go at his drink. He grabbed my arm and looked me in the eyes. Erick can look intense sometimes, and he scared me a bit.

"So, Adam, let me get this straight! Your hang up is that Christina had sex—coerced sex at that—with another man."

I felt a sharp pain wash over me. I nodded glumly.

"Jesus, you are a fool," he said with a sharp tone in his voice. He slapped his hand on the bar and shook his head.

"I'm a fool for trusting Christina," I said.

"No, you're a fool for thinking that you had no part in this," he said.

That made me mad. "Now look here—" I began.

"No, you look here. Anyway, do you think that, at our age, there are any girls left who aren't experienced? Let's say you divorce Christina; does that leave you with any better choices?"

I made a face.

"Yeah, scowl at me all you want, but you know I'm right. What with the birth control pill and all of that jazz, you try finding someone who's totally pure. There are not many of those out there. We're all human."

"I don't see what that has to do with me and Christina," I said. Erick was making me feel even more edgy, and I didn't like that.

"Everything, man," said Erick. He sipped at his drink for a moment, frowning at me. "And by the way, if you're thinking of dumping Christina, let me know."

"I will," I said curtly.

His face brightened. "She is one fine lady. I would take her—if she would have me—in a heartbeat."

His words had a bit of a challenge to them. He gave me one of his infamous smirks, but I knew that my friend Erick was quite serious about what he'd said. For a moment, I imagined Christina moving out, taking Chris with her, the emptiness of the house, my filling my days with work, Erick starting to come around, and me babysitting our son while the two of them went on a date. Over the sound of the bar, I could hear my life being lifted away from me, taken by the wind. And I wondered if I was going to be able to resist that, or if I would simply give in and let myself be swept away.

"Like hell you'll date her," I finally said. But we both knew that I had uttered it a little too late, just like everything else in our relationship.

Twenty-One

The Plea

Buck

DAYS PASSED, AND I CONVINCED MYSELF THAT I would at least hear from Christina—that she would call me on the phone and tell me that it was all a big mistake, that she hadn't meant any of it, and that she truly loved me. I thought about that a lot, in the morning when I woke up with the sharp rays of the sun stabbing me in the eyes, when I dragged my sorry ass into work, and when I went into the Good Times Club and drank until the joint closed and Zack had to tell me it was time to go home.

In some versions of the fantasy, the best ones, she would tell me that she was leaving her husband. She would show up on my doorstep with Chris on her hip, and her face would light up when I opened the door. And she would embrace me, and I would taste her sweet lips and feel her love for me, still beating pure and strong.

I felt devastated—undone. I'd made several starts at writing a letter to Christina as Zack had suggested, but I had ended up throwing most versions away, feeling that they were inadequate. Every time I sat down, I was reminded of the impending jail sentence before me, and I would break out in a sweat, a dread and malaise would overcome me, and I would have to lie down until it passed.

I couldn't believe I was falling apart so deeply.

I could have gone to my father for advice, I supposed, but what help would he have been? I wouldn't have been able to bear the deep disappointment in his eyes, the look that said I took more after my dead, weak mother than him, and his finally deciding to write me a check, because that was his answer to everything. Besides, he had played his part—it was his fault that Marilyn had hung on the way she had, and I was dead certain that had she not come into the picture, none of this would have blown up like it had. The thought of her approaching my Christina made me boiling mad, but I tried not to think about it. I hadn't gotten around to hiring a lawyer of my own, I suppose because doing so would have made everything that was happening to me more real, but I was sure that telling off Marilyn would only get me in deeper trouble.

Finally, one evening at the bar, Zack sat down with me and helped me put into words what was on my mind. I took notes on a paper napkin, and when I got home, I pulled out some expensive stationary that Marilyn and I had received as a wedding gift but had never used. I wondered why she hadn't taken it with her—she'd taken everything else—but I was happy to have it. The paper was a delicate cream color and felt fine in my hands. I cast about until I found an old fountain pen, and an hour later, I had what I would consider a suitable facsimile for Christina that was worthy of my missive to her.

Early the next morning, I pulled into the parking lot of the civic center and parked in the far tucked-away corner where she wouldn't see me at first. It wasn't too long before I saw her little Mustang pull into the lot and into her usual space by the door. Immediately, I began to shake so badly that I wasn't sure I could pull it off.

I wasn't sure how she would react. Things could go badly for me if she turned me in. I was well aware that I could get twenty to life for simply violating the plea deal—for simply talking to her.

But I had to take the chance; I wasn't much of a gambler, but if it went well, it could mean my whole life. A shortened jail term and a future with Christina.

But if she wanted to be hostile, even vindictive, she could turn me in. I would be toast.

I forced myself to get out of the car and to take a few deep breaths before I walked slowly her way. If I couldn't get a hold of myself, I would scare her off—perhaps forever—and I knew I couldn't bear to live if that were the case.

She popped out of her car, and my heart felt a pang, yet my pulse hammered at the sight of her—her blond hair piled so carelessly on her head, the nape of her neck looking so sweet and kissable—that I had to stop.

"Christina?" I called, though it came out more like a croak.

She turned instantly and regarded me warily, her whole posture telling me that she was ready to run.

"Buck, what are you doing here?" she asked, her gaze darting around the parking lot. "You're not allowed to see me. You're going to get in more trouble."

There was nobody there that early in the morning. I had counted on that fact to ensure some time with her.

I opened my palms toward her. "Look, I'm not going to hurt you," I said evenly. "I just wanted to talk to you. I just want to ask you for a favor. It will take just a minute of your time."

She folded her arms across her chest in a defensive posture that made my heart break a little bit more.

"I just wanted to talk with you about…about what's going on," I said weakly, taking a few steps toward her until we were mere feet apart. She hadn't fled yet, though she looked at me suspiciously. I drank in the sweet smell of her perfume.

I longed to embrace her.

Something about my expression must have warned her because she took a step back and said, "Buck, don't."

"I swear, Christina, I mean you no harm," I looked at her beseechingly, my big speech about talking to the district attorney and getting less jail time not top in my mind at the moment. "I love you."

She looked uncertain. "You can't love me, Buck," she said. Then a flash of anger crossed her face. "You assaulted me. You blackmailed me into having sex with you. That's not love."

The moment hung in the air between us. I felt deep sadness at how she had interpreted the events of our relationship. The photos had been an insurance policy; they meant nothing more to me. I couldn't see how she could take them so seriously.

"I loved you. And love you still," I began.

Her face looked stony. I needed to try a different tactic, I could tell, and I once more had to quell the urge to embrace her. My arms felt stupid, hanging there by my sides. I felt like a useless man.

"I realize that it's going to take you a long time to forgive me," I said. "And I'm really sorry if I hurt you in any way. I never meant to."

Her face softened a little bit, and encouraged, I went on.

"But in case you cared for me the least little bit, I wanted to let you know that I am going to go to jail. For a long time. Unless you help me." A sob welled up in me and came out, despite myself. "If Adam divorces you, we can get together after I get out of jail. We can have a great life together."

She looked concerned and startled. I had to take advantage of the moment, or it would pass.

"I need you to do me a favor and ask the DA for leniency. I am asking for you to help me get a lighter sentence—less jail time." I paused and added, "Maybe I could be paroled after six months."

Her expression hardened for a bit, and I could not bear the skeptical way she looked at me with her beautiful blue eyes.

"Hear me out, please," I said. "I couldn't bear to be in jail like that." I was beginning to feel a bit wild, and I stepped toward her, needing her comfort, but she took several steps back.

"Please, Christina, they'll…kill me in jail. I'll kill myself!"

I was insane then, clearly, but the closed look on her face made me feel in agony.

She turned and started walking away from me toward the door of the civic center. "Just leave me alone, Buck," she called over her shoulder. "Leave me alone, and I won't tell the judge you were here."

She was at the door, fumbling at it with her keys. She'd dropped her purse and the package she was carrying, and they had spilled on the ground.

I jogged over to her. I had nothing to lose. And that time I touched her on the shoulder, spinning her around.

"Christina, I'm sorry. I'm sorry," I cried, weeping openly then and ashamed. "I am in love with you. I didn't know any other way. I was obsessed. I was not thinking clearly. I'm sorry."

She looked at me with a new understanding in her eyes, and she took me in her arms while I sobbed on her shoulder, telling her I was sorry over and over and over again. I wet her shirt with my tears and felt the agony of being alive and being so close to the one I loved and yet so alone. I thought that I would die.

Then my crying stopped; it was all out of me, and I felt empty and bereft and dry. And she patted me on the shoulder and said "there, there" like she was comforting a child.

After a while, I wiped my eyes. The note I wanted to give her was still clutched in my hand, though it was a little tear soaked then.

"Buck, you just never seem to get that I'm already married and that I love my husband." Her tone was warm but her words were not. "You have forced yourself into my life and created so much conflict for my family." She regarded me steadily. "I don't care if you do rot in prison. I might just turn you in for contacting me."

I stood there, stunned.

"Just get out of my life," she said. The simple, straightforward way she spoke made me realize, more than anything, that it was over, that I probably had no chance with her, and that I would go to jail and rot there just like she'd suggested.

But still I thrust the note at her, even though I knew she could use it against me as evidence that I had contacted her. I'm a sucker for grand gestures, and I wasn't sure I cared anymore. "Just read this," I said, feeling myself getting weepy again. "Just read this and know…know I love you."

She took the note from me, looking bewildered. Her face was pale and frightened and sad all at once. I wanted to kiss her but did not.

Instead, I turned and walked away, my heart feeling heavier with each step. "What have I done, what have I done, what have I done," I mumbled all the way to my car. A light rain began to fall.

Twenty-Two

THE EVIDENCE

Christina

I STOOD THERE, SHAKEN, LONG AFTER BUCK HAD gotten into his car and pulled out of the parking lot. The rain fell all around me, but I stayed dry because of the underground garage. I had thought that it was all behind me—that I would never see Buck Johnson again. I had also thought everything was so clear in my life. Things were right and wrong, good and bad, and day and night. I was my husband's wife and my son's mother. I was not a mistress. I was the victim.

But then, seeing Buck fall apart in front of me and feeling such sympathy and…maybe even love for the man, however damaged he might have been, made me feel so very different. Changed.

It was like that scene from the *Wizard of Oz* where everything in Dorothy's world changes from black and white to full-blown cinematic color. Sure, it was beautiful, but it was also dangerous and filled with traps and deception.

I had loved my husband—I loved him still—but was it possible I had loved someone else? Even someone as dangerous, even as criminal, as Buck Johnson?

At last I realized I felt lonely in my marriage. I named it. My husband worked all the time. My husband neglected me. Worse yet, my husband took me for granted.

And I'd gone and shown him. But it seemed like things were worse than ever. My husband, as I had known him, seemed to have died. He had been replaced by the ghost of the man I had been living with who slept on the couch every night and had started going out again in the evenings with his friend Erick, drinking and probably carousing with women.

And it served me right.

I had changed everything by my actions, and I could not go back to my old world and my old life.

But what was this new world?

Dizziness struck me, and I sat down on a bench, not even bothering to unlock the door to the civic center. I closed my eyes and rested, or tried to, to make the overwhelming feelings go away. I didn't open them again until I heard the sound of Anna's voice.

"Christina? Lord, girl, are you okay?"

The rain had stopped, and the day had brightened. I opened my eyes and squinted up at my friend. She was faithful…in her own way. She stood there, the sun casting her face in a shadow, forming a bright halo that crowned her. She looked like an angel, and the thought made me start giggling.

"You're drunk or high, I gather," she said dryly.

"No, neither," I said, giggling some more. I reached my hand up to grab hers and pulled her down by me. She sat down with an "oomph" but didn't sound too put out by me.

"This is comfortable," she said. "What's going on with you?"

What did I have left to lose?

"Anna, I know we've talked, and you know things are happening, but I thought I would just give you an update on the situation in my life and on what's going on."

"Shoot," she said.

"The ballet is going well," I said. "That's not it." I rubbed my eyes. "I think my husband is going to leave me. He can't deal with the Buck problem."

She patted my hand. "He'll get over it. He's being a big baby."

"I don't think so," I said. "I think I'm going to be alone. Things are really strained between us. He spends a lot of time with his buddies and who knows who else."

Anna snorted. "I can't see Adam fooling around on you," she said.

"Why not?"

"He loves you!" she said. "Plus, he's a bit of a stick in the mud. I always wondered what you saw in him. I figured he must be a good lover."

"Anna," I said, but I laughed and swatted her on the leg.

"Is he?"

"I don't know," I said. "Not lately. He's been distant."

She frowned. "Just give him some time. He'll come around."

"I'm not sure," I said.

Anna said nothing. Sometimes I wondered if she was so opposed to marriage and found it so stifling and terribly old fashioned that she was willing to stand by and watch mine fail. But some conversations are too painful to wade into. She had been my dear friend for years and had stood by me, more or less. I wasn't willing to give that up, too.

We sat in silence for a bit, watching the rain resume and pool in little puddles in the parking lot. Then she asked, "How's Buck?"

"He was just here," I said.

"What do you mean? Doesn't he have some sort of restraining order?"

"Yes, but he was here anyway."

"Holy cow, Christina," said Anna. "No wonder you looked so spacey when I showed up." She looked me over with care. "Did he hurt you?"

"No, he just wanted to talk," I said. "Actually, he was pretty much a pussycat. He was crying like a little kid."

"What did he want?" said Anna. "What did he say to you?"

"He wanted me to go to the DA to get leniency. And to marry him after he gets out of jail."

"What? No!" said Anna. "He has a lot of nerve."

"He doesn't get it, does he?" I said.

"Well, if you'd played your cards right, you could have had two men courting you," she said.

"Anna, that just wasn't going to work," I said. "You know that isn't me."

"Well, you didn't give it a chance," she sniffed.

"It would be like the Mormons, only with several husbands," she said. "They could have been brother-husbands."

I had to laugh despite myself. Anna was a wild chick, and she was funny. I knew that she was just saying that because she didn't have anybody at all—just her poor, sick mother. I wasn't going to hold it against her.

"So are you going to do it?"

"What, marry him out after he's gotten out of jail?" I said, feeling suddenly euphoric.

"Well, that too," she said, laughing. "I meant are you going to turn him in."

"I don't know," I said, remembering the note in my hands. I showed it to her. "I have evidence if I want to."

She looked at it and started to snort with laughter. "He's not too bright, is he?"

"No," I said. "He's not."

We sat there awhile, laughing and talking as if we had the world by the tail and weren't two sad women who had major problems, until the dancers began showing up for rehearsal one by one. A few of them greeted us and stood off to the side, wondering, I suppose, why we were sitting there on the ground. Scott looked at us like we had lost our minds—and probably we had—but it didn't matter. Meg gave me a slight smile. I suppose she had heard some rumors about what was going on, but I wasn't going to give myself away. Even though it seemed likely that Adam was going to leave me, the ache that had settled into my chest was mine and mine alone. I wasn't going to mar the happiness of the group with my sob story.

I got up and gathered my stuff back into my bag, including the envelope Buck had given me, opened the door, and said, "Ladies and gentlemen, we have a show to do."

I should have tossed the letter.

The week of rehearsal leading up to opening night was so busy that I could hardly keep up with everything. Anna was a lifesaver, of course, and the new leads were doing a stellar job of keeping the company together. But still, I had the jitters. I tried to pass my feelings off as nervousness about my first real performance, my debut as an artistic director, and the stretching of my artistic wings from one who performs to one who exacts a perfect performance from others.

The scads of journalists didn't help. I didn't know there were so few women artistic directors in existence; we were such rare creatures that the media came out in droves. We were a stone's throw from New York City, really, so it didn't surprise me that the city pages covered our attempt. What surprised me was the cadre of callers from international newspapers. I hadn't thought they would bother with our tiny dance company, and it almost made me break out in hives when I realized that what we were doing was nothing short of groundbreaking.

But the papers sensationalized everything. They called me a "femme-fatale director," and while they seemed to be taken with the idea of a modernized ballet and a more daring and sensually expressive *Swan Lake*, they seemed to be a little…dare I say…titillated by the whole idea. They ogled the dancers during dress rehearsal, and it made a few of our ladies angry, I could tell. I had to tell Meg not to mind what the journalists thought as long as they gave us good coverage. Anna had watched the interchange and then had pulled me aside, smiled wickedly, and remarked, "I guess the coverage they give us will be inversely proportional to the coverage of our costumes." I had to laugh at that. I appreciated how Anna kept me looking at the humorous side of this whole situation.

The reporter who surprised me the most was a fellow from the Utah daily newspaper, who, I was surprised to learn, was one of the most influential dance journalists in the country. Utah was not simply a place riddled with Mormons, as I'd assumed and had made the unfortunate error of saying during our interview. He'd chuckled and proceeded to tell me about the long tradition of dance in Utah until Anna rescued me.

I got home late almost every night, and I was wrung out and exhausted when I did.

Adam would pick Chris up from my parents' house, get him dinner, and entertain him until I came home. Our son absolutely refused to go to sleep until he'd had some time with me. I tried to give Adam a few tricks for getting him to sleep, but the way he looked at me, with an expression that invited no suggestions, made me back away from him. Anna kept telling me that Adam needed some space, but I was beginning to wonder how much time it would take for him to forgive me—and if he ever would.

I would get Chris to bed and wolf down whatever was left in the house—directing was hard work—and Adam would disappear outside. He'd taken up smoking again, and I could smell it when he lit up, the odor drifting through the screen windows, making everything in the house smell stale and sad. It was getting chilly in the evenings, but he'd sit outside with a beer and a white T-shirt on, staring morosely into the yard. I'd finally go to bed, but he rarely joined me anymore. I'd find him asleep on the couch in the morning, his face creased in a pattern that matched the fabric on the sofa. He looked so peaceful and untroubled at those moments that my heart swelled with love and sorrow. At those times, I could touch him, stroke his brow, lean in, and take in his unique Adam smell of cigarettes, beer, and lavender cologne that he'd bought from a specialty shop in Brooklyn when he had had to take a trip to the city. The scent reminded me of my childhood.

Those were the times when I missed Adam the most.

On the eve of our first performance, I had to stay extra late; it was nearly 11:00 p.m. when I got home. The house was still, and most of the lights were off, including the porch light. I found Adam in the kitchen, standing there blearily, holding a beer as though he'd been sleepwalking and had just woken up. "Hey," he said unenthusiastically, giving me a perfunctory kiss on the cheek when I attempted to hug him. He told me that Chris was already asleep. There were some cold noodles with sauce congealing in a pot on the stove that I could have.

"Thanks, sweetie," I said. I threw my purse carelessly on the kitchen counter and opened a cupboard to retrieve a plate. When I turned around, I saw Adam standing by my purse and holding an envelope with a distinct look of dismay on his face.

My heart skittered.

He held it up. My name was printed prettily across the envelope in blue ink. Above it was written, "To my dearest."

"What's this?" he asked.

I'd forgotten I had that damn letter. But there was no way out of it. I couldn't lie to Adam. He already knew.

I'd better get rid of the thing.

I sighed and put down my plate carefully on the counter. I walked toward my husband, stretching out my hand to take it. "It's nothing important," I said as lightly as I could. "I haven't even opened it."

"It's from him, isn't it?"

I studied the floor, praying for a miracle. I could feel his anger rolling off of him. Anna always claimed we were energetic beings, so I tried to think loving thoughts, hoping he could feel how committed I was to him. "Yes, it is."

My husband was silent.

"He stopped by the civic center the other day." I paused, searching for the right words. "He wanted me to ask the judge for leniency."

Adam put his hands on his head. "That son of a bitch," he said. "I hope you told him to go to hell."

My husband's anger scared me. It seemed to be eating at him—to be destroying our marriage. "I don't think it does our relationship any good to carry a grudge," I finally said.

Adam looked at me in shock. "Then you did it. You did ask for leniency,"

"I did no such thing," I said, feeling defensive.

"But you will," he said. "That's the truth. You have feelings for him, don't you? Admit it? It wasn't just about him…"—he started pacing—"screwing you!"

I felt myself flush. "No," I said. "That's not it at all."

I must not have sounded convincing enough, because I did have feelings for that man, though they were confusing and shot through with rage.

"Why are you doing this to us?" he said, his voice cold. "Wasn't I enough?"

"I don't know what you mean," I said, feeling tremulous. I was starting to shake. "Of course you're enough." I felt myself start to shake and rubbed my arms. "I love you."

"No," he said, waving the letter in my face. "No you don't. Or you wouldn't have this."

I started to cry then. "I didn't have anything to do with that letter," I said. "I didn't even open it."

"That won't do," he said. "Don't you think it's rude not to see what your lover wrote to you?" I shook my head, the tears streaming down my face, but he continued. "Why don't I read this for you? How's that?"

"Let's just throw it away," I said. "How about we burn it?"

"If you feel that way, why did you keep it?" he asked.

"I don't know."

"You don't know anything, do you?" he said. "You don't know anything about being married or being faithful." He looked defeated and tired all of a sudden. "I guess I don't either."

He started walking out of the kitchen door to the dining room, and then he turned around and flipped the envelope at me. It flew in a neat arc and hit me in the chest. I let it fall to the ground.

"I need some fresh air," he said.

Then he strode away. I heard the front door open and close, and he was gone.

I stood there, shaking and crying. *My marriage is over*, I thought. I'd gone and lost him anyway. All of my resolve, all of the bravery I had shown in confronting Buck Johnson, in bringing him down, had all been for nothing.

What could I do to bring him back?

I thought awhile, and on impulse, I turned on the gas burner of the stove. I took the envelope and stuck one corner into the flame until it caught fire. Then I grabbed the plate in one hand, and, holding the envelope over it, walked outside into the dark backyard.

The moon was full enough to light my way. I set the plate down in the grass, sat on a lawn chair, and watched the envelope burn itself to ash.

I thought about redemption, about what it would take to have my husband's forgiveness, and about how to earn his trust. I figured that everything would take time.

I fell asleep. When I woke up, it was very dark and quiet in the neighborhood, but I was covered by a blanket. I took that as a good sign, but when I went into the house, my husband was nowhere to be seen. The light above the oven was on, and the nearby clock said it was nearly two in the morning. I had to put my worry aside; opening night was the next day.

Twenty-Three

THE OPENING

Christina

IT WASN'T THE LINCOLN CENTER OR THE KENNEDY CENTER, but I liked to think that Tchaikovsky himself would have been impressed. I was there early, having dropped off Chris while he was still half-asleep and run off without giving my mother time to start into me about my life and my husband. She had looked unhappy, but what was I to do?

I was early, but Anna was earlier. She tried to intercept me while I peeked into the auditorium to admire the set, and I was stunned to see workmen there and to hear the sound of sawing and nailing. "What's going on?" I asked, feeling my chest tighten. "Why are the set builders here again?"

"Well, we had a little problem last night," she said. "The main set piece fell down and broke a bunch of stuff, and, well." She waved her hand nonchalantly toward the stage as though the mess didn't matter. "They say they're going to be able to fix everything and make it right this time before the audience starts showing up."

That last part, she said very loudly while Paolo, the lead set designer, walked by us, and he merely smiled at her and said, "Don't worry, Ms. Anna and Mrs. Christina! We have it under control!"

"Thanks, Paolo," I called cheerily, though I was feeling as frantic as a fox being chased by a pack of hounds.

Just then, Mitch Carter popped into the auditorium, rubbing his hands together and grinning.

"Don't you look like the cat who ate the canary," said Anna. I rolled my eyes. Lately, her flirting seemed to have gotten worse.

He blushed and said, "I've got good news."

"What's that?" I said. "More big-name media coverage? Is Balanchine himself gifting us with his presence?"

"Better. We are sold out."

Anna squealed, and I clapped my hand over my mouth. I could have cried.

"For all four nights!"

Anna took the opportunity to hug him, and Mitch blushed even more.

"That's such a relief," I said.

He gave me a mock scowl. "I hope you didn't doubt me. I mean, I'm no Buck Johnson, but I know a thing or two about selling seats."

I felt myself blush.

"Oh," said Mitch. "I'm so sorry. I didn't mean to make you feel uncomfortable. I'm guessing that the company and Mr. Johnson has some sort of falling out, but I honestly don't know all the details."

"It's okay," I said, struggling to regain my composure. "I'd rather not talk about it, though. It's all behind us."

"Certainly," he said. He straightened his tie nervously. "Well, I need to make sure the box office is all squared away."

He offered me a hand and said, "Break a leg! Or is that just theater talk?"

"It works for me," I said. "Thanks for all that you've done. You're remarkable."

As he walked away, I looked at him glumly. I wasn't as excited about the sold-out seats as I had thought I would be. I was very nervous about whether the company would be able to pull it off, what with all the last-minute changes.

The costume designer looked around the corner. "Oh, there you two are," she said. "I've got some issues with some of the headdresses for the swan. Can you tell me what you want me to do?"

"Of course," I said. "I'll be with you in a moment. Anna, could you make sure everyone is warmed up properly? It wouldn't do to have any injuries."

"Will do," she said, fixing me a look that told me she needed more from me.

I looped an arm through Anna's. "How is our company?" I asked.

"A little nervous. I think they could use a pep talk from you."

"What's going on?"

"It's a lot of pressure, making history," she said. "We dancers are not tradition breakers."

"Bullshit," I said. "Balanchine?"

"Yes, my dear. But Balanchine's dancers weren't showing so much of their, how shall we say, private real estate?"

Ah, that was the rub again. The dance was actually innovative because it was so physical, demanding, and emotional. Our version of *Swan Lake* was going to go down in the annals of ballet history.

That is, if it didn't take a swan dive.

I frowned. "Are our principals in place?"

"Yes, ma'am," she said. "Shall we go rally the troops?"

I looked at my watch. It was roughly three hours until curtain time. "Onward."

To be honest, the bustle in the practice studio was bracing. My dancers scattered about the room, stretching at the bar and fussing with their ballet shoes. My principal ballerina had three different pointe slippers and seemed to be trying to decide what to wear. "You'll be fine," I said. "You can always change them at intermission."

"Yes, boss," she said, nodding.

Anna soon had them doing warm-up routines while I talked to the costume director about her headdress woes, suggesting we take out some of the weight.

"Oh mon Dieu," she said. "These will take me all night to fix."

"It's okay, Louise," I said soothingly. "I'm sure you'll have them ready to go by the time the swan is ready to take the stage."

She walked away, muttering in French, while her assistant pulled racks of clothing across the way and into the dressing rooms to be distributed. I heard the sounds of the instruments being tuned. The orchestra members had arrived.

The time flew by. Very soon, Mitch came and pulled me out into the lobby for the reception. "Your parents are here, and they wish to see you."

"And my husband?" I had blurted that out without thinking, and Mitch gave me a cautious look, patting me on the shoulder.

"I'm sure he'll be here soon. I heard the traffic was outrageous. And it's raining."

My parents exclaimed when they saw me, and they hugged and kissed me. I felt distracted when they peppered me with questions about how everything was going, and more than once, I found my attention drifting to the lobby doors whenever a new guest would enter.

Finally, my father said, "Just give him some time. His ego is hurt, and he's licking his wounds. He'll come around."

He took my hand in his and squeezed it. I gave him a nervous smile.

"Thanks, Papa," I said. "I love you."

"We both love you very much," said my mother. "Just concentrate on what you have to do tonight, and don't worry about the rest."

"How was Chris doing when you left?" I asked. They'd left him in the charge of a teenager who lived in the neighborhood and had watched him before. I was sorry that he couldn't come but even sorrier that he hadn't seen his father all day. Or me, for that matter.

"He's doing fine, sweetheart," said my mother. "Why don't you go mix and mingle. You're the artistic director. Go act like it. This is your night."

It didn't feel much like it, but I kissed them both on their cheeks and went about the room. I talked with donors and dignitaries and journalists who had flown in from parts far flung. I was a bit nervous about all the buzz that had been created. I hope that we live up to their expectations. I felt pretty sure that our dancers would give a flawless technical performance, but the heart and emotive energy were all important. A show could collapse easily based on a few missteps if the dancers got riled. And they were feeling the pressure of doing something that was a little daring, a little provocative.

I couldn't really indulge in second-guessing myself because before I knew it, I was being dragged away from the reception by Anna to give the dancers one last talk before the show commenced.

The dancers, who were scattered about backstage, looked stunning in their costumes, with a little glitter in their hair and makeup to catch the stage lights. Louise and her assistant stood off to the side, looking satisfied. Paolo was up on a ladder, fixing one last thing, apparently, which made me nervous, and I tried to ignore what he was doing. I hoped he was just being a fussbudget.

When I saw the spectacle before me, felt the vibrancy in the air, and saw their friendly and expectant faces, I became overcome with emotions.

"Thank you all for working so hard and for being so…beautiful and fluid…in not only your dance but also in your mind-sets," I said. "You have pulled together a show that is truly stunning," I said.

"And thank you," said Anna, walking across the room and handing me a huge bouquet of a dozen yellow roses. I took in a deep breath. My husband had remembered me—he had thought of me after all. I took the bundle and clasped it to my chest. "Thank you for working so hard to bring your personal vision to the Lockville arts community."

Anna hugged me and kissed me on the cheek.

"Did you see Adam?" I said. "When did he give you these? Why hasn't he come backstage?"

Anna's eyes widened for just a moment, but then she smiled. "Why don't you let me put these in water for you?"

"No," I said. "I'll do it."

She looked troubled. "Please, let me do this for you?"

"Nonsense," I said. "I'll only be a moment."

She shrugged and smiled at me pleasantly, but there was a sadness about her eyes that made my stomach churn.

When I walked away toward my office to fetch a vase I had seen stashed in the storage cabinet, I found out what was bothering her.

The card with the flowers was addressed to me, but it wasn't signed with my husband's signature.

It was signed, "With love, from B."

Twenty-Four

THE PAYOFF

Buck

THE ONLY THING LEFT TO DO THEN WAS GET Marilyn off of our backs and fulfill the last—well, almost the last—terms of the plea bargain. I still cared about my reputation, or at least I hoped to salvage it. And I wasn't willing to let Marilyn take down Christina. I simply wanted to serve my time and hoped that things didn't continue to blow up while I was in jail. I wanted to be able to track Christina down if I got out within six months to a year. With any luck, she and Adam would be divorced, and we could start our relationship off on the right foot. I believed in second chances.

That wouldn't be possible if Marilyn continued to run around and rock the boat.

It was almost nine in the morning. I shuffled through some paper work, but I couldn't focus on anything. All I was doing was moving the piles around on my desk. I tried to figure out whether I had time to return some calls before she landed on my doorstep, and I figured I didn't. I just wanted to get her in and out of there as quickly as possible.

The conversation with Marilyn wouldn't be easy. She still held a grudge, and she always wanted more out of the divorce than she had gotten. Things had gone pretty sour between us personally. It was not a happy time.

Finally, a few minutes after the hour, my secretary poked her head in the door and announced, "Ms. Johnson is here to see you."

"Send her in," I said. "And close the door behind her."

"Yes, Mr. Johnson," she said.

Marilyn came waltzing into my office like she owned the place. She was covered with makeup and wore a revealing blouse and a very short skirt. She pulled up a chair in front my desk and made herself at home.

"So, what's going on? What did I do to earn the honor of an invitation to meet with his majesty?"

I was really glad that I had made the decision not to meet her in public. I bristled at her overbearing attitude. "You never let up, do you?" I said. "You have been vindictive and resentful ever since the divorce." I glared at her sternly, but she just laughed.

"I don't know what you're talking about," she said. "And stop looking at me like you want to kill me."

I sighed. She was doing it again—getting under my skin. She'd done it during the marriage, and I hadn't been wise enough to see it as a red flag. But I needed to keep this simply business so that I could be done with her once and for all.

"Marilyn, you have finally gotten me. You never let it go, and now you have done me in."

My calm demeanor and my words must have gotten through to her. She sat up and scowled at me. "What do you mean, *done you in?*"

"You know what I'm talking about. You went to Christina and threatened her." I tried to keep my cool, but I felt enraged.

"So what?" she asked, looking at her nails. "I asked your latest lover to convince you to give me some money, you cheapskate. What's so bad about that?"

I took a deep breath. It wouldn't do to get my jail sentence doubled for assault, or worse yet, murder. "A lot. She went to the police. I'm in big trouble. I'm going to jail."

The shocked look on her face would have been satisfying if what I had said hadn't been true.

"What? What do you mean?" She leaned over my desk. "Why are you going to jail? I thought she was your lover."

"She was," I said. "But the first time wasn't exactly consensual."

She raised her eyebrows but made no remark.

"As part of my plea bargain, I have to pay you the twenty thousand dollars you asked for."

She sat back and fanned herself. "So when do you get locked up and for how long?"

I pulled the envelope with the personal check made out to Marilyn out of my desk and handed it to her. Then I pulled out a receipt for the money. "You have to sign this to affirm that you received this amount in full so I can give it to the DA."

"You're not pulling my leg, are you?" When she took the pen and paper from me, her hands trembled a little. She looked pale and decidedly less adversarial than she had when she had walked in my door. "Gee, this is bad—really bad. I had no idea. I'm really sorry."

"Marilyn, if you'd just left me alone, none of this would have happened."

She looked at me with pity. "And if you had behaved yourself, none of this would have happened."

I looked down. For whatever reason, what Marilyn thought of me still mattered.

"Yes, you're right. I have to take responsibility for what I did."

Marilyn seemed stunned. I know I seemed like I was a changed man all of a sudden. I was. I was quiet, even penitent. I had at one time thought that Marilyn was the love of my life, and when she hadn't been able to calm the demons inside me, we had parted with acrimony. Now that I had loved and lost Christina, I was nothing more than a shadow.

"I'm going to jail," I said. "You can go on with your life."

My face felt wet. I hadn't cried when my mother had died, but it seemed like I was making up for it.

Say what you'd like about Marilyn, but she wasn't heartless. Not really. Her getups, her airs, her jewelry, her couture collection, her makeup—it was all an act. I saw her guard slip—saw the woman who I had courted during what seemed like a lifetime ago.

She took a handkerchief out of her pocketbook, leaned over me, and began drying my face. "Oh, look, I am so sorry. I had no idea."

Her composure broke; her eyes were red and wet.

"How long will you be there?"

"My sentence is five years. But I could get it shortened to less than a year if Christina puts in a good word for me." I paused and rubbed my eyes. "But now she hates me."

A cold smile tugged at the corner of Marilyn's lips. "You need her to put in a good word to the DA for you? I could help with that."

I felt a coldness wash over me. My mood changed. I was tired. I valued Marilyn, but it was clear that she was a wild card. As long as she wanted something from me—or wanted me for something—my life would always be chaotic.

I grabbed her wrist and pulled her to me, close enough that I could smell the sweetness of her breath. I gazed into her eyes. "No, please do not interfere like that," I said. "I don't need those kinds of favors anymore."

"But, Bucky, I can help. I know I can persuade her."

I let go of her and took a deep breath. "No. If Christina won't help me of her own accord, it's not worth it. She has to do it herself."

My belligerence cost me. Marilyn looked more herself again: frosty, guarded, and composed. "Well, if you insist on doing it yourself, I guess there's nothing I can do."

"No, there's not," I said. I felt sad but at the same time relieved. I would make my own way in the world.

I felt clearer. I walked around the desk to give her a hug and felt a certain sense of peace. She wrapped herself in my arms and pressed against me with an uncharacteristic enthusiasm. When she disentangled herself from me, she said good-bye without looking me in the eyes. When she reached the door and turned around for a last look, she was crying.

"Marilyn," I said. "Let's not leave it like this."

"No, it's okay, Buck," she said, wiping her face. "You don't need me any-more. And I guess that means I can't need you."

She turned and walked through the reception area and out the front door of the building. I thought about watching her walk down the sidewalk but decided I didn't want to draw things out.

That chapter in my life was ending, and I needed to let it go. But there was one thing I wanted to do.

I debated all evening about whether I should attend the opening gala. An hour before the show, I pulled out my tuxedo and ironed my shirt. I looked at myself in the mirror and looked older and more fatigued than I ever had in my life, but I shaved anyway, using my old-fashioned straight razor. I took a steamy shower afterward and closed my pores with some bracing aftershave. I wished I had gotten a haircut—who knew what kind of barbers they had in prison. I put on my tuxedo and tied my bow tie, one of the few things about being a man that my father had taught me that I found I the least bit useful.

I was in luck when I found that the florist was open that time of night.

The lobby of the civic center was lit up like a store window at Christmas, and I had to go park in the far corner of the lot. I was lucky I found a spot, and I tried not to think about the last time I had been there, the last time I'd spoken to Christina.

I didn't know if I'd have the guts to speak with her, but I felt compelled to be near her, even if I didn't see her.

I tried to purchase a ticket at will call, but Mark Turner, the bastard, inter-cepted me. He took me gently by the elbow and steered me away to a quiet spot in a flower garden.

"What are you doing here, Buck?" he asked evenly.

"How much do you know?" I asked, feeling tired. I had promised not to talk about the charges against me or about the situation in general. But it seemed obvious by the way he was acting that something had leaked. I hoped I wouldn't be implicated.

His mouth twisted a bit as he thought about it. "Enough," he finally said. "Not everything, but I know that you and Christina have had a serious altercation that has involved the law." He shifted nervously. "And that you shouldn't be here."

"I just came to see the performance," I said. "I promise I won't cause any trouble."

"How do I know that?" he asked.

"I give you my word," I said. "Look, this will be my last night as a free man. Tomorrow they will pick me up and put me in jail. For a very long time."

"Jesus, you really screwed up," Mark said, looking shocked.

"Tell me about it," I said. "Don't trust a woman who says she loves you." I sounded a little bitter, and my voice was hoarse, but I was too far-gone to care about my pride. It was in the toilet. I took a white handkerchief out of my pocket and blew my nose. "Look, I just want to see the ballet. Can you give me that much?"

He scratched his head and meaningfully eyed the bunch of roses I was carrying. "You promise to stay away from Christina?"

"Yeah," I said, sighing. I thrust the flowers at him. "Just give them to her, will you? You don't even need to say they're from me. Say they're from a secret admirer. That will make her night."

Despite my bone-wrenching fatigue and my weariness with the world, the thought of her taking the roses and inhaling their sweet scent made me smile. She would look good with those roses, dammit. I wondered what she was wearing.

Mark gave me a funny look. "You're a lost cause, aren't you?"

"Better believe it. Siegfried never had it this bad."

"Well, don't make me sorry I let you in," he said. He nodded. "Wait until the lobby is thinned out a little bit before you go in. I'll save you a seat in the balcony. You can sit with me."

I felt my eyes welling up with tears. I was becoming a real crybaby. "Thanks," I said. "This means the world to me."

"Don't mention it," he said. "Seriously. Never mention this."

"Got it," I said.

He left me there, standing in the shadows. I watched the lobby, and at some point, Mark came out and beckoned to me. We walked up the steps to the private balcony. There were a few other board members already sitting there, and they looked at me curiously but didn't speak to me. I was beginning to feel like an attendee at my own funeral.

I sat down, and Mark leaned over to me. "Don't mind them; this is a knockout show. I consider myself a ballet aficionado, and I can truly say that this is a masterful production."

I nodded and said nothing. I already knew that my Christina was talented.

The conductor walked down to the orchestra pit to a scattering of polite applause from the audience. This was not a group of ballet goers who were acquainted with this company, and I sensed nervous anticipation and even a hesitation in their willingness to embrace the performance. I sent up a silent prayer.

The opening strains of Tchaikovsky's waltz played, and a lone figure, the lovely and star-crossed Odette, came floating onstage, making her way through a forest. As the story unfolded, Prince Siegfried encountered the beautiful swan queen, Odette, during his hunt in the woods. Christina's new ballet was underway. The performance was flawless. I watched the whole thing, mesmerized, until it came to its conclusion.

Mark had me wait until everybody was gone, and I watched in agony as Christina took her curtain call as the artistic director. For a moment, I hoped she'd look up and see me in the balcony and give me some recognition. But when she did, for the briefest moment, I stepped back into the shadows.

Mark was watching me curiously. "Seen enough?" he asked.

"Yes," I said. "Thank you."

Afterward, I decided to go to the City Club for a drink instead of the Good Times Club. I couldn't stand the thought of seeing Zack that night. I wanted to fade into anonymity.

The City Club was private and posh and about as different from jail as it could have been. The private, paneled bar was what you might call "cozy," and its customers were well-heeled businessmen and a few women who were obviously working girls or wives. They all had that same complacent look that you get when your life is set in course—when you know what you're going to do from one day to the next and when everything is simple and steady.

I didn't envy them. I would be experiencing that soon enough, and the thought of being locked up made me feel, for a moment, like I couldn't breathe.

Forcing myself to smile pleasantly and to act as if all was well, I sat down at the bar and ordered a drink from a nice older gentleman behind the bar who wasn't Zack, who didn't comment on how I looked or the mood I appeared to be in, and whose eyes only flicked over me curiously before he brought me my drink.

It was late enough that a few people dressed in tuxes and formal dress drifted into the bar area, bringing with them the lingering joy that comes with the arts. If anybody recognized me as the man who had funded the whole thing and had made their evening with *Swan Lake* and all its denizens and dancers possible, they didn't show it.

There was no disputing that Christina had done a fantastic job. She was grace under fire, that one, and it was amazing that she had brought the dancers together. I knew enough about the dance world to know that she had taken on the difficult task of not only assembling a company but also pushing it new directions. I had heard enough buzz in the lobby to know that she had succeeded and shocked many.

I was sitting there, nursing my drink, making the booze last, staring at the reflections in the bottles lined up in front of the mirror behind the bar, and trying not to notice myself, when I felt a man sit down beside me.

I glanced over at the same time he did, and I saw him looking at me with shock.

"You," he said.

My adrenaline spiked, but I gave him a sincere smile coupled with a hang-dog look—a look that admitted guilt—and said, "Yes, I'm afraid it's the terrible me. You must want to punch me. But first, can I buy you a drink?"

My ready admission of guilt and my offer to assuage his feelings with alcohol had done the trick, because Christina's husband looked confused for a moment but nodded cautiously.

"I suppose a drink before I rearrange your face wouldn't hurt."

I sincerely doubted he could do me much damage; he was small and thin, built like a dancer himself, and I had done a little competitive boxing in college, but I decided not to press the issue.

The love of my life's husband was sitting beside me, and I didn't know what to make of it.

I had, for the couple of years since my divorce from Marilyn, been trying to pay attention to signs. I wasn't religious by any means, but my mother had been not only a devout churchgoer but also a spiritual believer. She had believed there was meaning in everything—the picking up of wind, a chill over your arm, the family dog's slight change in posture—and she had been invariably right, though what her omens and portents had had to do with the Christian God, I never could figure out.

But the fact that God had, in his providence, put Christina's husband in front of me must have meant something.

I intended to find out exactly what that was.

The bartender took his drink order and brought it, and I was silent awhile, waiting for him to get a little liquor in him before I proceeded.

He didn't leave, which surprised me. I wondered if he was working himself up to slug me. I guessed it didn't matter. I didn't care anymore.

After a while, I turned to him. "Why didn't you go to opening night?"

Adam's ears turned pink. "What do you care?" he asked.

I shrugged. "I don't care. It's just that she's worked so hard for this evening. Made huge sacrifices, you might say. And I wondered if you cared."

He turned on his barstool to regard me. "Of course I care. I care a great deal."

I felt a little belligerent. Did he love her as much as I did? Hardly.

"You don't show it."

He frowned. "How dare you say that."

I put my drink down and leaned over to him. "Look, I'm just saying you don't show it. You're gone all the time in California. You don't stop by rehearsals. You don't even go to the opening night. What kind of husband does that?"

The distaste on his face spoke spades. "The kind of husband who's been cuckolded."

I shook my head. "That's your fault, buddy."

He started to stand up. "Now you've got a lot of nerve. I've held my peace with you and been civil, but I'm about ready to ask you to step outside."

I gave him a wolfish grin. "So we can settle this like men?"

He narrowed his eyes. "Exactly."

I held up my palms. "Well, simmer down there. The way I see it, you've already won. In fact, you had me beat the whole time, fair and square."

I could see that caught his curiosity, because he gave me a cool look and sat down. "How do you figure?" he asked.

"Well, I had to use persuasion to get her to spend time with me," I admitted. I sounded just bitter enough that Adam gave a rueful chuckle. "And the whole time, she didn't really want me. Not like I thought."

Adam gave me a sour look and nursed his drink. I took the opportunity to order him another. If he got drunk, he would be more likely to become belligerent and go after me. But he would also be less likely to do any damage. I paced myself and didn't drink as much. The evening was turning out to be interesting.

We sat in silence awhile, though it wasn't companionable. I finally broke it. "Say, I always wondered what she saw in you."

Adam looked down at his drink, silent for a long time. Then he said, "I don't know."

"Look, it was an honest question," I said. "I didn't mean to make you sore. It's just that we never talked about you."

The bartender walked over and brought another round. Adam gave me a surly look. "What exactly is it that you want?"

Without thinking, I said exactly what I wanted. "I want your wife."

Adam looked murderous. Drunk or not, he could have positively killed me right then and there. I was sure of it. But instead, he got off his barstool and took my shirt in his hands, drawing me up to his face. He was so quick about it that it surprised me. Then I saw that he was taller than I was and not as slight as he had appeared.

"Let me tell you this," Adam said, his voice low and menacing. "You'll never have her. If I have to kill you so that you never have her, I will."

I swallowed hard. The bartender came over and said, "Hey, that's enough of that, you two. This is a civilized joint."

Adam ignored him. "Do I make myself clear?"

I nodded.

"I love her." He let me go and looked at me, his face flushed, and I could see shame and pain in his eyes. "I screwed up. I admit it. I gave you the chance to slip in. But that's not going to happen again."

I felt odd, almost giddy at Adam's speech. When I got out of jail, he might still be around. But at least she would be taken care of.

After that, I swore, may the best man win.

Adam turned to the bar, drew out his wallet, and laid a wad of bills on the counter. "Your drinks are on me," he said without meeting my gaze. "You opened my eyes."

He walked out of the bar, and I realized I'd been holding my breath. Gradually, the voices of the other patrons swam into my consciousness, and I realized my mouth was bleeding. I'd bitten my cheek.

The bartender leaned over and tapped me on the shoulder.

"Why don't you shove off, mate, and don't come back," he said. "We don't like that kind of trouble around here."

I pulled up the collar of my jacket and walked out of the doors into the night. What was left for me in life was rapidly disappearing, but I had to cling to my hopes.

Twenty-Five

The Call

Adam

AFTER MY RUN-IN WITH BUCK JOHNSON, I FELT downright sick. I had wanted to at least hit him but hadn't been able to. In fact, I felt an odd sympathy for Christina; he was an attractive man, polite, and well mannered. She could have done worse.

And then there was the fact that he was absolutely, obviously in love with my wife. And his intensity was overwhelming, even to me.

Still, he couldn't have her.

Despite that resolve, despite my thinking about all the ways in which I loved my wife, all the things I missed since our relationship had become strained to the point of breaking, I couldn't bring myself to take steps toward her. It was as though I were lost in those magical woods of hers.

I remembered coming upon her a few months earlier when the whole show was being planned and seeing her sitting there late one night at the kitchen table, sketching a forest out in her notebook. I stood, mesmerized by the details: the intricate interlacing of branches, the way the path seemed to disappear into the fog. Until that moment, I hadn't realized—to be truthful— or fully comprehended what a visionary she was or how drawn to the story world of the dance she was. Ballet was something I appreciated for the sheer athleticism of the dancers and the pageantry and execution that went along with each show.

My wife had been so concentrated on her work that she hadn't noticed me standing there until she had looked up and jumped a little. "Oh, Adam, you startled me," she said. She was blushing a bit and went to gather up her papers, but I stopped her from doing so, touching her on the shoulder. "No, keep on with what you're doing," I said. "Is this a set from *Swan Lake*?"

She had looked at me shyly. "Yes, it's the forest where we see Odette wandering and where Prince Siegfried goes hunting with his friends and first sees the beautiful Odette."

"It's beautiful," I had said.

She frowned. "I hope I can get a fog machine to make everything look more mystical. And I'm concerned with being able to get all those trees on and off again in an efficient manner."

"You'll figure it out."

At one time, I'd been smitten with my life, newly in love with her, but I realized that I had let that fall away under the pressures of my work.

I knew all of that, but I hadn't slept at home since the evening I'd run into Buck Johnson. I had gone home, left her note, and then packed my bags and showed up at Erick's house. He had shaken his head when he had opened the door, but he had let me in without a word. He and I knew where we stood.

That was a few days ago. I went home this morning while Christina and Chris were still asleep. It was cowardly, but I didn't know what I was going to say to her. Somehow, I felt like when we did meet, I had to be everything she'd always wanted me to be. I carried the weight of our failed marriage in my heart, and it felt like I'd swallowed a stone.

The door wasn't locked, and the porch light was still on, so I knew that she had been waiting for me to come home. First I slipped into my son's bedroom, where he was sleeping with his hands thrown over his head, toys strewn all about his bed. He looked so innocent. Then I walked quietly into the bedroom that I shared with my wife. She looked peaceful too but pale in the early morning light. For a moment I felt like crawling into bed with her, but then I remembered what had happened, and I couldn't bring myself to do it.

The house felt large and empty with everyone else still asleep. I went in and made myself a cup of coffee. The morning papers were there, folded on the kitchen table, and when I opened the *Times* to read while I had a coffee, all the reviews popped out at me as though they were reproaching me.

The review from the *Times* said: "An innovative, brilliant mix of the classical with a clever element of enhanced character identity and a tasteful touch of sexual appeal, all choreographed to Tchaikovsky's beautiful score." The reviewer for the *Times* was not usually so effusive. He praised Meg Cameron for her portrayal of Odette/Odile, calling her no less than an actress. Scott Pierce was tagged as "brilliant" for his role as Prince Siegfried. Dennis Naby was praised for being "outstanding in his role as Von Rothbart, the wealthy, lecherous sorcerer who enslaves the swans."

I realized that I was familiar with the ballet but not with any of the people my wife had cast in it. In fact, I hadn't even popped by the civic center to see her rehearse. I had been lying to myself, it struck me. I had been rationalizing my belief that I wanted to give her the space to do her own thing, but I hadn't been interested enough in what she had been doing to take the time to go down.

And, in fact, I hadn't been involved in what she had been doing in any more than a cursory way since Chris had been born.

The sorry fact of my actions sat staring me in the face. No wonder Buck Johnson had managed to slip his way into my wife's life.

At that moment, the phone rang. I picked it up and said "hello." I heard the voice on the other end say, "Hello, Adam. Gloria calling. Do you have a minute? Can we talk?"

I groaned to myself. I had so far avoided having any conversations with my in-laws. They were lovely folks and had embraced me like a son. But I hadn't wanted their pity or support in this. I had been upset that Christina had told them what was going on. I felt that our private life was our business, not theirs.

It wasn't their fault. So I tried to sound friendly. "Oh, hello, Mom," I said, the moniker sounding foreign and strange in my mouth. "I have some time." I felt somewhat nervous, so I added, quite unnecessarily, "Good to hear from you."

"Thanks, Adam dear," she said. By the tone of her voice, I could tell that she was quite happy with the term "Mom" and my friendly manner. "I won't beat around the bush. Tonight is the grand finale."

I felt sick to my stomach. "So it is," I said.

"Everyone is so disappointed that you haven't attended any of the performances. Christina so wants you to attend. She's done such a good job, and it would be so sad if you were to miss it."

I didn't know what to say. For some reason, the ballet had been inextricably tied, in my mind, to her affair. I let the silence hang there awhile.

"Adam, would you please? If not for my Christina, would you do it for me? We have an extra ticket for you. Won't you please join us?"

I knew that it must have taken a lot for Gloria to call me, let alone to beg me like that. I exhaled. I wanted to lie to her—to assure her that I would be there, that everything would be okay, and that I would be her daughter's dutiful husband until death do we part. But I wasn't sure anymore what was going to happen. Even if I did want her. I didn't know if I had it in me to find my way back to her—to our marriage.

"Mother, I'm trying to get my head screwed on right. I haven't been myself. I'm trying to come to terms with and understand what's happened," I said.

"Yes, dear, I understand. I really do," she said. "You know, though, it really is the right thing, attending the performance. Regardless." I could hear her disappointment through the line, but I also heard a steady resolve. Christina's parents had survived the war and were made of stern stuff. They seemed steady and always there; perhaps that was one of the reasons I had neglected her sometimes. They were there, and I figured they could step in to fill any gap I left by traveling so much.

She plowed ahead. "There's going to be a reception following the performance. It would be so nice if you would come. All of the dancers and many dignitaries will be there."

I took a deep breath and counted to ten. I suddenly felt a little snappish, but I didn't know why. "I will think about it," I said, sounding stiff, even to myself. I tried to sound a little warmer. "No promises. But I appreciate the call."

"Oh, Adam, Christina does love you so much." Her voice quavered as though she were about to cry. "Please come tonight. We would so much love to see you there."

"I know," I said. "That's not the issue."

"Well," she said more briskly. "I have a ticket for you that I will leave at will call."

"Thanks, Mom," I said gently. "Good-bye."

When she hung up the phone, I looked at my watch out of habit. I had to go to work that day, but I thought about calling in sick. For some reason, I knew if I didn't go that night, our relationship would be over.

Was I willing to let it be over?

Just at that moment I felt a presence at the kitchen doorway. Christina stood there, wrapping her robe around herself, looking at me in surprise.

"You're home!" she said.

"Yes," I said, feeling a little sheepish then for having gone off and slept at Erick's house for a few days. But then I felt a tinge of self-righteousness.

"Oh," she said. She moved into the kitchen to pour herself a cup of coffee too. "I was worried."

"I'm sorry. I should have called."

"Well, you left me a note," she said.

I nodded. She sat down on the kitchen table and looked at me warily. There were dark circles under her eyes.

"So did I hear the telephone?"

"Yes," I said.

"Well, who was it?"

I looked at her. "Were you expecting someone?"

"No," she said, looking chagrined. "I just wondered who it was."

I was silent for a moment, rearranging the papers on the table and pretending to look at them. Finally I said, "It was your mother."

"Why didn't you wake me up?" she asked.

I sighed. "She wanted to talk to me."

Christina looked a little nervous. "Oh, Gee, sorry about that. I told her not to meddle."

"No, it's fine," I said. "She just invited me to go with her and your dad to your ballet tonight."

Christina looked at me with a mixture of worry and hope. "I would love it if you did," she said shyly. "It is the final performance."

"Yes, I know," I said, looking at the newspaper again, though it just swam in front of me.

She said nothing, but I could see her watching at me.

"Look, stop staring at me like that," I said, putting the newspaper down. "I don't know if I really want to go to the ballet. I want to support you and all of that, but I'm uncomfortable about the whole thing."

She looked at me in surprise. "Why do you feel uncomfortable?"

"I'm trying to come to terms with everything, and the ballet, frankly, reminds me of him."

She looked down at the table for a moment, as if praying, and then looked up at me with a very serious, sad look on her face. "I am so, so sorry, Adam. I didn't mean to hurt you. In fact, I thought I was protecting you."

"Well, you did hurt me," I said, feeling a raw bit of anger boil up that I couldn't seem to let go of. "And it's going to take some time to get over it. And I'm trying to understand what happened. But I'm having a hard time."

"What can I do to make it up to you? Looking back, I know I used bad judgment, and I got trapped in the situation. I wanted to get out of that terrible situation without anybody knowing about it."

"But me?" I said. "You couldn't have talked to me?"

"Oh, Adam, you would have seen those photos. They were so humiliating that I didn't want anybody to see them. I just wanted to get the negatives, get it over with, and get out of there. I couldn't bear to have you see me that way." She wiped her eyes. "He kept them in a stamped envelope that was addressed to you at your workplace."

I put down the newspaper, but I just couldn't respond to that. I still felt so confused.

She was crying then. "I am so sorry about how everything went. I don't want to ruin our marriage, Adam. I was trying to save it, but I messed everything up so terribly. I am so sorry. I feel so stupid."

She sat there and wept, and I went over and stiffly hugged her for a little while. Then I kissed her on the forehead, went out to the porch, and sat down to think. After a while, I realized I wasn't getting any closer to coming to terms with the problem, so I decided to go to work after all. I wished I could understand why I felt so hurt.

I popped in to say good-bye to Christina, but I couldn't answer the question that was in her eyes.

Twenty-Six

THE FINALE

Christina

THE ORCHESTRA WAS BUSY TUNING THEIR instruments, creating an ordered chaos of voices and notes that added to the excited buzz of the civic center. The audience slowly filed into the auditorium, the ladies in their finest and the men in suits and ties, although there was a scattering of casual dressers in blue jeans and long-sleeved shirts. Here and there, there were a few mothers accompanied by their daughters, aspiring ballerinas all with open faces, looking eager for the performance to begin. I saw many dignitaries from the local arts community: Mitch Carter, Mark Turner, Frank Wichman, some wealthy patrons, and others; all had front-row seats.

I watched all this from a vantage point in the wings. This was the part of the ballet that excited me the most: the thrill of anticipation and the energy of the audience.

But I watched that night, in part, with a feeling of fear in my stomach. And the fear didn't come from the performance or worries about whether we would have technical difficulties or the reviews would be bad or the audience members wouldn't find themselves transported.

The past week had gone by in a blur. When I had gotten home after opening night, Adam had been gone. I'd found a note that said he'd gone over to

Erick's house. That was it. He hadn't signed his name with "love." There had been no more information.

I had spent the night restlessly tossing and turning. But there was no more crying. I was done with tears. I accepted the fact that I'd made the hugest mistake of my life by getting into an entanglement with Buck Johnson. I had effectively ruined my marriage. Adam had every right to leave me. I would have to accept that and move on with my life.

Many women were divorced these days. It was becoming acceptable, not like in the old days. But I swore I wouldn't become bitter. Or hateful. I had to be myself.

Maybe someday, if I continued to be a loving mother to Chris and if I could turn my marriage into at least a friendship, I could redeem myself.

I had to believe in the power of love. If Adam and I were meant to be, he would come back.

I believed we were meant to be. I just had to have faith and the courage to accept the things that I couldn't change, just like the serenity prayer stated.

Nevertheless, the days were agony. I kept busy with Chris. At nights, with the performances, I had something to distract myself.

At opening night, I felt a certain fear that *Swan Lake* was going to be over. What would I do with myself after that? I was fairly certain that the ballet could make enough money to support me, so that wasn't my main concern.

But I wanted my husband back. I admit it. I wanted it all.

But if Adam didn't show up that night, would he ever? I somehow had put a lot of extra pressure on the grand finale. I knew that it was unrealistic, but it somehow seemed magical—potent. The curtains would come down on my show, but I didn't want them to come down on my marriage. The show was a fleeting thing. My marriage was supposed to be until death do we part.

I sighed and looked out at the audience, trying to drink in the energy, letting it sustain me. Then I saw my mom and dad enter and slowly walk down the aisle to their seats. I craned my head so I could see better, hoping to see a familiar figure with them. I scanned the crowd behind them; perhaps he'd gotten separated in the press. But I didn't see him.

I waited a few moments while my parents got seated, and I stepped out so they could see me. They looked a little unhappy, and my mom answered my raised eyebrows by shaking her head "no." My dad gave me a forced smile.

Some more people sat in their row until there was only one empty seat. And to my heart, that one empty seat gave me an empty feeling that hung like a dark cloud over the evening.

Adam wasn't coming.

I felt Anna walk up beside me and take my hand in hers. "Oh, there are your parents," she said, surveying the audience.

"Yes, there they are," I said as cheerily as I could.

"Christina, where is Adam?" she asked, apparently just then taking in the empty seat beside them. "Is he really going to snub your great and grand event?"

"Oh, Anna," I said, turning to her. "Things are pretty bad between us now. I don't know what's going to happen." I knew my mother had called him this morning and hadn't gotten anywhere. She had told me as much at the early dinner we'd had together a few hours ago.

"I'm really sorry, hon," she said. "Do you think it's…" She hesitated, but her dark eyes studied mine.

"Over?" I said, finishing her sentence and smiling wryly. "I desperately wanted him to come, and I'm hoping we'll get back together. But it's out of my hands. It's up to him. There is nothing more I can do."

"Well, keep smiling, Chrissy. For now you can relish in what you've accomplished here and now." She patted me on the hand. "Things will work out, I'm sure."

"Let's just focus on this evening's performance for now," I said.

Together we walked backstage to summon the dancers for their final instructions. I wanted to be sure that their energy was up. The final performance was going to be the one that was most remembered in the arts community. We'd done extremely well so far, and I wanted to make sure that nothing slipped. There were many people in the audience—including luminaries from across the world—who were watching to see if we could pull it off.

The dancers gathered around me backstage, and I surveyed them with pride. "You are making history here. You have revolutionized an art that will flow downstream and become a new standard in ballet," I said. The dancers looked pleased.

"It's time," said Anna, touching my arm.

"Thank you, Anna, for all you've done," I said. I turned to the dancers and announced, "Let's finish strong."

And then the orchestra started to play.

I wanted to slip into the audience to see the final performance, but I was needed backstage. I could already tell that the evening was going to be flawless. The cast was more relaxed and more comfortable in their roles. It was obvious they were having fun and didn't want it to end. Scott and Meg performed some difficult lifts that had given them some problems in earlier performances, though the audience was none the wiser. Naby's presence as the sorcerer required some strenuous passages, but he wasn't even winded when he came off the stage and gave me a big grin as he walked by. The opening number was spot on, the the ensemble was perfectly synchronized, and the White Swan Pas De Deux was breathtaking. The audience errupted with applause.

I had never felt so happy, even though I felt as though my life was crashing around me. I tried to put off any thoughts of what would happen to Chris and me. I resisted walking over to the stage door to look out into the audience to see if Adam was there, because my presence as a director was needed. I couldn't keep watching like that; I had to come to terms with what my stupid mistake had cost me.

Somehow, the story of *Swan Lake* made me more emotional than ever. I could feel Odette's longing, and though I knew it had a happy ending, I felt like weeping nevertheless. I was happy but not happy. I had found fulfillment, but it had come at a great loss.

And then the performance was over. It seemed as though everything had just begun.

I felt an emptiness overcome me once again. There was no dancing or music to fill it. No Adam.

The dancers milled about backstage, getting themselves in order for the final curtain calls.

I could hear the audience applauding and whooping.

I watched from the wings. The supporting cast ran out onto the stage first, followed by the secondary characters. The audience whistled and cheered.

"You're up, kids," I said, beckoning for Meg and Scott to take their place on the stage. As they ran past me, Scott gave me an impulsive kiss on the forehead. "Thank you for believing in this," he said. They danced on into the lights and took their bows.

The rest of the main characters danced out on stage and took their bows. The applause swelled the room, and the audience was filled with goodwill and appreciation.

It was several minutes before it was my turn to go on stage. Anna went out, and there were a few whistles and catcalls, which made her blush.

Finally, it was my turn to go on. I walked out onto the stage to take my bow. I felt overwhelmed by the outpouring of goodwill. I drank it all in: the applause, the cheers, the standing ovation, and the support of the arts community of Lockville. I knew that the future of the ballet company was ensured; I would have a job. I could do more dances.

But even as I stood there, blinking in the bright lights on the stage, I felt a lump in my throat. I told myself that this wasn't the time to cry. Too many people had counted on me and had helped get me there. I'd sacrificed too much.

And then I saw, out of the corner of my eye, a well-dressed man carrying a dozen roses walking onto the stage. For a minute I didn't recognize him.

Then I wasn't sure I could believe what I saw. I must have been hallucinating. It couldn't have been true.

But my illusion came closer until I could see that he was real and that I wasn't dreaming. He had a smile on his face. "Congratulations, my dear," he said. "Fantastic performance."

I started to tear up. Was he there for show, or did this mean something?

Then he handed me the roses. "These are for you," he said.

"Adam," I said. "You came."

He ducked his head and blushed for a moment before he raised his face to look at me. His eyes told me everything I needed to know. "Of course I did," he said. "How could I not?"

"Does that mean you forgive me?"

He nodded and gave me a searching look. "If you forgive me."

He didn't wait for my answer; he simply took me in his arms and held me. I was crying full on then. He gave me a long, deep kiss. I could hear the audience go wild.

For an instant, everything was bathed in radiance. I saw my husband, standing by my side, his face filled with love and longing. The dark forest was behind me, the corrupt sorcerer had lost, and I had found my way back not only to my prince but also to myself. In the end, there was redemption after all. I had been granted a second chance. I didn't know what we would find, but I was looking forward to it.

"Let's get out of here," Adam said. I nodded, and he proffered his arm. I tucked my hand in his elbow, and we bowed to the audience before walking off the stage together, side by side.

Acknowledgments

I keep trying new things to stay alive; writing a book is one of the challenges I undertook at the age of eighty. I hope this is the first of other books in my literary career and that you enjoyed it.

I owe the utmost to my lovely wife, an accomplished ballerina who inspired my appreciation for the art of ballet. Thank you for supporting me in all my endeavors, even when you felt I was traveling in waters out of my depth. You have been my life partner, and we have conquered all challenges together, and for that, I am grateful.

I picked up invaluable support and training from my writing coach, Lori DeBoer, who was instrumental in helping me bring my ideas to life.

Thanks to my son, Rick, and my friend David Harrison, who offered support and encouragement.

Thanks to the people at my company who said they wanted to read my book and kept me going.

I am also grateful to my neighbors, who, during our weekly breakfast get-togethers, asked me repeatedly when this book would be done. I'm pleased to deliver it at last.

About the Author

N. F. Steiner grew up on a farm in Kansas. He graduated from Kansas State University with a degree in mechanical engineering and worked in the aviation field for more than fifty years. He learned how to fly a plane at an early age and still owns his own airplane. He started his company out of his basement in 1987, and after he retired in his eighties, he decided to launch his dream of being a writer. He comes to his love for the ballet by his wife.

His next book will be a memoir about his life and times.

For more information, email him at bluevirgapublishing@anvpartners.com.

Fiction

Former ballerina Christina Cramer has it all: a doting husband, a beautiful son, and her own fledgling ballet company. But when art patron Buck Johnson sets his sights on her, she becomes ensnared in a series of liaisons that could destroy her marriage. With her husband, Adam, increasingly absent, Christina struggles to stand up to Buck, her blackmailer, to manage her dancers, and to make her way back to her family. Set in the 1960s against the backdrop of a production of *Swan Lake*, this debut novel by n. f. steiner probes into the dark side of love, the cost of human frailty, and the unpredictable path to redemption.

www.ingramcontent.com/pod-product-compliance
Lightning Source LLC
Chambersburg PA
CBHW071140260626
47162CB00003B/868